The Body in the Dam

TB Brown

Published by TB Brown, 2022.

Table of Contents

Prologue...1
Chapter 1... 11
Chapter 2... 15
Chapter 3... 28
Chapter 4... 33
Chapter 5... 41
Chapter 6... 51
Chapter 7... 57
Chapter 8... 62
Chapter 9... 72
Chapter 10 77
Chapter 11 87
Chapter 12 94
Chapter 13 102
Chapter 14 108
Chapter 15 117
Chapter 16 121
Chapter 17 130
Chapter 18 140
Chapter 19 146
Chapter 20 155
Chapter 21 159
Chapter 22 164
Chapter 23 172
Chapter 24 176
Chapter 25 183
Chapter 26 193
Chapter 27 199
Chapter 28 206
Chapter 29 211
Chapter 30 218

Chapter 31 226
Chapter 32 231
Chapter 33 235
Chapter 34 240
Chapter 35 244
Chapter 36 248
Chapter 37 252
Chapter 38 259
Chapter 39 268

For Valerie:

Thank you for putting up with me

Thank you to the many contributors who had the grace and
patience to support this effort: Val, Chad, Pat, David,
Bruce, and countless others.

Thank you to John Paine for splendid editorial services.

Prologue

ROSIE WAS A GENTLE man, and he had retired to the Woodlake Resort and Country Club for a peaceful lake experience. Since then, too much had changed. The last straw had come last week when a longtime member of the community Board of Directors had resigned, and the board needed a new volunteer. Fred Akers had stepped forward, but he was so new nobody knew him. If elected, he would be the vote the Army goons needed to approve gasoline-powered boats on Lake Surf.

Fred wasn't even retirement age, and Woodlake had always been a retirement community, Rosie thought. It was designed for golfing in the morning and cocktail parties in the afternoon. The long summer weekends were a time to sail around the lake and perhaps take out the lazy battery powered pontoon boats for a booze cruise.

But Fred was too young, especially for the board. He was only in his mid-forties, and he had a young family. His wife Jill was even younger. Rosie had to admit, she looked great in a bikini. Fred had just retired from the U.S. Army after 27 years, another one of the entitled swine from Fort Bragg. More and more of them were moving in. These soldiers were not interested in a quiet retirement. Thanks to them, the summer weekends had been filled with loud music, lakeside volleyball, and endless parties going late into the night. Now they'd be filled with the roar of motorboats and disruptive wakes churning the lake into a stormy sea, damaging the shoreline and eroding the earthen dam.

Rosie pulled into the gravel drive of the modest ranch house around nine o'clock Tuesday morning. Set on a one-quarter acre lot in the gated community, and flanked on one side by an empty lot and on the other by a lot being cleared for construction, the house had a surprising amount of privacy.

Fred must have known Jim Devaney, Chairman of the Board of Woodlake, from his time at Fort Bragg. Devaney had been commander of the 82nd Airborne Division Artillery. Rosie knew that Devaney was all for power boats on Lake Surf. He probably recruited Fred Akers to fill the vacancy on the board.

Walking up the drive, Rosie heard someone banging a hammer behind the house. The sharp raps echoed in the morning air. He rang the doorbell but got no response. He rang again. Nothing. He rang again, this time jabbing the button so the doorbell sounded repeatedly. In a little while a younger man answered the door. This man might be early forties. He looked fit. He wore work clothes, a framing hammer in his hand.

"Good morning. Can I help you?"

"I'm sorry to bother you. I'm looking for Fred Akers."

"You found him." Akers reached out and shook hands with a firm grip and friendly smile.

"They call me Rosie." He didn't like the nickname, but it had stuck. He was used to it. He did not bother to explain it. "Do you have a few minutes to talk?"

"Sure," said Akers. "Come on in. I'll get you a cup of coffee. We can sit out back. I could use a break."

Rosie followed him through the foyer into a large open living room with a cathedral ceiling and floor-to-ceiling windows looking out over Lake Surf. The morning sun shone brightly into the living room, nearly blinding him. The room was clean and tidy, but the furniture was worn.

Akers appeared from the kitchen with two cups of coffee, and Rosie followed him out onto the back porch. They sat in wicker chairs and looked out at the lake.

"You have a beautiful view."

"Yeah, thanks. I love the lake in the morning. Sometimes it's so calm you can see the reflection of the branches in those trees over there"—he pointed with his coffee cup— "like a photograph on the water."

"That is sort of what I wanted to talk to you about, the lake," said Rosie. He hesitated, rubbed his palms together. "I hear you are running for the Board of Directors. You're the only candidate, so you're guaranteed to win." He tapped his chest. "I'm on the board. Have been for ten years. We've had some turnover, but not me. I've been to every board meeting since I moved here. I'm like the, uh, unofficial memory of the board and the community. Well, me and Deloris Hitchcock." He sat up straighter. "We protect this community."

"I am glad you stopped by," said Fred. "I might need some tips on how to get things done."

"I can help with that," Rosie nodded. A pause. "What I wanted to talk about was the, uh, the board. I don't know how much you know about our history here, and our community."

"I'm learning something new every day," said Fred.

"This community was built with a vision. We have fantastic amenities, a great clubhouse, championship golf. The restaurant and pub at the golf course serve great food, great drinks. Everybody knows everybody else. The gates keep out trouble, the streets are quiet. Everybody drives around in their golf carts, even home from the pub." Rosie winked and smiled warmly.

"It is a great place to live, and relax. We have great fishing, and a nice lake for cruising or sailing. We have beautiful sunsets. The board has worked hard for a long time to preserve the atmosphere here, and the lake is a big part of that. Sitting out on your porch in the evening to enjoy sunset, to really feel the peaceful lake experience. Nothing better."

Fred smiled and nodded.

"The thing is, this new push to open up the lake to motorboats. We've never had motorboats on the lake," he continued. "I mean, everybody gets out on the water, of course. We have a sailing club, very active. I'm in that. If you want to meet some fun people, that's a great place to do it. We have kayakers and paddle boarders. A few rowers. Lots of pontoon boats. People love to cruise the lake at sunset. We get the best sunsets. It's a special place." He paused and spread his hands. "But we've never had powerboats."

"There are battery-powered boats on the lake now," said Fred. "I see them out, and I see them at the marina, too. All the pontoon boats."

"Sure," said Rosie. "But that's not the same. They're not real motorboats, not like the gas-powered boats. Can you imagine? All the noise, the exhaust, the waves." He scoffed. "Motorboats would ruin the lake."

Fred thought for a minute.

"I don't think so," he said. The lake is plenty big enough for motorboats. My wife and I, we bought in here last year so our girls could grow up on the lake, with a boat. Like I did when I was a kid. There are more and more young people moving in here. More and more kids. Even the older folks have grandkids. I've talked to a lot of people. Plenty of folks want motorboats on the lake. People have been pushing for it, but frankly, the board has been resistant. It's not going to last. Things are changing. It's time. People want motorboats. Skiing. Wakeboarding. All that."

"Who have you talked to, if I may ask?"

"Jim DeVaney, for one. You know he has a brand-new grandbaby girl?"

"Yes, I heard, but I have not met her yet," said Rosie.

"Yup. A baby girl. Sarah, I think he said. He said he's getting a fishing boat with a big outboard to take her tubing when she's a little older. And Jim's not the only one. People are frustrated. Everybody says the board meetings are held during the day, during the week, when nobody with a job can go. Well, now there is a vacancy, and I have time. I am willing to volunteer. A lot of people here want change, and I think we can make some progress. The lake is plenty big enough for powerboats, and there is room for everyone. I mean, look at it."

The lake remained perfectly calm in the morning light.

"It's almost always like that. Completely calm. When we get motorboats in here, it'll still be like that most of the time. Nobody goes boating on a weekday morning. Nobody goes boating in the winter. It'll be quiet and still most of the time, motorboats or not. There'll still be plenty of time for a 'peaceful lake experience.' Motorboats won't change that."

"That's not true. The lake is not big enough," said Rosie, a little heatedly. "You look at it." He leaned forward and turned toward the water. "The birds, the fish, the peace, the quiet. Motorboats will ruin all that. And if we let them in, we will never get them out."

"Nah," said Fred, also leaning forward. "They won't ruin anything. There's plenty of room. Other communities do it. Heck, it'll probably increase property values. The lake is our biggest draw. I've talked to guys who specifically did not buy in here because of the motorboat ban. Once its lifted, demand for property will rise. Honestly, I expect that by the end of this summer, we will be able to get that done. Let me show you something."

Fred walked out to the dock. The visitor followed. He could see signs of Fred's morning work. A builder's square, a box of nails, and a crowbar lay on the shore near a tarp with some lumber scraps. At the dock, Fred pointed to the new construction.

"I'm buttressing the dock to put in a boat lift. This thing will hold six thousand pounds. I'm planning to have a ski boat in here this year before the weather gets cold."

"Do you really think we are going to let that happen?" said Rosie, anger rising.

"Oh, I think it's a done deal. We have the votes." Fred turned his back and pointed out into the lake. "We'll probably put in some buoys to mark a ski area, to keep the boats far enough—"

Rosie didn't really mean to do it, but the crowbar felt solid in his hands. When Fred said "It's a done deal" and turned to the lake, Rosie bent over and picked it up. It was right there at his feet. The crowbar had a nice heft and balance. Reminded him of a golf club. He didn't swing hard. The well-crafted and streamlined tool made a slight whoosh as it sliced through the air. He didn't feel much in his wrists as the crowbar came down square on the back of Fred's head. It made a dull ringing sound, but it did not vibrate in his wrists at all.

Fred dropped like a stone. He fell sideways and landed face up. Rosie still held the end of the crowbar. It twisted as Fred fell, and pointed down at an angle to the man on the ground, the claw buried deep in Fred's brain. The eyes were open, moving a little, but he couldn't get any words out. He grunted a little. That made Rosie uncomfortable, so he wiggled the end of the crowbar. The four-inch claw in Fred's brain wiggled in direct proportion, and red blood oozed around the black steel. That stopped the grunting and dimmed the eyes. In a little while the lights went out, and just like that Rosie was a killer.

Oops, he thought. I wonder why that just happened.

He was not excited. He felt calm and clear.

I did not really mean to do that. It just sort of happened, on its own. He had it coming, though. You can't just come in here and change everything. Look at how his eyes are open.

Rosie had read in books where the dead eyes of a murder victim were supposed to stare relentlessly at the murderer. "Look what you've done to me," they were supposed to say in silent reproach. He thought Fred's eyes didn't say much. They just looked dead. Dull brown, and dead. The color of dog shit. Shit colored eyes for a shitty morning. He had definitely had a shitty morning.

Just then a duck splashed noisily in the lake a few feet off Akers' dock. The splashing snapped him out of his reverie. He broke eye contact, shook his head and looked around. The lake remained calm. The sky remained clear. There was no one in sight. The houses across the lake looked quiet, no sign of anyone about. The duck bathed.

Fred had been using a brown tarp to catch construction scraps. It was lightly covered with oddly cut wood scraps and a few bent nails. Rosie pulled the tarp over the body. He thought about the conversation, wondered if he should have handled things differently. He felt no remorse, only a calm sense of purpose. He did not know if anyone else was home. He didn't think so. It was that time of morning when mothers might be taking their kids to school.

He grabbed up his coffee mug and went back into the house. On the way he stopped by the wicker chair where he had sat and inspected it. He couldn't see anything, but might there be fibers from his clothes on the chair? Did wicker take fingerprints?

He grabbed gloves from his truck, then went inside to the kitchen. He cleaned every surface he remembered touching. He washed his coffee cup and carefully put it back in the cabinet. He couldn't figure out what to do with the wicker chair, so he took it outside and put it in the bed of his pickup.

At the dock, he wiped the crowbar clean of blood, brain matter, hair and fingerprints. He swung it round like an Olympic hammer thrower and threw it far out over the lake. It sank with a small splash. The duck paid it no mind. He wrapped Akers in the brown tarp. The body made a tidy roll. To his eye it looked like someone had bundled up a dead body in a brown tarp, but he might be biased. It also looked like a brown tarp rolled around some garbage.

The rolled-up tarp fit nicely into the bed of the pickup next to the wicker chair. One final walk through the house and the yard. He had not left anything for anyone to find. He climbed in his truck and drove away. Through it all, no one noticed anything. The lake remained peaceful.

Rosie drove the speed limit to the back gate. The front gate was manned by a security guard 24 hours a day, and there was no need to tempt fate. He turned left out of the gate and drove to the dump. It always surprised him, how busy the dump was. People were messy and liked throwing things away. The supervisor came over to say hello. They were always too damn friendly, thought the killer. He smiled and said good morning.

"What you got there," asked the dump man. He was dressed in a dark green shirt with a name patch over the right breast, and a rumpled grey cap. He looked eagerly into the bed of the pickup.

"Old chair," said the killer. "Don't have any room for it, just need to get rid of it. New furniture coming, you know." He grabbed the chair and made for the trash compactor.

"Hold on," said the dump supervisor. He took the chair and inspected it with squinted eyes, then set it down near the garbage compactor, at the end of a small row of heavily used items. An old cooler. A sooty grill. A banged-up chest-of-drawers. People loved to recycle the garbage of others. Made them feel frugal, and clever.

"Somebody might want that chair," said the dump man. "What else you got in there?" He was looking at the rolled-up tarp. Maybe stopping by the dump was a bad idea.

"Oh, that's just some scrap lumber. I'm keeping that for spares," Rosie said. He thanked the man and drove away.

Where do you put a dead body? The lake? They might drag the bottom. Or Akers might float. Did bodies float? He'd seen something on TV about that. As he drove, he passed a dead deer on the side of the road, hit by a car. It would start to stink soon, unless someone buried it. Now, there is an idea, he thought.

He parked at a gravel parking area near the dam. There were a few walkers out, but no one within a hundred yards. He could smell the freshly turned dirt of recent earth work. In light of recent weather events, there had been some concern about the integrity of the dam, and the engineers had agreed that some work was needed. Fortunately, it was not too much, or too costly. The community agreed that maintenance of the dam was everything.

Trucks and earthmoving equipment were parked on the dam where the work was nearing completion. Several scars from the new work were visible on the large back slope of the earthen dam. Rocks covered the freshly turned areas to prevent erosion, but the earth beneath still bore signs of recent digging. Perfect. He just needed to wait until nightfall.

He walked and planned how he would do it. First park the pickup in his garage, and get the tools. Shovel, pick, gloves. Maybe some rope if he needed to tug the body. A headlamp would be useful, but he must be cautious with light. Maybe one of those lamps with a subtle red setting designed to protect night vision. That would be best.

It might take a few hours, and he had to start late in the night. Unlikely to be disturbed then. Drive over, turn off his headlights a quarter mile out, and coast into the parking area. Move the body and the tools to a suitable spot on the back of the dam. Clear the rocks from an area three feet by seven, or so. About the size of a grave. Dig deeply. The fact that the earth had recently been turned would help. Lay Akers in the grave, then cover him with earth. Erase any sign of his presence. The recent work on the dam would conceal his work. At dawn, he would be first on the dam for a walk, to inspect his work in the light of day.

As it happened, his plan came off perfectly. The next morning, he saw no trace of his nocturnal activity. He drove back to the landfill and threw away his gloves, clothes and tools, then he drove home to shower. It was turning into a nice day.

Chapter 1

Twenty Years Later

THE HURRICANE STARTED as an ill-defined low-pressure area in the atmosphere off the west coast of the African continent near the Cape Verde islands. Cool moist air from the Gulf of Guinea rose to meet dry Saharan winds to form a trough of low-pressure air moving west over the Atlantic Ocean. As a large high-pressure region over the eastern North Atlantic kept the trough over the moist air of the tropics, it began to organize and strengthen. In the vast empty ocean, the storm began to rotate and pick up speed. When the sustained winds topped 39 miles per hour, it acquired a name: Miranda.

Skippers at sea took notice. Smaller vessels altered course to avoid the storm. Some brave captains of larger ships, with cargo to deliver and bonuses riding on getting into port early, put on speed to get through the storm before she grew stronger.

In the great emptiness of the tropical ocean and still far from land, Miranda began to rotate more quickly, in a counter clockwise direction. As her intensity increased, her winds reached 74 miles per hour, and she became a hurricane. The lonely surface of the sea bucked and heaved and salt spray peppered the whitecaps. Far from the storm, surfers began to reap Mother Nature's rewards as the swell picked up near shore. It was then that she showed up on the morning radio broadcasts in the Carolinas, but no one paid her any mind.

She continued on a direct path towards coastal North Carolina, picking up strength and moisture as she grew. Hurricane warnings began to sound along the southeastern coast of the United States, from Georgia to Maryland. When coastal evacuation orders came for regions of South Carolina, North Carolina and Virginia, shelves at Wal-Mart and Dollar General emptied of bottled water and loaf bread.

A large fine zone of high pressure over the eastern United States began to push back against Miranda's progress, and her path westward slowed. She waxed and waned in strength, but she inched toward the coast.

When she made landfall on September 12th at Wrightsville Beach in North Carolina, people were relieved that she had weakened into a category 1 storm, but she was still a hurricane, and she uprooted trees and knocked out power. She crept slowly inland, coming to a virtual standstill in eastern North Carolina, dumping rain over the soaked earth. Catastrophic flooding occurred in the low-lying plains in the eastern part of the state.

About a hundred miles inland, the ground begins a slow rise which continues all the way to the escarpment of the Appalachian Mountains and highlands of western North Carolina. This wide piedmont of rising land was largely spared significant flooding from the September rains of Miranda. Largely, but not entirely.

At the Woodlake Resort and Country Club, at the eastern edge of Moore County, North Carolina, residents had a longstanding quarrel with the community management. Residents accused the absentee owners of Woodlake Dam of negligence. The dam held back Lake Surf, a 1000-acre impoundment known for fine fishing and beautiful sunsets. The community sported an 18-hole golf course, a nice clubhouse and restaurant, playgrounds and a pool, and all the amenities of a private gated community.

The centerpiece of the community was the shallow and vaguely rectangular Lake Surf. The large earthen dam had been inspected repeatedly for years and found wanting. Plans were drawn up for repairs and maintenance, but they were never completed. There had been a spate of work on the dam a couple of decades ago, when times were good, but the dam had languished since then. The absentee owner, a mysterious individual, or perhaps an ownership group from somewhere in Europe—somehow nobody was quite sure—claimed to be broke. According to ownership's mouthpiece, an attorney from the state capital in Raleigh, there was no more money to maintain the dam. Neither the community residents nor the ownership was willing to pony up the cash required. The community had seen more than its share of infighting over the use of the lake, and no one was willing to pay until those issues were settled. The state did not mandate repair, either because they were satisfied with the work done long ago or because of budget cuts at the Department of Environmental Quality. The US Army Corps of Engineers was silent. The dam languished.

Eastern North Carolina sticks its nose out into the Atlantic Ocean directly in the path of northbound Atlantic hurricanes and is one of the most hurricane prone coasts in North America. On average, a tropical cyclone will strike the North Carolina coast about every 2 years. The early years of the twenty-first century proved to be amongst the most active in recorded history. By the time Miranda arrived, Woodlake Dam had been roundly battered, and the lack of maintenance was beginning to tell.

When Miranda stalled over the state and dumped three days of record-breaking rain into the Lake Surf watershed, the lake swelled beyond containment. The flood proved too much for the old earthen dam. The spillway began to crack and overflow, and the dam began to fail. The failure was not the sort of catastrophe that suddenly washes away homes and families, but the dam failed nonetheless. The earth surrounding the spillway began to wash away.

Downstream residents were evacuated, mostly the poor and disenfranchised. The Corps of Engineers and Department of Environmental Quality finally took note. Residents of Woodlake went on Channel 5 News out of Raleigh to point fingers and wring their hands about declining property values. The television crews loved to juxtapose these well-off homeowners complaining about property values with the poor and poorly spoken evacuees from downstream. The governor made a statement.

The local media loved it; it made for good copy and better television. A major engineering firm was called in from Raleigh, and heavy earth moving equipment showed up. It all got even more exciting when the first body washed out of the dam.

Chapter 2

DERWOOD FLYNN HAD A good morning, by his standards. Mondays never bothered him. He awoke before dawn with a foggy head, but his sleep was undisturbed by nightmares of killers he had not killed. The bourbon had seen to that, as it usually did. The fresh ground coffee was hot, and the morning air on his back porch was cool. His tablet was charged, and he opened the *Times*. Derwood had always been an early riser, but ever since he got out of the army, he refused to set an alarm clock. He awoke each day to the rhythm of his body.

Today was a special day, his first day on his new job. His old friend Martin Sinsley, a detective with the Sheriff's Office, had convinced the Sheriff that Derwood should be deputized as an investigative assistant. Sinsley knew of Derwood's past in the army and thought getting involved with law enforcement was a good idea. The job was unpaid, but Derwood did not need the money, and the Sheriff's budget was already strained to the limit.

Derwood poured coffee and went out on the back porch to watch the sunrise and catch up on the morning news. It was cool outside still, so he put on slippers and turned on the patio heater. It fired up after a couple of adjustments, and he settled in to read the news.

When the weather permitted, he started all his days on the back porch overlooking Lake Auman. He moved to Seven Lakes, North Carolina, when he was in his twenties, young and full of piss and vinegar. He was on active duty in the army then, stationed at Fort Bragg. Seven Lakes was one of several nice communities within driving distance of his work, and it had by far the nicest lake, Derwood thought, even if it was a little further drive than Woodlake, the other local lake community.

He liked living on the lake. He liked the views, and he liked the peace. Out by the island he could see bald eagles. A couple of them nested somewhere out there. Deer roamed the woods, and he liked them too. The wildlife made him feel peaceful. Derwood worked hard to feel peaceful, like the therapists from the army said he should.

He settled in on the back porch to read the news. It was a slow news day. Rising tension over Israeli settlements in the West Bank, concern about rebel enclaves in Syria, thousands of acres of uncontained wildfires in California, a Hollywood movie producer on trial for sexual assault, and hand wringing over the three-game losing streak for the Atlanta Braves headed into October. He came upon a nice piece on the generosity of strangers. Hurricane Miranda had hit North Carolina hard, and there were flooding, power outages, and damaged lives. The *Times* reported several stories of one group or another volunteering time and money to help. The paper published a link where readers could donate to a relief fund.

When he was finished with the *Times*, Derwood refilled his coffee and pulled up the *Town Crier*, the local paper that covered all things Moore County. The lead story got his attention. The rains of Miranda had flooded Lake Surf, and the Army Corps of Engineers had been called in. After assessing the damage, the Corps decided Woodlake Dam was not sound. They recommended draining the lake. But before that could be done, the spillway began to fail and the dam began to wash downstream.

'Residents of the Woodlake community on the shores of Lake Surf, already reeling from the impending drainage of the lake by the Army Corps of Engineers, were stunned to learn the buried contents of Woodlake Dam overnight. As the swollen reservoir crested and churned through the spillway, the dam began to erode. A group of high school students watching the flood noticed something odd. Closer inspection revealed a human arm, and the flow of water over the dam gradually uncovered a body buried in the back side of the dam.

"'We were just watching the flood over the dam, you know. Then we saw this thing. This arm. It was like he was trying to crawl out to the ground or something. Totally Walking Dead and everything,'" said local teen Heather Clark."

Derwood put down the tablet and sipped his coffee. He gazed out over Lake Auman, a light wind rippling the surface. Overhead, the morning sun highlighted a jet contrail, a glowing yellow streak shining in the sky before the sun's first rays brushed the surface of the lake. He imagined himself sitting sleepily in a window seat aboard the airliner, off to some unknown destination, about some important or perhaps not so important business. A life outside his own, with a different set of wants and needs and problems. A life of sound sleep, with no nightmares.

His detective friend Martin Sinsley would probably be there this morning, and Derwood got dressed. He was headed for the door when it swung open from outside. It had to be Lizzy. No one else would enter his house without knocking.

"Hi, Daddy," said a young woman as she studied him head to toe. "You look better this morning. Less hungover."

The last time his daughter had swung by in the morning before school, he had been sporting a hangover, and she had shown her disapproval. She vowed to solve her father's problem.

The two had been semi-estranged for most of her young life. Lizzy's mother, his ex-wife Kate, had seen to that. She had begged Derwood to open up about his experiences in Middle East, but when he had told her of the things he had done, she recoiled. Her reaction put a stop to any further sharing. She decided he was dangerous. Kate's imagined fears became reality one night when Derwood put her supposed guy "friend" in the hospital. Even through the sober lens of time, he felt his actions justified. Kate disagreed.

Their time together had been intense but brief, two untethered souls colliding at a time when neither knew what their futures held. Elizabeth was the only real reminder of their relationship. When she thought about it, Kate objected to Derwood's presence in the girl's life. She thought he was a bad influence, and dangerous. Luckily, she rarely thought of him at all. As far as he could tell, she did not think much of Lizzy, either.

Since Derwood's retirement from the army and the subsequent reduction in his deployment schedule, he had tried hard to become part of Lizzy's life. At first, she had rebuffed his efforts with the petulance of a seventeen-year-old girl, but his persistence had paid off.

"Gee, thanks, Lizzy," said Derwood. "Tell me how you really feel."

"I feel like you're trying to bury your memories at the bottom of a bottle." She smiled sweetly. "I think you can do better."

"Yeah, thanks for sharing. I love you too. Don't you have somewhere to be?"

"I just came by to say good morning. I'm on my way to school." Lizzy was a senior in high school, and she was into all sorts of activities. Derwood was still trying to keep track of her schedule.

"Any big plans today?" she asked. "I'm free this evening after band, if you want to grab some dinner." She seemed suddenly hesitant.

"Maybe," said Derwood, grateful for the change of subject. "I'm headed over to Woodlake. Marty has some work this morning."

"Oh yeah, the new job. Right," she said. "What's happening this morning?"

"Some kids found something in the dam. The rain washed it up overnight. I'm going to check it out."

"Well, you have fun with that, then," said Lizzy.

He chuckled. "If we get together tonight for dinner, I'll tell you all about it."

"I can hardly wait!" she said. "We'll play it by ear, but don't forget. There is something I want to talk about. I have, uh, this thing. This... problem." Definitely hesitant. "Maybe you can give some dad advice."

"Is everything okay, Lizzy?"

"Oh, sure," she said quickly. "It's no big deal. Just, you know, a thing. I'm glad to see you look better this morning, Daddy. See you later. We'll talk tonight."

Just like that, she was out the door. Derwood was grateful for her attention, even if he sometimes felt like her latest project. Maybe he should buy her a puppy.

He climbed into his pickup truck and drove the half hour to Woodlake. When he pulled into the winding entry lane, framed by mossy oaks with landscaping reminiscent of the low county, the gate guard shack was unmanned and the gate was open. What was the point of a gated community if the gate was left open? Maybe Woodlake had more pressing problems, or maybe they had run out of money.

Heavy machinery rumbled on the dam, widening and controlling the leaking spillway and draining the lake. Derwood saw a state patrol vehicle and two Moore County Sheriff's cars. Cones blocked access with newly hung yellow tape. CRIME SCENE DO NOT CROSS CRIME SCENE DO NOT CROSS. He crossed.

He walked up to a Sheriff's deputy, a short stocky man dressed in civilian clothing, a conservative suit and tie. The man had dark hair, shot through with gray, and an ample chin. His complexion was ruddy and good-natured.

"Good morning, Marty."

Martin Sinsley looked up from his notepad. "Derwood Bartholomew Flynn. As I live and breathe. Oh, wait!" Sinsley stood to attention, adopting his best military bearing. "Good morning, Deputy Flynn!" he said, a broad smile on his face.

Derwood returned the smile. "What can I say, Marty? Deputy Flynn reporting for duty." He had to stop himself from saluting.

The two old friends shook hands. "We don't really do all that military stuff in the Sheriff's Office, Derwood," said Marty.

"Good to know," said Derwood.

"You miss it, I can tell. I think it's boredom. You miss the army. You're not getting enough stimulation. You need excitement." Sinsley knew about Derwood's past, but nothing of the doctors' advice to avoid excitement and stimulation.

Derwood scoffed. "Yeah, right." He looked over the back of the dam. "What do you have here?"

"Not sure yet. Human remains. Don't know who it is, how long it's been there, or who put it there."

"Huh," said Derwood. He was no stranger to scenes of violent death, or to basic forensics. His time in service had not been in the investigative service or military police, but part of his role as a team leader on scene had been intelligence.

Once a scene was secured and threats neutralized, his team had to scrub the scene as quickly as possible, taking any useful information. Documents, pictures, computers and hard drives, maps, receipts, brochures, anything that might shed light on the enemy's plans. Sensitive Site Exploitation, they called it. Often, it meant taking prisoners, if there were any left alive when his team was done storming a position. Sometimes, they had left people alive.

He surveyed the scene at the back of the dam. Blue sky overhead washed crystal clear by the recent storm, the morning still cool. Near the flanks of the dam, trees showed signs of the recent hurricane. Some were stripped of foliage, some bent at odd angles, and a few were blown down. Overall, not too much wind damage. But then, Miranda had carried more rain than wind. The gravel road across the dam where Derwood stood was partially washed out. Lake Surf was still high to overflowing, waves lapping the top of the dam. The lake poured over the emergency spillway in a stream several feet deep.

The spillway was about fifty yards wide, forming a shallow depression in the top of the dam. It was originally lined with rock and gravel, but years of neglect let a thin layer of dirt and sand settle in the depression. When the lake crested and began to flow over the dam, the soil was quickly washed away, and gravel, rocks and clay followed soon after. On the back of the dam, the water left the poorly maintained channel and flared out into a broad stream, eroding the remaining structure.

In one area halfway down the back of the dam, water piled up and there was a modest fan of spray thrown a few feet skyward. In the midst of the spray, like a sculpture in a fountain, a human arm reached toward the sky. The skeletal hand was slightly clenched, as if reaching for help. Derwood thought any help would be too late.

"Aha!" he said. "A clue."

"See? You're getting the hang of this already. I'm going to take a look," said Marty. "You coming?"

Marty had donned boots and knee-high gaiters. Sinsley was always prepared. Derwood glanced down at his own shoes, comfortable and worn leather sandals, thick wool socks.

"I think I'll just stay up here and listen to the play by play. You go ahead."

Sinsley shrugged and picked his way carefully down the back of the dam, moving in the moist and muddy areas just outside the water flow, where the footing was better. He made it down near the body, but he could not approach and simultaneously stay dry. He glanced up at Derwood, who was looking down at him with a big grin, waving him on. He scowled and stepped into the water.

The body had been buried, and rocks placed over the gravesite, but the soil beneath the rocks had washed away. As the earth and rocks moved, the water tugged at the bony arm until it pointed to the sky. A solid band of unadorned gold encircled the fourth finger of the left hand. A man's wedding ring, loose on the bony finger, held in position by a combination of the knuckle, gravity, and luck.

Sinsley took a few photos with his phone. The flow of water was increasing, and the erosion along with it. He snapped on a pair of latex gloves and slipped the ring from the bony finger and put it in a plastic evidence bag.

Back atop the dam, Sinsley said, "We have to move the body."

He gestured to a uniformed deputy. "The crime scene folks won't like it, but it's better than letting it wash away completely. We can preserve the chain of evidence if we record it." He handed Derwood his cell phone.

Sinsley and the deputy took an emergency stretcher back down to the scene and began to lift the rocks that held the body in place. The remains were wrapped in a shredded and rotted tarp and still wore disintegrating clothing. Using gloved hands, Sinsley and the deputy were able to move the remains and any fabric or material they found onto the stretcher and bring it up to the top of the dam. When they finished, they were soaked head to toe.

While they waited for an ambulance to take custody of the remains, they studied the pile of bones, fabric, and dirt on the stretcher. "I pulled this off his hand." Sinsley held up the evidence bag with the gold ring. His clothing dripped water.

"Man's wedding ring?" said Derwood.

"Looks like."

"He's been in there a while," said Derwood, taking in the decomposed corpse and rotted clothes. "I wonder who he was."

"We'll know soon enough," said Sinsley.

The ambulance arrived, and the crew loaded up the remains. The local morgue was in the hospital basement, and eventually the coroner would give them some answers. The ambulance crew drove away. They did not mind this kind of call. For once, they were not in a hurry.

"How old is this dam?" asked Derwood.

"I want to say it was built forty, fifty years ago. Before my time anyway. It's caused a lot of trouble over the years. It gets in the news every so often, with people worried about maintenance and safety."

"Huh," said Derwood. "Do you have any open missing-persons cases going back that far?"

"We weren't computerized until the 2000s. The earlier files are in storage. I don't know how far back they go. We can check the cold cases and see what pops up," said Sinsley. "You want in on this one?"

"Maybe," said Derwood. "Let's see how it plays out."

"Aw, hell, Derwood. You know you want in. You need a reason to get up in the morning. You're already getting a double chin. Plus, you were interested enough to drive over here this morning."

He had a point. Ever since Derwood got out of the army, where the demands of his unit and his job had forced him to maintain top fitness and a razor's edge of readiness, he had let himself slide. He had gained forty pounds, and slowed down considerably. Last night's bourbon and the comforts of his back porch often kept him from the seven-mile jog around Lake Auman. He made his excuses, said his farewells and drove home.

SINSLEY CHANGED INTO a spare set of dry clothes he kept in his car, then followed the ambulance over to the hospital morgue, where the body would be kept until it was moved to Raleigh for the state coroner's office to perform an autopsy. At the morgue, he had a closer look.

A pendant hung around the skeletal neck on a tarnished silver chain. The pendant was entirely black and smooth, as if made from polished stone. It was in the shape of a broken-edged triangle, with a blade piercing the triangle from bottom to top. The top of the blade was affixed to the chain by a small ringlet.

Sinsley recognized the emblem, but he could not imagine how someone wearing it would end up buried in the back of the Woodlake Dam. Soldiers like that, from Derwood Flynn's old unit, were hard to kill. He walked back out of the hospital to the parking lot, where his cell phone had reception. Derwood answered on the fourth ring.

"I think you are going to want to be involved in this one, Derwood. Our dead body might be one of yours. He was wearing a Unit pendant."

DERWOOD DROVE TO THE hospital and met Sinsley in the parking lot. The morgue was in the basement. Inside, they waited for the elevator, and when the doors slid open, the two were confronted by a waist-high blocky device on wheels. The strange box had locked drawers on the sides and a blinking light on top. It motored out of the elevator unassisted, but a foot directly in front of Derwood, the rolling box stopped. The light blinked and the front wheels rotated left and right, seeking safe passage. The box motored backward, trying to turn around. Someone had glued a wig to the top of the rolling box and hung a name tag off the front. The nametag read "Bonnie."

"Huh," said Derwood.

"That's Bonnie, the lab robot," said Sinsley. "She collects and delivers samples all over the hospital. Non-urgent samples, I guess. Labor saver."

The elevator doors slid closed until the bumpers hit Bonnie. The robot shook slightly as the doors bounced back open. Derwood, still directly in the path of the robot on wheels, backed out of the way. After a moment the robot camera eye detected a clear path, and the box haltingly started forward and whirred away down the hall and around a corner. By the time he returned his attention to the elevator, the doors had closed and the empty carriage departed for the basement.

A minute later, they exited the next carriage at basement level, and wound toward the morgue. The hospital basement corridors were lit with bare fluorescent bulbs and lined with painted concrete block walls. The paint was chipped and the linoleum floor stained with the grime of years. There were none of the decorative prints or soft pastel colors that adorned the public facing areas on floors above.

As they waited by the locked door of the morgue for a hospital employee to admit them, a plastic cart rumbled into view, pushed by a large man wearing earphones. He continued on, not seeming to notice the men in the hall by the morgue door, but he stopped when the cart was about a foot away from Derwood. His face held a blank smile, and he did not make eye contact. He dropped his hands from the cart and stood vacantly, bobbing his head in time to the music in his ears and silently mouthing unknown words while waiting for his path to clear. His nametag read "Billy."

"Huh," said Derwood.

"That's Billy, one of the hospital janitors," said Sinsley as the two men backed across the hall. "He takes out the garbage. Never complains. Perfect employee, they say."

Once the path was clear, Billy slowly trundled the cart around the corner toward the loading dock.

At last a member of the pathology department arrived wearing a knee-length white coat. She waved her ID badge at the reader next to the door, and the door clicked open. Inside, the morgue was cold. Standing next to the body, Derwood bent and looked hard at the pendant, still draped around the corpse's neck. Sinsley had been careful not to disturb it.

Twenty years before, when he first arrived at the Unit, there was a recently retired operator in another squadron named Fred Akers. Derwood did not have to search for the name. Everyone knew the story. Akers had vanished. Most thought he had gone off his rocker, found himself the most powerful man in some Central American jungle hellhole, seduced by the appeal of power and autonomy. Most thought he had gone into the Heart of Darkness, full Apocalypse Now.

Sergeant Major Akers had been a highly decorated team leader in assault Squadron D, 1st Special Forces Operational Detachment-Delta. He retired after a long career at the sharp end of America's spear. His career was in the days before the Global War on Terror took over the entire military culture of the United States, back when politicians still worried about Central and South American drug lords and communist rebels destabilizing American puppet regimes.

After his military retirement, Akers had moved to Lake Surf at Woodlake and taken a job as a civilian contractor for the Unit. He became a recruiting machine for Woodlake, always talking up the good life on Lake Surf, trying to get Unit guys to move to the neighborhood.

One morning his wife came home from running errands to find him gone. He did not show up for work the next day, and had not been seen or heard from since. Local police investigated, and the Fort Bragg Military Police looked into the case, although they had no jurisdiction. The Combat Support Squadron and the Clandestine Operations Group from the Unit had poked around as much as they dared. Operators from Squadron D had even canvassed the area.

No trace of Akers had ever been found. The army concluded that he had tired of the rhythms of daily life in a gated community. It was too normal, too tranquil, and he fled for the less refined pleasures of Central America.

But now a body had washed out of Woodlake Dam wearing a black triangular Delta Force pendant. Derwood had not known Fred Akers well; he had vanished not long after Derwood arrived at the Unit. But he remembered the man's hopeful predictions about a utopian community full of retired Unit guys, where the party never stopped.

"Well, that's a Unit emblem," said Derwood. "But no self-respecting operator would wear one of those things. Our guys don't advertise where they work. They leave the public glory to the SEALS. Our guys keep a low profile, and keep their mouths shut."

"A retired guy might wear one," said Sinsley.

Derwood looked at him sideways, lips pressed together. He saw doubt in Sinsley's eyes.

"What are you not telling me, Derwood?"

Derwood shook his head, "Nothing, Marty, but you are right about one thing. I do want in."

Chapter 3

DERWOOD TURNED OUT of the hospital and wound around the Pinehurst traffic circle, Moore County's most recognizable landmark. The locals hated it because it was the source of a daily traffic jam. In this rural county nearly every route from north to south or from east to west led through the circle.

His mind wandered as he drove through the quaint downtown of Southern Pines, past the boutique shops, restaurants and bars, and turned toward Fort Bragg. He was coming to track down the retired Unit operator missing for twenty years, vanished without a trace. Could Fred Akers have been in the Woodlake Dam for twenty years? It had to be him.

He drove through the back entrance to Fort Bragg, a lightly travelled crossroads where the landscape turned from manicured horse farms to lonely pine forests, with occasional dirt roads running into the woods and scattered signs warning drivers not to linger at the roadside. Traffic was light, and he drove leisurely. After his doctors came down so hard on him, Derwood never rushed, not anymore.

Fort Bragg, a sprawling installation nestled in the sandhills of North Carolina, covered in endless forests of loblolly pine, was home to nearly 50,000 U.S. military personnel. Large parts of the installation hosted artillery ranges frequently used for training the big guns, and residents in surrounding communities often had to look to the sky to determine whether they were hearing thunder or the thudding guns of the US Army. Signs along the road warned "LIVE RANGE, KEEP OUT."

Ironically, the forests and artillery ranges host at least two endangered species. The conservation lobby went bananas when the red cockaded woodpecker came under the protection of the US Fish and Wildlife service, nearly shutting down training on Bragg until a compromise could be reached. The woodpecker's habitat was protected, but the shells could still rain down on the areas inhabited by the tiny St. Francis Satyr butterfly. Maybe butterflies don't enjoy the same public adoration as woodpeckers. Maybe they need a better public relations team.

As a result of these peculiarities, large swaths of Fort Bragg were virtually untrodden by human feet. He drove through the peaceful outlying areas before arriving several miles later at a fenced compound tucked into the woods.

Derwood pulled up to the security gate and showed his ID. After a thorough inspection of his pickup by a gate guard and his dog, the MP waved him through. He turned left into the Unit compound, and parked near the command building. He went inside and found the office of Command Sergeant Major Lawrence Simpson.

Simpson was a large black man with a gleaming bald pate. His biceps erupted from the rolled-up sleeves of his uniform, and his forearms were the size of tree trunks. Simpson glanced at the newcomer and immediately stood up.

"Derwood Flynn. How the hell are you?" The two men knew each other well, and saw one another often, but the huge yet affable Simpson had a habit of greeting all of his old friends as if they had not seen each other in years. They shook hands, and Derwood sat across from Simpson's desk.

"You look good, Derwood. Rested." Derwood was wearing his customary loose-fitting clothing and leather sandals. Simpson peered at him. "How are things? How are you sleeping?"

Derwood waved him off with a dismissive shrug. "It looks like some local teenagers found Fred Akers."

Simpson's eyes widened as he sat back in his chair.

"Lake Surf flooded, and Woodlake Dam washed out. The Corps of Engineers came in to deal with it. Last night some teenagers were on the dam watching the show, and they found an arm sticking out of the back of the dam."

"No shit?" said Simpson.

"I watched them pull it out. The body was pretty well decomposed, been in the ground a good while. Maybe decades. But there was a pendant around the neck. A Unit emblem. One of those black stone ones you see sometimes. Active-duty guys don't wear them, but some retired guys do."

"And you think it was Fred Akers."

"It has to be. Same neighborhood. The condition of the body suggests the timing might be about right. The pendant." He shook his head. "Too big of a coincidence to be anyone else."

Simpson leaned back and looked at the ceiling, silent for a while before he spoke.

"Do you remember when we first got here?"

Derwood nodded.

"Fred Akers." Simpson shook his head and chuckled. "He had just retired, and he was trying to get everybody to move out to that country club neighborhood he found. He said it would be a nonstop party. He and that wife of his. What was her name?

"Jill."

"Oh, yeah, that's right. She was so hot, she could boil water in her hand. They were gonna turn Woodlake into the home of the beautiful people. He almost had me believing it, too," said Simpson. "Cherise and I looked at property over there. It was beautiful."

"Why didn't you buy in?"

"There was some weird stuff going on over there. I like my marriage, and I wanna keep it."

"What kind of weird stuff?"

"The kind where couples trade partners for the night. Or clothing optional parties, maybe. That kind. Still, sometimes I wish we had bought in. We'd be sitting on a mint."

"Not anymore," said Derwood. "They're draining the lake. All that lakefront property is going to be hit hard."

"Hmm. Maybe so. We thought pretty hard about it. But they had a lot of restrictions in that neighborhood. You can't do this; you can't do that. Fred swore he was going to change all that. Then he vanished. Just gone one day. Everybody looked. Police, MPs, even Unit guys. We figured he'd gotten bored with retirement and gone back in country. He was into some pretty heavy shit down south. We figured he'd suited back up and gone over the border to bring justice to the wicked in El Salvador or some other shithole. I'm sure you've heard the rumors."

Derwood nodded.

"Anyway, once he vanished it took the shine off that neighborhood, you know?"

Derwood nodded again. "I need a look at Akers' old file. Sheriffs are taking the body up to the state crime lab in Raleigh for an autopsy. They'll collect DNA, and it won't take long for them to identify him. If it's him, they're going to come knocking on the wire." Derwood hesitated. "I've started working with the local sheriff, just a bit. You know, to... ahhh," he shrugged uncomfortably, "to get out more, I guess. And since they'll be coming here anyway, better me than them, right?"

Simpson gazed flatly at Derwood. He was one of the few who knew of Derwood's nightmares. As the top enlisted man at the Unit, it was his business to know everything about his soldiers. In the deserts, Derwood had lived in a windowless soundproof storage container. Every evening at sunset, he woke and his team was given a target list. Every night, they went out to hunt and kill violent men. During the days, Derwood slept. His box provided perfect conditions for deep and dreamless sleep, and his nocturnal excursions provided a crystalline sense of purpose. His life was a cycle of sleep and violence, turned on and off like a light switch.

He expected to return to the States unscathed, but IED blasts and roadside bombs continued, and he became fixated on targets his team had not eliminated. His sleep deteriorated, and he dreamt of the horrors inflicted by the targets he had not killed. His doctors told him it was post-traumatic stress disorder, except he was not troubled by the things he had done or the people he had killed. He was kept up nights by the assholes that got away.

The shrinks had prescribed a quiet life, cultivating calmness. The doctors said if he could avoid remembrances, the nightmares would fade in time. Simpson knew he was trying, but the quiet life was not in his nature. Simpson knew these efforts had not helped yet, and he knew of Derwood's mixed results from his ongoing trial of self-medication with Kentucky Straight Bourbon Whiskey. Simpson was the one who suggested that Derwood devote some time to local law enforcement. It would give him a purpose, a mission. A guy like Derwood Flynn needed a target. Simpson was encouraged to see his old friend try a new strategy. Plus, thought Simpson, some assholes need killing.

"Larry," said Derwood, "if that is Fred Akers' body, some retribution might be in order."

"Sure, Derwood," said Simpson. "Sure."

Chapter 4

DERWOOD LEFT SIMPSON'S office and took the elevator two floors down to the personnel office. He did not use the stairs. His knees were fine; he just didn't want to work up a sweat. Doctor's orders.

He sat at a desk in a corner and flipped through the thick file. Akers had been with the Unit since its inception in 1977. The first part of the file read like an unofficial history of the founding and early operational activities of the Unit as well as of modern special forces.

Akers had survived the original selection and quickly found his place as an operator. He was on the Unit's first official mission, the April 1980 debacle known as Operation Eagle Claw, the failed attempt to rescue the U.S. embassy hostages taken by rebel Iranian students in 1979. Derwood shook his head. The institutional embarrassment over the disaster was deeply ingrained in his psyche.

Over the next decade, Akers had seen extensive action in Central America. He had been all over the region, from Guatemala to Panama. He had been an in-country advisor to El Salvador's infamous Atlacatl Battalion, later implicated in some of that country's worst human rights violations. Parts of Akers' service in El Salvador were redacted, even here in the secrecy of his personnel file behind the wire at Fort Bragg.

Derwood knew of El Salvador's bloody history of civil war and insurgency, and he knew of the violent tactics employed by all sides in that conflict. He had never pretended that human rights should trump the need to win. The stakes were too high. But even he grew uneasy thinking of El Salvador's death squads. What the hell had Akers been into down there?

He somehow missed out on the Grenada invasion, but he spent two years on the ground in Nicaragua, and he left only after the Eugene Hasenfus story went public in 1986, eventually revealing the full extent of the U.S. involvement in the Contra–led rebellion against Nicaragua's Sandinista government. The arms-for-hostages deal with Iran and funds diverted to bankroll the Contras in Nicaragua had nearly brought down Ronald Reagan.

Over the next few years, Akers made repeated trips to Central America, but details were spotty. He was involved in the rescue of American hostage and CIA agent Kurt Muse from a prison in Panama City just before the U.S. invasion in December 1989. He was in Colombia in December 1993 when drug lord Pablo Escobar was gunned down, but Derwood found few details about his mission.

Akers continued his frequent trips to the region over the next few years, but his role changed from direct action to more administrative functions, although again details were sketchy. Derwood stopped at one peculiar note of an arrest in the Chiriquí Province of Panama. Akers was involved in a violent incident at an alleged brothel, but the charges were later dropped because no witnesses could be found.

Akers' military career eventually wound down towards retirement, and he left active duty when he was forty-five years old. The remainder of the file summarized the investigation into his disappearance. He always seemed to have money, and as with many former operators, there was no shortage of fat civilian job offers. He took a lucrative offer as a contractor, and he had maintained his close ties with the Unit until his sudden disappearance in the last week in May two decades before.

His last known whereabouts had been his home in Woodlake on that Tuesday morning. His wife left that morning to take the kids to school and run errands. She said Akers planned to spend the day building a dock in the backyard. It was his top priority, and he was trying to get it done before the end of summer. She did not know of any enemies or of anyone who might want to cause him harm. She did not know where he might have gone. She had met a few of his relatives, but she said he was not close to his family. She said his real family was the guys in the Unit. She knew little of his military service, but she knew a few of his close friends from the Unit.

The police interviewed the neighbors as well. No one knew anything. They went through Akers' financial receipts and pulled his phone records. A few of the numbers had been redacted from the file, but the lead detective had not identified the redacted numbers anyway. Several operators from the Unit had gone out to canvas the neighborhood, walking all over the area looking for clues and knocking on doors. They found nothing.

The case hit a dead end. After a few weeks there were no leads, and after a few months it fizzled. The file concluded with pure speculation. The investigators thought he had gone back to Central America, where he had developed many contacts over the years, and where he could easily blend in if he chose. Opinion was divided over whether he bought his own private island to live like an expatriate king, or whether he became operational, pursuing ends known only to himself. Nobody believed Fred Akers had been taken against his will or put in the ground by someone with a grudge.

Derwood sat back and closed the file. Would Akers leave his wife and two young children without a word, after loudly talking up his new neighborhood and trying to get a bunch of friends and colleagues to move there? Derwood did not buy it. Judging by Akers' career, any number of people might want him dead, but they would all be a continent away, separated from the tranquility of Woodlake by multiple international borders.

Derwood returned the file and drove back toward his home in Seven Lakes. He had been at Fort Bragg longer than he expected, and it was early evening by the time he got home. He sent a text message to Lizzy and set the charcoal alight in the grill on his back porch. Charcoal was good for slowing down the day, and he loved the smell. It reminded him of long summer evenings.

He looked in the liquor cabinet at the half empty bottle. As he reached for it, he paused. Lizzy would be here soon, and she would not be pleased. Maybe she was right. Maybe he was drinking too much. But a quick one would not hurt.

Who was he kidding? Of course he was drinking too much. But her admonitions were having an effect. He was cutting back. He had been sleeping a little better lately, keeping things better under control. He put the bottle back in the cabinet just as he heard her at the front door.

"Hi, Dad! You won't believe it! You know how Woodlake Dam is washing out and all that? You won't even believe what they found!" She tossed her bags on the couch as she went through the living room toward the porch. Derwood was amazed at the accessories required of the modern high-schooler. She had a bookbag stuffed full and straining at the zipper. It must weigh thirty pounds. She had a second bag for her band gear and various other accoutrements.

"What happened to lockers?" he asked.

"Huh?" She looked confused.

"Lockers. Where you put your books and stuff overnight."

She scoffed. "Nobody uses lockers, Dad."

"When I was a kid—" he started, but stopped when Lizzy threw back her head in exasperation.

"Oh my god! Here we go with the geezer stories! 'Back in my day," she mocked with a warbling voice. "Get with the program, old man! You will never believe what they found at Woodlake! Mike told Jen that Sophie heard that Laura and Heather found..."

"...a dead body!" they shouted in unison.

"You know already?"

"I know things, kid," he said.

"The new job. Right. Of course you know. Crazy, right? I mean, right here in Moore County! Murder most foul! Something is rotten in the state of North Carolina!

"Well..." she paused expectantly. "Tell me all about it!"

He did, over supper on the back porch in the fading light.

"Can I help?" she asked. "You know how we've been trying to spend more time together?"

"And you think bonding over a murder investigation is quality time, huh?"

"Well, maybe I want to be a cop when I grow up."

"Uhh ... I don't think so, Lizzy. Stick with band for now." He paused, then prompted, "This morning you said you might need some dad advice."

"Yeah," she said, drawing the word out and putting her head down, but she did not say more. He waited.

Finally she spoke. "How old were you when you and mom met?"

"Lemme see." Thinking out loud, he said, "I think I was twenty-eight. Your mother was younger. Maybe twenty-five?"

"So you were not each other's first, you know, uh, experience?"

She had his full attention. "Are you talking about sex, Lizzy?"

"Ummm, maybe," she said, avoiding eye contact.

"No, we were not each other's first experience."

"How old were you when, you know, you did it the first time?" she asked.

He sighed. Maybe he should have had a stiffener of bourbon, after all.

"Sixteen," he said, and waited.

After a bit she asked, "Did, uh, did anything ever go wrong?"

"I'm not sure what you mean, darling."

Her eyes were very moist. "Dad, I think I'm pregnant." A sob escaped her then, and tears spilled onto her cheeks.

He did not know what to say, so he said nothing. As she sobbed, he reached for her and hugged her tightly. He stroked her hair gently and after a while whispered, "Shhhh. It's gonna be alright. Shhhh. I've got you, sweetheart." She cried into his shoulder.

After a while, her sobbing eased. She went inside to clean herself up, and while she was in the powder room, the doorbell rang. Derwood looked through the peephole before answering and saw Lizzy's mother outside, his ex-wife. He could see her clenched jaw, narrowed eyes, and tight face – all but steam coming out of her ears.

He leaned back against the wall and shut his eyes. He swallowed dryly. He should have had the bourbon.

Kate pressed the doorbell again. Derwood hurried into the kitchen and opened the liquor cabinet and helped himself to a hearty swig, before opening the front door. By the time he did, Kate stood just outside with crossed arms, tapping her foot, lips clenched.

"You know I could hear you come up to the door and walk away," she said.

"Hi, Kate," he said.

"Let me talk to Lizzy."

The powder room door opened in room behind Derwood, and Lizzy spilled out, all traces of her earlier breakdown washed down the sink. She approached the door and stood just behind Derwood. When she recognized her mother standing in the doorway, she looked surprised.

"Oh! Mom! Hi. Uh, what are you doing here?" she said.

"Looking for you. You shouldn't be here. Time to come home."

"But mom," Lizzy started before Kate cut her off.

"Don't you 'but mom' me! We talked about this! I told you to stay away from him! Now get in your car! I'll follow you home!"

"Aaaaaaaggggggggghhhhhhh," Lizzy whined. "Fine!" She stomped back in the house to get her things.

"And you!" said Kate, jabbing Derwood in the chest with her forefinger. "Stay away from my daughter!"

He put his hands up and took a step back. "She's my daughter, too, Kate," he said.

"That didn't seem to matter to you back when she was just a baby."

"That's not how it was, and you know it, Kate. You did the leaving, not me. You took her."

Kate took a deep breath and let it out in a huff. She stared at Derwood's face and eyes for a moment.

"You had no right to do what you did. Nobody was getting hurt. Not until you stepped in and did your goddam Rambo impression."

"People were getting hurt. I was getting hurt. Lizzy would have gotten hurt, eventually."

"Yeah, well," said Kate, "she got hurt anyway, didn't she?"

"Who got hurt?" said Lizzy as she walked into the foyer carrying her heavy school bags, less annoyed than only moments before. She looked from her mother to her father and back again. They continued to glare at each other, ignoring her, but she seemed oblivious to the tension in the air.

"Who got hurt?" Lizzy said again.

Derwood and Kate both turned to stare at her. Neither looked happy.

"What?" said Lizzy.

"Get in the car. We're leaving," said Kate.

Lizzy looked at her father. "Go with your mother, sweetheart," he said. "Go home. I'll talk to you soon."

"No," said Kate, "you won't." She turned to Lizzy. "I told you to stay away from him. You don't know him like I do. He's not what he seems. He's dangerous."

Now Derwood and Lizzy looked at one another for a moment. Finally, he nodded and with a tilt of his head said, "Go home."

Later after she left, he remembered the bourbon. Facing tomorrow morning with a clear head was worth considering, but he knew that he would not feel clear in the morning no matter what he did tonight. With enough bourbon, he might not get restful sleep, but at least he would not dream.

And what about Lizzy? He did not see what he could do about her, except just be a shoulder to cry on, someone to talk to. His shirt was still damp from her tears. Kate was a problem. They had ignored each other for years, but now with Lizzy and Derwood spending time together, Kate was getting increasingly ramped up. She still saw herself as a victim; she had never been able to acknowledge her own complicity in their breakup years ago, and on the rare occasions they saw each other these days, she continued to blame him. When he reflected on the past, he thought maybe he had overreacted. But he had been young then, back when he was special and the world was his. He had mellowed since those days.

He had not really promised Lizzy he would not drink, had he? He filled his glass. Outside on the porch the night grew cooler, but the bourbon kept him warm. Eventually he toppled off to bed. The bourbon did its work; he did not dream.

Chapter 5

THE NEXT MORNING DERWOOD went out on his back porch with a steaming cup of coffee. The morning was clear and cool, with a touch of humidity that promised a beautiful day. As he sat down to read the news his cell phone vibrated and blasted forth the opening E-flat minor chords from Richard Wagner's opera *Götterdämmerung*. He liked the ringtone. He'd started listening to more classical music lately in an effort to find serenity. Doctor's orders.

The caller ID showed Martin Sinsley. "It's pretty early, Marty," said Derwood.

"Yeah, well, it feels pretty late on my end. I've been up all night going through old files. I don't know the last time anybody was in this basement, but I should have worn a hazmat suit, and I still need a shower. Dust everywhere. Bugs, too. Spiders. I hate spiders, but I found some interesting stuff. Might have a line on our corpse. Have you ever heard of a man named Fred Akers?"

"Ah, hell, I was afraid you'd say that," said Derwood. "Yeah, I've heard of him. Met him, actually, must be twenty years ago."

"Well, well. Look who has been keeping secrets. You probably know the story better than I do. What else are you not telling me, Derwood?"

"Cut me some slack, Marty. It's still early. I went out to the Unit yesterday and did a little digging. Akers was into some pretty bleak stuff in the eighties." Derwood outlined what he had uncovered in the files at Fort Bragg the day before, careful to gloss over the classified elements.

"When I met him, he'd just retired. He'd been stateside for a few years by then. I don't know exactly what he'd been doing in the jungle. He was just a newly retired guy interested in making a life for himself after the military."

"You think he is our guy?" asked Sinsley.

"It would be a big coincidence if he wasn't," said Derwood. "How about you? What did you find?"

"I read through the original investigation," Marty said. "There was no physical evidence. None of the neighbors knew anything. His wife was the last one to see Akers the morning he disappeared. She said he'd been acting normally, nothing unusual. No old contacts reaching out, no recent travel. He planned to spend the day working in the back yard. She was pretty insistent that the investigators talk to the Woodlake Board of Directors. Apparently, there was some big controversy about lake use brewing in the community at that time. Fred was gunning for a spot on the board of directors. His wife thought his vote might be important, like a tiebreaker. She said people in the community were divided, and some were pretty angry."

None of that was mentioned in the file Derwood had seen yesterday.

"What was the issue?"

Derwood heard a rustle through the phone as Marty flipped a page in the file. "It was lake use. One faction wanted to open the lake for boating and the other didn't. Like power boating. Skiing and stuff."

"Yeah, so?" asked Derwood.

"Exactly. It doesn't seem like a big deal, but tensions were pretty high about it. His wife thought it was important. The investigators talked to everyone they could. It turned out to be your typical neighborhood squabble, a real first-world problem. A bunch of people wanted to open Lake Surf to motorboating and skiing and stuff, but a vocal group of longtime residents wanted to preserve the lake just the way it was, without gasoline-powered boats. They wanted to keep it for non-powered boats like sailboats or kayaks, and battery-powered boats for cruising around the lake."

Derwood knew without asking which side of that issue Fred Akers would have been on. Any Unit guy, really. Except him. These days he was striving for a peaceful lake experience. Doctor's orders.

"So, Akers was running for the Board of Directors, and his vote might have been decisive in opening the lake up to motorboats?"

"Yup," said Sinsley.

"Huh. Doesn't seem like a very good motive for murder, does it?"

"Have you ever met a sailor?" asked Sinsley.

Derwood thought about the Lake Auman Sailing Club. He thought about how they reacted when a surfboat put a huge wave through their Saturday morning regatta.

"I see your point," he said.

"The problem I have is, it's been twenty years. The case is ice cold, and we just don't have the manpower to dedicate to these cold cases. No one is going to care too much about a vanished former military operator, missing for twenty years. I'm the only investigator this case is going to get, and I'm only going to get a couple of days before the sheriff puts me on something with higher priority. Here's where you come in, Derwood. Maybe you can see if any of these folks are still around. You know, talk to them, see what you can find out."

"I suppose I could do that."

"Listen, I'll text you the list of witnesses from the case file. Why don't you go talk to them, and let me know what you find out?"

"What are you going to do?" asked Derwood.

"The case is too cold. The Sheriff is only giving me a couple of days before she reassigns me. Right now, they're still digging up the dam. I'm calling a few of the state crime scene folks in to help. I'm just going to keep snooping around, see what turns up."

"You got a hunch?"

"Call it what you want. You never know what you might find unless you look."

The file gave Derwood a list of names to track down, topped by Jill Akers, Fred Akers' wife. It was about a half hour drive. On the way he texted Lizzy.

Dinner tonight?

Her reply came back as he pulled in to Jill Akers' house.

Probably. Play it by ear. Heart emoji. It made him smile.

The house was a tidy gray on white cape cod with a loop driveway and no garage. The yard was well shaded by tall pines and covered in pine straw. Derwood approved. His idea of effective landscaping meant little to no maintenance.

When he rang the bell, a dog immediately began barking inside the house. Peeking through glass on the door, Derwood was relieved to see an aged golden retriever bounce into the room. Harmless, he thought. Behind the dog came a woman wearing yoga pants and a formless yellow sweatshirt with 'APP STATE' stenciled across the front. She stopped before answering the door, and Derwood could see her silhouette through the door as she paused to glance at her reflection in a wall mirror. Her sandy blond hair was swept into a ponytail, and she had no need for makeup. She wore it anyway. He adopted his most congenial face, with a friendly smile and open body posture.

"Good morning. I'm Deputy Derwood Flynn with the Sheriff's Office." He flashed his shiny new badge, but the introduction felt strange on his tongue, like a lie. "I am looking for Jill Akers. She used to live here."

"What is this about?" asked the woman, curiosity replaced with guarded eyes.

"I'd like to ask Mrs. Akers a few questions about some things that happened a long time ago. Shouldn't take too long."

"It's him, isn't it?" she asked. She meant the body in the dam. It was a sensational story for this sleepy part of rural North Carolina. Everyone was talking about it.

He nodded. "We think so."

"I suppose you'd better come in. I was headed to the gym, but that can wait." She opened the door and Derwood followed her into a large open room, where she gestured for him to have a seat at the dining table.

She offered him refreshment and retreated to the kitchen for a moment. He saw a bookcase with a framed picture of the woman and a man he recognized. They were standing on a dock overlooking a lake, wearing bathing suits. She was much younger in the photo, but it was undeniably the same woman. Simpson had been right. The bikini clad woman in the photo could have been a model. The man was Fred Akers. There were other photos on the bookcase also. Pictures of her with another man, and with children.

Jill returned, and he noticed she had pulled off the sweatshirt. The yoga pants were now fully exposed, topped by a form fitting tank top that left little to the imagination. She had not lost much since the photo on the shelf, and she wanted him to notice. Derwood tried not to stare as she handed him a cup of coffee.

"That is the only picture of Freddy I keep out. It was taken just before he went missing. It was Memorial Day weekend. We had some friends over that day." She smiled. "The picture reminds me of him."

"Who are they?" asked Derwood, pointing to the other photos.

"That is my family. My husband Bob, our kids. We met a few years after Freddy..." She paused, not knowing quite what to say.

"Died," suggested Derwood quietly.

"Maybe so. I suppose so. But you never really know, do you." She turned from the bookcase and walked to the table.

"People going missing is just so cruel. You don't know whether to be sad or hopeful. You tell yourself all kinds of stories, but as time passes and nothing happens?" She shrugged. "You just have to move on. But you never really know. I wonder every single morning, even now, will this be the day Freddy comes home?"

Her words were smooth, rehearsed, as if she had been through this before.

"I'm sorry," Derwood said.

She forcibly brightened her affect and dabbed her eyes. Derwood had not noticed any tears.

"Well, it was a long time ago. Did you know they told me he ran off? They said he went back to Nicaragua or Panama. Or maybe Costa Rica." She shook her head. "They were so sure, but they couldn't even tell me which country."

"What do you think happened to him?" asked Derwood.

"I think he was killed." She spoke slowly, as though dragging up painful memories. "For a long time, we waited while the police searched. Some guys from the army came around too, but nobody ever found anything. It was a bad time."

Derwood waited for her to continue.

"Years later, I met my husband Bob." She scoffed. "I call him my husband, but he's not, not really. Legally I'm still married to Fred, since he's never been declared officially dead. How screwed up is that?"

Derwood didn't say anything. He took a sip of coffee. Simpson had mentioned permissive practices in Woodlake back in the day. Derwood knew something about that. When he was a younger man, before Lizzy was born, he had seen couples swap partners while still married. It was a marriage killer, as he knew firsthand.

"Where did you meet Bob?"

"At the gym. He is a personal trainer."

"Ah. And you met after Fred died?"

She glanced away. "Yeah. Well, I think so. It's been a long time. We might have seen each other around before, but we did not get together until years later."

"Uh huh," said Derwood.

She fidgeted in her seat before changing the subject.

"He disappeared on a Tuesday. The day after Memorial Day." She gestured to the picture on the shelf. "It was near the end of school. Everyone was gearing up for summer. Freddy had the day off. It was a beautiful morning, the kind you get around here in spring, after the pollen is gone and everything feels hopeful and new. I took Sam and Micki to school, and stopped by the grocery store on the way home. When I got back, Freddy was gone. That's it."

"Was he acting normally that morning? The week before? Do you remember anything different?"

"It's been twenty years. I told the police everything I knew at the time."

"Maybe he really did just leave," said Derwood. "Go back south. Some of the things soldiers do can leave a mark." Derwood paused.

"No." She shook her head quickly. "If he were leaving, Fred would not have left his tools laying out in the yard. He was a stickler for taking care of his equipment. He always said you had to keep your tools clean and ready. It's just not like him to leave them laying out."

Derwood thought of the old rifleman's creed: "I will keep my rifle clean and ready." It had not been a big part of his military training, but Akers had come along a generation before, and he had probably learned it in basic training. As a Unit operator, he would have been meticulous in taking care of his equipment.

"He loved his family. He loved me. He loved his children." Her voice held no doubt, but her eyes were less convicted. She wanted it to be true, he thought. She wanted him to believe it, too.

"I knew him, you know," said Derwood.

Jill looked surprised.

"He was older, but yeah, I knew him. The reason I asked when you met Bob is because, well..." He paused for a sip of coffee. "This is a little awkward. Back then, there was some, uh, infidelity."

A flash of surprise lit her face, but then she leaned back onto the couch with a smile. She crossed her arms beneath her breasts. The gesture drew attention to her already considerable decolletage. Derwood did not glance down, but maintained eye contact. Discipline mattered.

"So you know about that. Well. That Unit out there at Fort Bragg, it's made up of a bunch of psychos. They want loyalty to the Unit above all. They want guys who will 'do whatever is necessary.'" She made a sarcastic show of air quotes.

"When we would get together with the other guys and their wives or girlfriends, it felt like a big family. You were either in or out. Once you were in, there was this huge separation between you and everybody on the outside. You were special."

Derwood nodded. He had lived it.

"But that was an illusion. At least it was for the wives. The real relationships were among the men. The wives were..." She waved her hands looking for the right phrase. "Expendable. Interchangeable. I don't know. We were at all the social events, barbecues and parties and stuff. But there were always inside jokes you didn't get, and there were always quiet conversations off to the side that you weren't part of. There was a lot of stuff the guys couldn't talk about. And they could be cold."

Now it was her turn to pause, staring into space. After a moment, she turned back to stare into his eyes. She leaned forward.

"Infidelity? Yeah, there was infidelity. We did what we had to do to belong. Have you ever been expendable?"

Derwood had been a soldier; soldiers were expendable. He had also been married to Kate, but he kept his mouth shut.

"Well, that's what we wives were. Expendable. Interchangeable."

"Maybe you didn't like that." Derwood gestured to the photo on the shelf. "Maybe you went to the gym and got your personal trainer to do something about it. Bob there looks strong. Maybe you got Bob to teach Fred a lesson."

Her gaze was intense, full of some emotion Derwood could not identify, but then she suddenly barked a laugh and sat back again, sinking into the cushions.

"You're funny. And you're wrong. Bob wouldn't hurt a fly. Plus, what makes you think I didn't like it?" She looked him up and down like a spider contemplating a fly.

"No, it wasn't the swinging. Turned out, that was the best part. It was neighborhood politics. Fred had this idea that Lake Surf would be like a playground for military families. He wanted to get as many of the old Unit guys out here as he could. But there were problems from the start. Those guys weren't interested in gardening or pinochle. They wanted action and excitement. That meant change in this community. More people coming in; people speeding around the perimeter road; loud parties; people floating on tubes on the lake drinking beer; motorboats; wakeboards; lake surfing. Not your peaceful lake experience anymore. And our ideas about, uh, you know," she gestured as she searched for words, "relationships did not necessarily fit here.

"Fred decided to run for the Board of directors. Everybody knew his vote would be decisive between the older crowd and the younger crowd. The status quo crowd and the change crowd. But the old guard did not want change."

She put her palms on the table and looked Derwood square in the eye again, full of confidence. "There was a big vote coming up. Open the lake to gas powered boats, or keep them out. Change, or status quo. That vote would've opened the lake. Four-three, in favor.

"That's what happened. Somebody killed my husband, to stop that vote." She finally fell silent, but continued to stare hard at Derwood.

Her voice and eyes were unified in conviction. She wanted him to believe. He watched her for a long moment, and finally shrugged.

"Who?" he asked.

"I would ask Deloris Hitchcock," said Jill.

The name was in the old file. She was a member of the board of directors when Fred disappeared. She had been questioned, like all the board members.

"Why her?" asked Derwood.

"She's been here forever. She must be seventy now. She was on the board for forty years, if you can believe that. She knows everything that's ever happened behind these gates. She was on the board when Freddy vanished. Plus, she knew Fred." Her eyes flashed with hidden anger, only for a moment, then it was gone again, buried in her past hurt and grief.

"How would she have voted?"

"Oh, she hates change. She's stuck in the past. I guess when you're her age, the past is all you've got."

Chapter 6

THE DRIVE TO THE HITCHCOCK home offered glimpses of Lake Surf. The Corps of Engineers was still at work on the dam, draining the lake. All along the shore, receding water left a mud flat. The lake had already retreated beyond the ends of the docks. Birds waded and hunted in puddles left behind. Lake Surf had always been shallow, not much more than fifteen feet at its deepest, but the rectangular lake was slowly turning into a large mud puddle surrounded by expensive homes. Derwood found it sad that Fred Akers' dream had come to this.

Castleberry Drive split a thin half mile long peninsula sticking out from the center of the western shore into the middle of the lake. The peninsula was narrow, with houses on either side of the road, and the lake just beyond in both directions. He came to a large house at the very end of the peninsula, straight off the end of a cul-de-sac.

The house was a two-story brick contemporary design, clean and attractive but not ostentatious. Before the storm had come through, the location would have been glorious. Now, with the shrinking lake and the recent macabre discovery in the dam, it felt a little desperate, like dreams destroyed by death and weather. He rang the bell.

An ageless woman opened the door. Long dark greying hair framed a thin face. Faint wrinkles tightened by high cheekbones pointed to thin lips, a perfect nose and clear deep eyes. She wore light makeup. Gold spangled earrings draped from still shapely ears towards a pale-yellow smock dotted with white flowers that hung loosely to her knees, a young woman's dress. The only tell was the loose and mottled skin of her neck.

"May I help you?" she asked with a gentle drawl.

"My name is Sheriff's Deputy Derwood Flynn, and I am looking for Deloris Hitchcock." He showed his ID. The title rolled more easily off his tongue this time.

"An unusual name. I have not met a Derwood since I was a child," she said.

"My father liked the name. He was old fashioned." He had learned to ignore comments about his name.

"Well. I am Deloris Hitchcock." She looked Derwood up and down, her face remaining smooth and tight. "Perhaps you should come in."

Derwood followed her through a foyer into a large room opening to expansive views of the lake in the background. In the distance, the earth moving equipment rumbled over the dam.

"Great view," he said.

"It used to be," she said. "Of course, you will have heard about what is happening here." She dropped her terminal 'r's when she spoke, a tidewater accent. "Those people from the government are destroying the dam, draining the lake, and digging up dead men." She spoke with disdain. "But we will put this nastiness behind us. We will restore the lake, put things back in order. Now, Mr. Flynn, what could you possibly want with an old woman like me?"

"I'm here to talk about the body in the dam."

"I see," said Deloris. "Before we start, allow me to offer you some tea. William! William!" she called out. "Tea for our guest."

Into the room came a large man. Not just tall, although he was tall. Several inches over six feet, Derwood thought. But he was broad also. He must have weighed over three hundred pounds. He wore loose-fitting clothing, so it was impossible discern whether his bulk was muscle or flab. He had dark hair cut close to the scalp in a uniform length, and a dark unkempt beard obscured the lower half of his round face. His eyes were set close together above fleshy cheeks. His face was slack, the affect flat. Derwood felt sure he had seen the man somewhere before, but he could not place him.

"Yes, Mother," he said as he passed through into the kitchen.

"William is my son, a great comfort to me," said Deloris.

Derwood had just had coffee at Jill Akers' house. He did not want tea. He did not care for it, particularly in the South, where tea was usually served so sweet that it could rot your teeth in minutes. It was no wonder there was a dentist on every corner in affluent southern communities. The less well-off just had to make do with tooth decay, because nobody could do without sweet tea.

When he had been in the deserts, conversations over tea with village elders had been important events, trading donkeys and money for information and goodwill. Smiles and lies all around. He did not refuse the tea. It gave him a good reason to settle in on the couch and stay awhile, and the ritual of tea might make the old woman more talkative.

After a few minutes, William returned with a teapot on a serving tray and two cups. He set the tray down and left. He did not make eye contact, nor did he speak, even when Derwood offered thanks. He moved quietly back down the hall whence he had come.

"William is a quiet boy," Deloris said. "Ever since he was a child. He doesn't take to strangers, but he has a good heart. He takes care of his mother, and an old lady cannot ask for more." She heaped spoons full of sugar into the empty cup before pouring in the hot liquid. "But you are here to talk about the body in the dam. I don't know what I can possibly tell you, but please, proceed."

"We think it's Fred Akers," said Derwood.

"I see," said Deloris.

"Do you remember him?"

"Yes, of course I remember him. A young hothead." She smiled and set down the tea. "Younger than me, anyway. I thought he ran off. That's what the police said. Some men do, you know."

"Some," agreed Derwood. "But it turns out Fred Akers never left Woodlake after all. You were on the Board of Directors when he disappeared."

"Yes."

"Do you know of anyone that wanted to harm him?"

"Probably half the community," she chuckled. "At least they wanted to block him from the board, but I do not know of anyone who wanted him dead," she said.

"Did you have a relationship with him?"

She smiled. "I don't know whether to be flattered or outraged, Mr. Flynn. The man was twenty years younger than I was at that time."

"Not all relationships are, uh, intimate."

"That's true. And you want to know whether I knew Fred Akers, and if so, in what capacity. I see."

Derwood waited.

"Yes, I knew him. I knew his wife, too, poor woman." She took a long sip of tea. "He was not what he seemed." She set her cup down on the table, content to sit quietly looking at Derwood.

After a moment, he said, "What do you mean?"

Deloris looked down and sighed and finally said, "I guess it cannot do any harm now. The man has been gone twenty years." She looked up again. "Fred and Jill Akers were what they call swingers. Do you know the term?"

"Wife-swapping?" said Derwood.

"That's what they called it when I was a baby. Maybe that is a politically incorrect term these days, but yes. Wife swapping. Jill was not interested in the lifestyle at first, but Fred pushed and pushed until she agreed. Then, she took to it like a fish to water. Of course, those things never end well. How she hated him after that."

"Huh," said Derwood, and after a moment, "Did you have a relationship with him?"

"Persistent, are you? Mr. Flynn, I never kiss and tell."

He stood and walked to the large picture window and stood next to a baby grand piano. The piano was positioned such that the pianist would have a broad lake view while playing, but the player's back would be to the room and any potential audience. Odd, he thought. On the music rack above the keyboard rested several pages of a complex piano score. The score was incomplete, apparently a work in progress. The symbols were written in pencil on prelined staff paper, although there were few eraser marks or strike-throughs. A yellow wooden pencil lay with the score on the rack.

Deloris ghosted up behind him and spoke. He had not heard her approach.

"Do you play, Mr. Flynn?"

"No, not piano. This looks like a tough piece. Are you composing?"

"Not me. My son. He has a talent. He is quite musical. He transcribes these pieces by ear. It is remarkable, really, and it gives him purpose, his raison d'être. But he does not compose."

Just then Derwood's cell phone sounded in his pocket, the bold E-flat minor from the tiny speaker warbling thinly into the room. As soon as she heard the horns blaring from his pocket, Deloris' eyes widened in surprise. He took the phone out to answer the call as the old woman stared at the device and backed away. He turned to the window and put the phone to his ear.

"Hey, Marty." He listened for a moment. "Okay. Let me call you back in a minute."

When he disconnected the call, he saw that Deloris was near the entrance to the hallway, whispering quietly to the large man who had brought the tea. He was agitated, staring at Derwood, the vacant expression replaced by an inexplicable urgency. She took his hand and whispered quietly, and the large man abruptly relaxed, turned, and disappeared back down the hall. He did not speak. Deloris turned back to him.

"I think you'd better go now, Mr. Flynn. And please, excuse us. My son is feeling unwell, and he needs to work." She gestured to the piano. "It helps him to focus and clear his mind." She led him to the door and wished him good afternoon.

No sooner had he stepped on the porch than the door shut solidly behind him. At that moment, an image flashed into his mind of an awkward lab robot, then a large man pushing a cart near the hospital morgue. Before he could knock and ask Deloris if her son worked at the hospital, the deadbolt lock clicked firmly into place.

He had not paid enough attention to William, but the body size and shape were right. He could have been the same man he had encountered in the hospital, Billy, the perfect employee, buried in his headphones and smiling vacantly.

William did not seem to like Derwood's ringtone. The man liked music, that was clear. Maybe the unscheduled and unsolicited interruption of the cell phone trilling derailed the music in his head. Or maybe he just did not like Wagner. A lot of people didn't.

Chapter 7

AS THE MAN IN THE PICKUP pulled out of the driveway, Brandi Hitchcock glided into the living room. High cheekbones and clear eyes, her reflection in the large picture windows overlooking the lake was an image of the older woman.

"Who was that, Mother?" she asked.

"He said his name was Derwood Flynn."

"What did he want?"

A hollow bell sounded, ringing dully throughout the house.

"Everything in its proper time, dear. Wash up now."

"Yes, Mother." The young woman retreated.

Just because a hurricane had torn through the community and destroyed the dam holding back her beloved Lake Surf was no reason to foster disorder. Deloris Hitchcock served meals precisely at the same time every day. She thrived on routine. At ten minutes before meals, the bell gave everyone fair warning that service would begin soon. There was no last-minute washing of hands or rushed scramble for a glass of water. It had been that way for as long as the children could remember.

They were not children now, of course. William was in his thirties, and his younger sister Brandi in her twenties. But she still considered them children. They gathered at Deloris' house at least weekly, Brandi from her apartment in Cary about an hour away, and William from his room down the hall.

Today promised to be a good day; her children were home. Brandi had come for the weekend and had Monday off from her job as a pharmacist at the hospital in the city, and William lived with her still.

He'd had trouble holding a steady job when he was younger. His listless personality around strangers and his taciturn nature turned away customers and coworkers, and he did not last. Deloris had worked with him, though. As part of their program, she encouraged him to wear headphones while he worked. Something about music soothed him and kept him calm. Music had been the key to most of the successes in his life. Once he realized he could keep his music with him wherever he went, he was able to shut out the distractions of the world around him and concentrate on the rhythms, notes and scales that echoed in his mind. Things outside the home were better for him after that. He could push a broom or empty a trashcan in peace, and some jobs were a perfect fit.

Deloris opened the conversation as always.

"William, tell us about your plans for the day. And sit up straight."

The large man repositioned himself in his chair, brought his shoulders up from a habitual slump.

"Yes, Mother," he said. He spoke slowly, avoiding eye contact. "I am exploring La Campanella. I started it last week, but tonight I will really begin."

Deloris approved. It had taken years to cultivate goal-setting and task dedication in the boy. When she found him, he languished in the foster care system and had difficulty with social interactions, speech and nonverbal communication, and even his play was stilted and repetitive. People in the foster care system thought him stupid and slow, but Deloris suspected there was a powerful mind behind the curtain of awkwardness. She chose him because his apparent lack of social skill reduced the likelihood that he had been subject to excessive outside influence in his early childhood, and he represented as close to a blank slate as possible given that he was already six years old when she found him.

Deloris tried many ways to reach the boy, and she began to lose hope. At the birth of her own natural child, she considered discarding him to focus her efforts entirely upon her infant daughter. But one day while working with the girl she played a piece of music, a Wagnerian opera. The baby girl did not seem to notice, but the effect on William was electrifying. The music grabbed his attention and brought him into sharp focus. He hummed the piece obsessively for days after. He sat at the piano and picked out notes. Before long, he was able to recreate his own elementary version of the complex piece. The music unlocked something within him, and Deloris had found the key to access his inner life. Deloris began his conditioning, and William began to blossom.

"That's good, son. But what about work? Do you work today?"

"Yes, I work today, Mother. Right after breakfast. But tonight, I will do what matters. I expect to have it ready for you next week."

"Do you expect any difficulties?" asked Deloris.

"La Campanella" was a notoriously difficult piano piece, and learning it was a painstaking task. She had tried to cultivate creativity in the boy, to somehow get him to produce original work, but so far he had only succeeded in mimicry, regurgitating the work of others. Even that was quite an accomplishment, Deloris knew. He had a rare gift.

"No, Mother," he said. "It will take some time, though."

"And work? Any difficulties there?"

"No, Mother. I like it. It lets me concentrate."

"Thank you, William." Deloris turned her unblinking eyes towards her daughter. "And you, darling? Tell us about your plans."

Brandi paused to line up her silverware and straighten her napkin, all right angles and triangles. She took a sip of water, then refilled the glass from the pitcher on the table. A quick glance reassured her that all three glasses were filled to the same level. Symmetry mattered.

She tapped her fingers lightly to emphasize each word, and she spoke slowly. "I have no specific plans today. I will drive to my apartment. I work at the hospital tomorrow."

Deloris frowned. The girl was doing it again, counting her words. Even, never odd. She had been obsessed with patterns since childhood. Deloris approved of order and regularity, but her daughter carried it too far. A habit Deloris had never been able to train out of her. She suppressed her irritation.

"Other than work, do you have anything lined up for the week?"

"No, Mother. Nothing yet," Brandi said more quickly than before, her fingers tapping time on the table. She smiled. That last bit was easy. "Just work," she added with delight.

Now William rolled his eyes and began to fidget at the table. Mother was not the only one who tired of his sister's idiosyncrasies. Deloris pinned him with her gaze. "Be still, son."

"I don't like it when she talks like that, Mother."

"I know you don't, son, but it is her turn to speak. Everything in its turn, dear."

Brandi said nothing, but the press of her lips conveyed displeasure at the interruption.

"But it makes me angry, Mother," said William.

Brandi glared at William with a poison smile. "Play the Wagner, Mother," she said.

William's eyes grew wide, but Mother intervened.

"That is not necessary, my darlings," said Deloris. "Let us take a little time out, calm ourselves. We will eat in silence for a few minutes."

The children obeyed. They had always had a complicated relationship. Despite the differences in age, they sometimes acted like best friends. William lost his awkwardness and isolation around his sister, and she seemed to relax around him, too. But at other times they treated one another with disdain.

Once she judged the children had regained emotional control, Deloris asked, "Have you heard the news today? A body washed out of the dam yesterday."

Brandi smiled and clapped four times. "How exciting! How frightful! A body!"

Once she got going, the symmetry was easier for her, and other people barely noticed. Except her family. They always knew.

"Whose body? Do we know whose dead body it is? Do you, dear brother?"

"How would I know?" he said. "I don't follow the news."

"The body has not been identified," said Deloris. "That man was here asking about it. He thought it might be a man named Fred Akers."

"Did you know him?" asked Brandi.

"I knew him once, long ago. He has been missing a long time."

Memory is a funny thing, Deloris thought. With enough effort, you could cloud memory and nightmare, until it was impossible to tell what was real anymore. She had worked hard for years to bury the past. And still somebody had sent the man to her.

Things in Woodlake had been quiet and stable for a long time, but the hurricane had changed that. Now there were police crawling around on the dam, and Lake Surf itself was being drained. She looked out the window past her own reflection, to the sun-dappled water beyond. An icy feeling of dread settled low in her belly. She did not like change, but change was coming.

Chapter 8

ONCE HE WAS BACK IN town, Derwood climbed out of his pickup and called Sinsley back.

"Hey Marty, it's me."

"The victim is definitely Fred Akers. Dental records confirm it."

"So, he didn't run off," said Derwood.

"Nope. He's been here the whole time."

"I talked to his wife. She said he was killed, and she was right. She also said the murderer was someone right here in the neighborhood. She might be right about that, too."

"Maybe she did it," said Sinsley. "The coroner said the cause of death is probably a head wound. Can't be sure after twenty years, what with all the soft tissue gone and not much physical evidence, but they found a hole in the back of the skull. Maybe an inch across, and there was a groove of depressed bone leading to it like a trough. He was probably hit from behind. Something with a handle, like a hammer or a pick. Something heavy, where the tip pierces the skull, and the handle strikes the head."

"Sounds like it would hurt," said Derwood.

"I doubt he would have felt much at all, but it sure would do the trick. Knock him down and out with one blow. But who knows? Might have been a lot of other injuries to soft tissues. No sign of those after twenty years. Not much soft tissue left. Only one strike left any physical evidence still visible on the skull after all this time. There were other injuries too, older injuries in other parts of the body, but those had all healed. Old breaks, that kind of thing.

"We would normally have gone over the grave site in more detail with a crime scene team, looking for bullets and other evidence, but the water prevented that. At least we have an ID. That's a start."

"How is the dig at the dam going?" asked Derwood.

"They're going as fast as they can, but nothing interesting so far."

"Ok, Marty. Thanks. Keep me posted."

The next name on his list of subjects was Willem Smits. Smits now lived in an assisted living complex in Southern Pines. Derwood climbed in his pickup for the drive over to Pinelands Estate, the Taj Mahal of senior living.

Southern Moore County was lousy with the aged. The fine weather, outstanding golf, and surprisingly robust medical community made the area famous as a retirement mecca, anchored by the world-famous Pinehurst Resort. The sandy soil supported thin pine forests with little undergrowth, creating a dry and sunny environment with soft forgiving footing, perfect for horses. The area was drier and warmer than the rest of the surrounding state, and the lovely weather made an attractive retreat from the harsh winters of the north. The pine forests were said to emit a special ozone that helped consumptives and those with other infirmities live into old age.

As he drove, Derwood considered what he had learned. Jill Akers was trying to convince him the crime was tied to Woodlake itself and the politics of a gated community. Not much motive, killing a man over motorboats, but people could surprise you. Jill's relationship with her murdered husband had been complicated. It was hard to see her bashing his head in, but maybe she had motive enough. Maybe she recruited her personal trainer, now boyfriend or husband or whatever he was? His photo identified him as strong and fit. Maybe he got the better of Fred Akers? And Deloris Hitchcock sure seemed strange enough.

People related to the world as it involved them, and most were ultimately selfish creatures. People would kill for surprisingly small amounts of money. He'd once read of an outlaw who murdered a man in his sleep for snoring. He doubted that one, but people could surprise you.

Most murders were rash and impulsive, and it did not require a strong motive to pull a trigger. With a gun, the act of murder was as simple as clenching a fist. Guns eliminated the distance between thought and action. Easy to use and lethal, a dangerous combination.

Beating someone to death was different, more personal, more brutal, more committing. It took real effort. You had to really be feeling it to beat someone's brains out.

Wife swapping. Maybe Akers swapped with the wrong guy. But who was likely to win a confrontation with a man like Fred Akers? Guys like Akers tended to win fights. Not this time, though. Maybe someone he trusted had gotten behind him. Maybe he swapped for the wrong woman. Maybe he swapped the wrong woman. Maybe Jill Akers hated him as much as Deloris Hitchcock said.

Derwood pulled into the main entrance to Pinelands Estate in late afternoon. Thick thunderheads were roiling overhead but still holding back the rain. He went to reception and signed in the visitor register.

Assisted living and skilled nursing facilities dotted the Moore County landscape. Pinelands Estate was one of the most sought-after facilities. If space opened in Pinelands, it never lasted long. The facility spanned the gamut from independent living in an elder community all the way to full memory care with a dedicated Alzheimer's unit. Pinelands had housed generations of wealthy elders from wealthy families. The facility was private, exclusive and expensive.

According to the information Marty had given him, Willem Smits had moved in when his friends agreed that his mind was going, a few years ago. His dementia had progressed rapidly. He graduated first from the independent living into assisted living, then to skilled nursing and finally to the memory care unit. That would be his last stop on this side of the grass. Since moving to Pinelands, the rapid progression of the disease had slowed, but by the time Derwood went to see him, he was wheelchair bound and only rarely able to glimpse through the veil in his mind to remember his earlier life.

A nurse informed him that Willem Smits liked to spend his days sitting outside in his chair under a blanket, beneath an arbor on the edge of the green, which was where Derwood found him. He appeared comfortable in his chair, head leaning slightly forward, eyes closed. Smits was about seventy years old, and the years had not been kind. His white hair was thin and wispy, cheeks were hollow and sunken. Sallow flesh hung from his thin neck, and his body was swallowed within clothes and a jacket that hung off him. His hands were buried beneath a red, white and black throw quilt emblazoned with the logo of North Carolina State University.

A fresh-faced redheaded girl sat on a stone bench next to him, reading aloud from a book. She glanced at the pregnant sky, probably gauging when the rain might fall. She could not have been much out of her teens. She wore a blue and white uniform with a nametag that said SARAH in all capital letters, and beneath in smaller print Sandhills Community College. Derwood took her to be a student, perhaps a student nurse or nurse's aide, or even a candy striper from the local high school, here to gain some experience working with elderly patients in need of care and companionship. She read aloud as Smits appeared to doze.

Derwood approached and broke the illusion. She stopped reading, and Smits raised his head and blinked.

"Good afternoon." He turned to Smits and introduced himself. "I'm sorry to intrude, but I just need to ask a few questions."

"I don't know if that's a good idea." The young redhead spoke with an authority that belied her years. "Uncle Willem gets confused. He gets upset easily." She turned to her charge. "Don't you, Uncle?"

Smits did not reply.

"Are you related?" Derwood asked. The girl looked confused for a moment, then chuckled and shook her head.

"Oh, I see. No, everybody calls him Uncle Willem. I don't know why."

"I don't want to upset him, but it's important that I speak with him. Let's give it a try," said Derwood.

"I'm not supposed to leave him alone," said the girl.

"No problem. You can stick around. May I sit?"

Derwood took her place on the bench. He put down the umbrella he had brought from his pickup in anticipation of the rain. The electricity in the air announced that a thunderstorm was coming. Smits looked at him without curiosity, eyes sunken and cloudy, vacant.

"Willem, my name is Derwood Flynn," he said again. "I am a deputy sheriff."

Smits looked confused. "Sheriff?" he said thinly. Derwood waited. Smits did not speak again.

"You used to live out at Woodlake, right?" He waited some more.

Smits looked around and blinked.

"Ahhh mubble hubble," he said. His head tilted slightly to the right, bobbing lightly on the thin neck.

This was going nowhere fast. Derwood decided to try a different tack. He picked up the book the redheaded girl had been reading. Agatha Christie's *By the Pricking of My Thumbs*.

"I've always loved Agatha Christie. How about you, Willem? 'By the pricking of my thumbs, something wicked this way comes.'

Where were we?" He flipped though the book, and it fell open to a natural crease about a third of the way through, and Derwood began to read. He had not gotten far when Smits spoke.

"Sarah already read that."

Derwood looked up, surprised. Although slow and quiet, the words were clear. Smits' mind was largely wrecked, but there was a glimmer of awareness.

"Oh. Sorry. Were you further along?"

Smits did not say anything. Derwood looked at the girl, who quietly mouthed the word "further." Derwood flipped ahead in the book and started to read again. Smits listened in silence and gradually his head slumped forward and his eyes drifted shut.

Derwood wondered how to break through the walls around the older man's corroded mind. The reading had seemed to spark some interest, but he could not tell if Smits had really processed the location in the novel or if it was a random utterance. He read for a while, then put the book aside. When he did, Smits stirred again, opened his eyes and looked around. He blinked as if he did not quite know where he was. He looked toward Derwood.

"What did you say?" Smits asked, again slow and quiet, but clear. Overhead, thunder rumbled from the darkening sky.

Derwood leaned in close, grabbed his hands from beneath the blanket and looked him in the eye. "Willem, do you remember Fred Akers?"

Smits head snapped back, and his eyes widened. The fog over his countenance was burned away by a new intensity. He stared hard at Derwood and his lips curled into a snarl. The redheaded girl's eyes grew wide.

"What are you asking me about that for?" he snapped, harsh and clipped. "What do you want me to do about that?"

He pulled a hand free and struck out feebly. Derwood made no effort to dodge the blow, letting it land harmlessly on his forearm.

The girl looked concerned. Derwood waited, but Smits said no more.

"Fred Akers," said Derwood.

At the second mention of that name, Smits' eyes cleared for a moment before the curtain dropped again.

"You do remember Fred Akers," said Derwood.

Smits began to fidget, then to speak. "No, no, no. No, you cannot." His voice started low and soft, but rose in pitch and volume. "You will not. No, no, no, not here, not now, not ever."

"Calm down, Uncle," said the redheaded girl. "It's okay."

But it was not okay. Louder and louder, Smits began to scream. Spittle flew from his lips. He shouted and hit, feeble still but emotional intensity and rage giving him the strength of ten octogenarians.

"No! No! No! No! No! No!"

Derwood grabbed him by the wrists, and the girl tried to soothe him, but Smits continued to struggle.

"Go! Go! Go! Go! Go! Go! Go! Go!" He barely paused for breath. "Go! Go! Go! Go! Go! Go! Go!"

"What did you do, mister?" The redhead said. "You better go!" She gestured frantically. "Move! Go! Leave him alone!"

"Go! Go! Go! Go!" Smits' eyes bulged and glared in hatred as Derwood stood and backed away.

"Now Uncle Willem, you've got to calm down, sweetie. You're going to hurt yourself, and you're scaring me. Please, calm down. It's me, Sarah. We're best friends. I'm here now. This man is leaving."

"Go! Go! Go! Go! Go!"

She glared daggers at Derwood and jerked her head over her shoulder in the direction she wanted him to go. He took the hint and backed farther away as she started to coo to the old man and sing a lullaby.

"Go! Go! Go! Go! Go!"

Derwood went. As he got further away and turned out of Smits' direct line of sight, the old man began to calm down and the redhead embraced him in a gentle hug. The old man's shoulders shook as he wept, in concert with rumbling thunder overhead. Derwood had just made it back to his pickup when the first fat drops of rain began to fall.

Derwood still felt groggy and hungover. He did not want to make dinner, and he had not heard from Lizzy today. On his way home he stopped off at the Lake House Bar and Grill, a local watering hole in a shack off a back road. It was one of those buildings that housed many tenant businesses over the years, but the Lake House had been the one to survive. The beer was cold and the food was hot, and the waitresses knew everyone's name. The locals loved it.

Derwood wedged himself into an open stool at the bar, where the bottle blonde behind the bar said, "Hey, Derwood. Man of Law?"

She meant Man of Law IPA, one of the increasing numbers of local brews that was gaining traction in the Sandhills. When he came in to the Lake House, he often had the IPA. Derwood didn't normally drink beer, but tonight he figured he needed a night off the bourbon.

"Hey Angel. Man of Law'd be good, thanks."

She filled a pint and set it on the laminate bar, and Derwood called Lizzy. They talked a bit, and she reminded him that she still needed money. He knew what it was for. Why else would a pregnant seventeen-year-old girl ask for money? He was not the moral police, and he did not claim any special knowledge or high ground, but he knew a lot about killing. He told her to sleep on it.

Three beers and one cheeseburger later, stuffed with meaty fat and grease, Derwood headed home. The beer had taken the edge off his hangover, and it was late enough in the day now that he thought he might get away with an early night. He went home, and went to bed. He left the bourbon in the cabinet.

SARAH SMALLS IGNORED the man as he left her and Willem Smits under the arbor. She focused instead on her charge. She had never seen him this upset.

"It's okay," she said and gently embraced him. "He's gone now. He won't come back."

But she was not sure that the man would not return. In all her days sitting with Smits, this was the thing she dreaded above all. The man in the suit – the one who first brought her the money that got her out of foster care, and that continued to flow as long as she came here to sit with Smits – the man had been clear. She was here to watch and report what she saw. Whoever was behind the money that gave Sarah her independence wanted to know if anyone ever came around asking questions about Woodlake long ago.

And now this man showed up asking exactly those questions. Sarah's continued independence depended on her making a phone call. That's all they wanted. Only for her to report what she had seen. She did not know who was behind it, nor why they wanted to know if Smits received this visitor.

Over the years, Sarah had struggled with her feelings. Despite herself, her animus had diminished towards Smits, Pinelands, and elder care in general. She had feared that the foster system had burned all feeling out of her, but her time at Pinelands had rekindled it. She felt some tenderness towards the old man in the wheelchair. Sympathy maybe, or pity. Like you would feel about an old dog that belonged to someone else. Some days she wished he would die already, so she could be free and move on, but other days she felt kindness. Those days she even felt kindly towards bovine Jenny at reception.

The man was gone now, and the first drops of rain were marching across the lawn. She gathered up the book and escorted Smits back inside before the rain caught them out. She was conflicted, but once she got him inside and comfortably seated in the activity room, she excused herself. She had to place a call.

The call went to voicemail, but before long she received a return call. The number was blocked. She did not recognize the man's voice on the other end of the phone, but she told him about the visit from Derwood Flynn.

"Is that all?" Sarah asked.

"That's all," the voice said.

"What do I do now?"

"You know what you have to do now." The line went dead.

Chapter 9

THE KILLER DROVE SLOWLY to the Needles golf course, bordering Pinelands Estate. The parking lot and course were dark and deserted in the middle of the night. The killer wore matching clothing, dark but not black. It would not do to get stopped and have to explain an unusual wardrobe. A hat covered the head, hiding the hair, and a small pack was slung over the shoulder. The ensemble was completed by a hiker's headlamp, which cast a small circle of red light on the ground.

The killer climbed out into the rain, nestled beneath a large golf umbrella, and walked across the wide expanse of a driving range, through a narrow band of trees, and across the fourth fairway of the golf course to the wall surrounding Pinelands. The ten-feet privacy wall was made of red brick topped by wrought iron fencing. There were a few small maintenance gates in the wall, and the killer made directly for one situated near the building that housed the memory care unit. A small crowbar made short work of the lock, and the rain hid any sound as the gate swung open and the killer moved inside the compound.

A thin line of trees softened the exterior wall before the grounds opened to a lawn. The lawn was wide and open, dotted occasionally with trees and landscaping. The night sky was blotted with rain, but the red glow from the hiker's lamp gave enough light to make out the contour of the ground.

The killer had been here before, and knew the grounds well. They were only a shadow in the storm beneath the umbrella and neither hurried nor crept, but walked at an easy pace, silent and invisible in the night. There was no one about to see.

The locked fire escape door on the south side of the large building led to a stairway that climbed to the roof, accessing each floor along the way. The figure pulled out a rigid plastic card and soon the door was ajar. They smiled, relieved that the crowbar could stay in the pack for now. Pale light from the landing shone into the night.

The killer silently entered the building and pulled the door gently closed. Water dripped onto the floor. The memory unit was on the top floor. This arrangement had been discussed by Pinelands management. The top floor made egress more difficult in the event of a fire, but it also lessened the possibility that an addled senior would wander out at night if unattended. Management had also discussed alarming the doors, but that gave the impression that the clients were prisoners rather than paying customers, and management felt that was the wrong image.

The figure climbed silently up the stairs. The door to the memory unit was at the top, the last before the roof access. It was unlocked. Through the window in the door, the figure could see that the wide well-lit hallway was empty. A nurses station guarded the far end, but no staff were in sight. They softly opened the latched door and smiled. There should have been an alarm.

The figure crept quietly in and moved to the first door on the right. The knob turned easily and the door opened without difficulty. Inside was a spacious room, reminiscent of an efficiency apartment. A nightlight glowed dimly, bright enough to wash the room in a soft glow but not likely to disturb a heavy sleeper.

There was a kitchenette with a sink and microwave and coffee maker. A small sofa and reclining chair fronted a flatscreen television on the wall. A sleeping man lay on a double bed on the far side of the room. The figure crept quietly across the room and flicked on the light on the bedside table. Next to the light on the table was a copy of *By the Pricking of My Thumbs*.

"Uncle Willem. Uncle Willem. Wake up, Uncle Willem." The killer gently rocked the slumbering man by the shoulder until he grunted awake. "Hey Uncle, sorry to bother you. I came by to read to you."

"Oh, it's you." said Smits, voice thick with sleep. "That's nice. Thanks for coming. I like reading." Smits' eyes fluttered shut again.

"Uncle Will. Uncle Will." They gently shook the sleepy old man again. His frail body rocked on the bed like a scarecrow. "Before we read, I need to give you your shot. Wake up, Uncle Willem."

He slowly rose from the depths of sleep. "Another shot? Oh. OK. What's this one for?"

"It will help you rest. You had a hard day, and you need to rest."

"Oh. OK."

"We'll read right after the shot, and you must be still and quiet, to hear me read."

"OK," said Smits.

The figure took off the backpack and drew out a syringe and a small vial of clear liquid. The bedside lamp illuminated a blood red top and orange label with black print that read "Succinylcholine chloride injection USP 1,000 mg TOTAL (100mg/mL)." They drew up two milliliters in a syringe and briefly considered Smits' shoulder. The old man was thin with little in the way of subcutaneous fat. They selected an inch-long 27-gauge needle, and prepared the syringe.

"Now, don't make a sound, Uncle Willem."

"OK," he said again.

"Mosquito bite!" said the figure and slipped the needle gently in the deltoid muscle on Smits' upper arm and pushed the plunger, sending 200 milliliters of succinylcholine in the old man's body. It would not take long. The figure rubbed the injection site to take away the sting, and put the needle away.

Smits did not make a sound. He took the injection without a whimper. Within a few seconds, his body began to feel an unusual warmth, then he felt a tremor starting.

The figure noticed the expected fasciculations as they took hold. Succinyl choline was a depolarizing neuromuscular blocker, commonly used in emergency departments to chemically paralyze patients in need of immediate respiratory support. The drug took effect quickly and caused a massive depolarization of the nerve cells controlling all voluntary muscles in the body. The depolarization led to a brief period of uncontrolled shivering. It would stop when the depolarization burned itself out and the muscles lost the ability to contract until the drug wore off.

Succinylcholine arrested all voluntary motor function including breathing for a period of five to ten minutes. This period of complete paralysis gave doctors perfect conditions to slip a breathing tube into the throat and quickly put someone on a ventilator. Succinylcholine possessed no sedative properties of its own, and doctors usually sedated patients before its use, as it was considered inhumane to chemically paralyze someone while they were awake and conscious. The killer knew this, but Smits would be dead in a few minutes anyway, so why bother?

They read aloud softly from the Agatha Christie as the old man's body began to tremble in response to the drug. He was able to utter a quiet grunt before the paralysis took hold, and his eyes came fully open in the last moments. They were filled with a burning light of panic as the muddled mind behind the eyes came to realize that death was at hand. A few minutes more and the light in the eyes winked out.

The killer sat at the bedside and read on to the end of the chapter before putting the bookmark back in the book. Agatha Christie really was the best. They put away the needle and medicine vial, searched quickly and found no leavings, then gathered up the backpack and went to the bathroom for a towel to wipe every surface that had been touched, turned out the light and went to the door.

All was quiet in the hall. The figure stepped out and shut the door gently and went back into the stairwell, careful to wipe the door handles and knobs. Down the stairs and out the same fire door. The blessed rain still fell, hiding activity from prying eyes. Across the lawn to the gate and out across the golf course toward the car parked a quarter mile away. Once there, the killer drove away.

Chapter 10

WEDNESDAY

DERWOOD SLEPT FITFULLY and crawled out of bed when morning came. He was not hungover, but neither was he rested. The IPA did not have the nightmare-killing effect of bourbon.

He stumbled into the kitchen for coffee. The rain which had started the day before had come in intermittent showers throughout the night and gradually faded to a light and steady patter on the back porch. The lake was misty, and the shroud of rain blurred the far shore into an impressionist blend of colors.

Derwood's phone erupted into the E-flat of *Götterdämmerung*.

"Hello."

"Is this Mr. Flynn?"

"Who's calling?

"Oh, this is Sheila from Pinelands Estate. You left your umbrella here yesterday, and we thought you might want to pick it up. I got your number from the sign-in log. I hope it's okay I called."

He had left in a hurry just before the rain started yesterday, and he must have left his umbrella on the bench where he met Smits. He would not have bothered, as they were cheap at the local dollar store, but he had gotten that particular umbrella at the U.S. Women's Open Golf Championship the last time it was in Pinehurst, and it was his favorite.

When he got to reception at Pinelands, the umbrella was waiting for him. He thanked the receptionist and turned to leave, but then turned back. "How is Mr. Smits doing today?"

"Oh, you didn't hear? He died in his sleep last night."

Derwood gaped at her, walked back to the desk. "What?"

"Oh yeah," she said, excited to inject a little drama into her morning routine. "He went to bed last night and never got up this morning. It happens fairly often around here, I'm afraid. It's a pretty good way to go." She affected nonchalance. We see death up close here, we can handle it, her body language said.

Derwood's mind raced. Could Smits' death be a coincidence? The man had been confused yesterday, and he was frail, but he had moments of vigor and he did not look like a man near death. On the contrary, he had gotten agitated and aggressive when Derwood asked about Fred Akers. It was too much for coincidence. But who knew about his visit? Who cared?

The receptionist sensed his bewilderment. "Are you family?"

"What? No, no, not family, I'm with the Sheriff's office. He seemed fine yesterday. It just seems strange." Derwood thanked her again for the umbrella and walked out. He punched Martin Sinsley's number into his phone.

Sinsley answered on the first ring.

"Good morning, Marty. We need to talk. Where are you?"

"I'm headed to Woodlake Dam right now. They found something."

"I'll meet you there."

SINSLEY WAS ALREADY walking down the paved road on the dam when Derwood arrived. Drizzle fell from the gray sky, gently soaking everything and everyone. At least Derwood had his umbrella.

The heavy equipment was still in place on Woodlake Dam, where the Corps of Engineers was still at work draining the lake. On his first visit two days earlier, Derwood had noticed how low the water level was, but he was surprised to see that the lake still had a long way to go. From his vantage point on the dam, it did not look like the water level had fallen appreciably in the last couple of days. Maybe the engineers had gotten better control of the flow, and had slowed the drainage to protect the downstream watershed. Or maybe the rain over the last day balanced the water draining out through the expanding spillway with water running into the lake from the surrounding countryside.

Derwood and Sinsley met on the dam near a white van from the state crime lab. The back of the dam showed signs of Sinsley's search. Yellow rope cordoned off the ground into a grid of many squares, numbered and labelled with small flags in the ground. The squares nearest the spillway had green flags indicating they had been searched and cleared. Orange flags were areas not yet searched. Red flags marked parts of the grid where radar had indicated an anomaly of interest.

Ground-penetrating radar was not a perfect tool. It was excellent at locating bodies in a graveyard, but finding a body in a graveyard is like finding hay in a haystack. Out in the real world, radar had limitations. Sometimes it could not distinguish a large rock or buried tree trunk from human remains. Cadaver dogs made a good adjunct.

Several of the red-flagged grids had been worked by the dogs, but all had turned up empty until this morning. The radar had hit upon a mass buried a few feet in the sandy soil of the back of the dam, and the cadaver dogs had gone nuts when they were brought in for a closer look.

"Damn dogs are amazing," said Sinsley. "I had no idea. Did you know they can smell a body buried fifteen feet underground? Or under thirty feet of water? Or even after thirty years?" He shook his head.

"They got a hit right down there, and we're about to start digging. Looks like something is buried a couple feet down. Since you're here, may as well grab a shovel."

"I don't really think that's a good idea," said Derwood. "My doctors tell me to take it easy, you know." He put a hand on his low back. "So, doctor's orders. You go ahead. I'll supervise."

"Mmm-hmm."

Sinsley grabbed a shovel from the van and joined a crime scene technician at the search grid square that caused all the excitement. They started to dig. The shovel work was vigorous, and soon Sinsley was soaked with sweat and rain. The soil gave way until the shovels reached the buried object. The men put the large shovels aside and pulled out smaller hand trowels. They were forced down on hand and knees, to clear the last few bits of earth from the buried object.

Sinsley looked up the slope to catch Derwood's eye atop the dam. He nodded solemnly. He pulled out his phone and snapped a quick photo, texted it to Derwood standing above. The photo was grainy and out of focus, but Derwood could make out the empty stare of a human skull.

An hour later, the Moore County sheriff herself arrived on scene, with the district attorney accompanying her. Sheriff Susan Blanchard had been a fixture in the local political scene for years. DA Margaret Kidd, by contrast, was new to her post. Although separated in age by nearly a decade, both were honest, tough and respected. They were also sisters.

They had worked closely together for years, supporting one another's rise through the ranks of local law enforcement and each encouraging the other's venture into elected office. Sheriff Blanchard had helped pay for her younger sister's path through law school at the University of North Carolina. Both were well respected by their staffs and the community at large, although Derwood had met neither woman.

"Okay, Marty, got your text. You found another body. We're here, and it's raining. Show us what you got," said Sheriff Blanchard. They ignored Derwood.

"Sure, Sue. Hey Maggie," Sinsley said to the younger woman. "You said I had a couple days to find something, and I found something. There is another body in the dam."

"Yeah, I inferred that from the picture of the skull," said Blanchard drily. "That makes two so far. Any indication who this is?"

"I have a good guess," said Sinsley, turning to Derwood. "Akers wasn't the only person to vanish from Woodlake. A little over two years later, in fall of 2002, there was another disappearance, an entire family this time." He paused as the others reacted to this terrible news.

"Amanda and Jason Hinrichs and their eight-year-old son vanished. Nobody saw anything, no physical evidence. No trace. But here is the kicker. Amanda was running for the Woodlake Board of Directors."

"Huh," said Derwood.

"Her neighbors said she was going to vote to open the lake. But before she actually made it on the board, she disappeared.

"It was the first day of school, and Jason Junior didn't show up. Jason Senior did not show up for work either. Amanda was an interior designer. Jason Senior was an accountant. Young family, well liked. No red flags. Not a trace of them since, and no bodies were ever found."

"It's always the husband," said Derwood. "He probably met another woman. Didn't want to be bogged down with a wife and kids. Threw them down a well somewhere and headed west."

"Maybe. But if he did, he's keeping a low profile. He hasn't used his credit cards, never drew any money out of the bank, never called or visited any family or old friends. Just gone." Sinsley snapped his fingers.

"And you think the Hinrichs' disappearance is related to Fred Akers."

Sinsley started counting on his hand. "Same community, both running for the board, both on the same side of a contentious local issue, both disappearing without a trace." Four fingers extended.

"So," the sheriff said, pointing down the slope, "you found them?"

"Well, there's only one body in this location, so it's not the whole family, but it could be one of them. One of the adults, at least. The remains are too big for a child. We won't know until we get it up to the state lab for identification." He paused to wipe away a rivulet of water running off the brim of his hat.

"When I was looking through the old records, I didn't see any other open missing persons cases from Woodlake here. This body is decomposed just like the first one. It's been in there a while. Hell of a place to bury a body, but I suppose if it worked once, why not try it again?"

"Hmm. Looks muddy," said the sheriff.

"Ah, come on, Sue," said Margaret Kidd. "A little mud's not going to hurt you." She turned and began to clamber down the rocky slope to the open gravesite.

"I'll just wait up here," said the sheriff. "You let me know how it looks."

Sinsley followed the DA down the slope. Susan Blanchard turned to Derwood.

"Hello." She looked him up and down, her critical eye noticing the casual dress, the sandals, the untucked shirt. She had not seen him since swearing him in as a deputy, and she had not expected much from the unpaid part-timer. His shoes and pants were still clean below the knee, if increasingly damp from rain spatter. She looked down the slope where Margaret and Marty were kneeling in the mud beside the body.

"Not interested in a close-up?" she asked.

"I can wait."

"From what Marty tells me, you've probably spent enough time in the mud to last you awhile, huh?"

He nodded, and they made small talk until Kidd and Sinsley returned, trudging back up the hill through the mud and rain.

"Well, Susie," said Margaret. "That body has been there a while. It's badly decomposed. Can't tell if it's a man or a woman." She moved under the large golf umbrella Derwood held in his hand.

"You don't mind?" Her foray down the slope in the rain had left her a little bedraggled. Her light brown hair was short cropped beneath a damp Durham Bulls cap, and a streak of mud crossed one cheek. The bill of the cap shaded her eyes. High cheekbones blended into rounded cheeks that promised deep dimples if ever she smiled. The faint shadow of the cap fell across full pale lips.

"No, sorry. Of course not," Derwood murmured. He was not used to standing close to women these days.

"The guys from the state will dig it out, get it up to Raleigh, and identify it if they can. With any luck, we will have more to go on in a day or two." Kidd spoke with assurance, obviously comfortable discussing dead bodies on a rainy morning.

"Something's going on around here, though. Or at least something was when these people were buried here. Any ideas?" She looked from Sinsley to Blanchard. She grabbed Derwood's umbrella hand and moved the canopy to better cover her head from the rain.

"The best theory so far is that Fred Akers was killed by somebody local and buried here twenty years ago, over a dispute about boating rights on Lake Surf that has been going on and off for years," said

Marty. "We've started to interview some people who were around back when he disappeared. I'd guess this new body is related, unless all the local killers hit on Woodlake Dam as a good burial spot. If we can find out who this is, we might be able to get a clearer picture. Derwood has been talking to the locals."

"Huh, is that right?" said Maggie as she turned to Derwood with interest. "Are you a cop?"

"I'm learning," said Derwood. "I watch a lot of television. How hard can it be?"

Maggie smiled and her face was transformed. Her eyes lit up and the promised dimples took full shape. Slightly crooked teeth just touched her lower lip in a faintly lopsided grin. The clouds parted and a beam of bright sunlight fell on the umbrella. Or maybe Derwood had imagined that last part.

She looked him in the eye, then slowly took him in head to toe, then back to his eyes. "You're funny. All right then," she said, smiling, "why don't you tell us what you've found out so far?"

Derwood read playful mockery in her tone and serious inquiry in her eyes. He fumbled for words, "Uhhhhh..."

"Cat got your tongue?" She turned to Sinsley. "Marty, is he with you?"

"Ah jeez, Maggie. Don't start." Sinsley rolled his eyes. "He's with me." He slapped Derwood on the back. "This is Deputy Derwood Flynn. He's been helping out with the investigation. Sue made it clear we had to find something else here, or move on. I'd rather investigate murder than larceny, so I've been here looking for bodies. Derwood's been out talking to people. He's not as helpless as he looks." He looked meaningfully at Maggie and lowered his voice. "Or as harmless."

Maggie kept smiling as she looked Derwood up and down again. "I hope not," she said.

Derwood addressed the Sheriff. "I've talked to several people who were around back in Akers' day," he said. "I've been through his military records."

"What military records?" said Maggie.

Blanchard spoke up. "Akers was a special ops soldier out of Bragg. Derwood here was, too."

Maggie glanced at Derwood, her smile replaced by a more thoughtful expression. Interest perhaps? He couldn't tell.

Blanchard continued. "Akers was into some heavy lifting in Central America in the eighties. The original investigators thought he probably left the country."

Maggie sniffed. "Wrong," she announced. The others ignored her.

"I talked to Fred's wife Jill Akers," said Derwood. "She never bought that theory, says Fred wouldn't run off without his family. She says somebody local killed Fred. Back then there was a big dispute about the best use of Lake Surf, and tensions were pretty high. She thinks somebody who disagreed with Fred's point of view killed him. I wasn't sure what to think. She had motive, and its always the spouse, right?" He glanced at Maggie. "At least on TV."

She hid a smile. The sheriff sighed.

"But why would Jill Akers kill that person?" He pointed to the open grave, and turned back to Maggie. "You're right that there is some weird stuff going on around here. That body is just more of it. We're going to find a connection between whoever that is and Fred Akers. And these killings are not just old news." Derwood's gaze swept the entire group. "The killer is still out there, still active."

"Oh, whatever!" said Maggie, rolling her eyes. "It's a cold case. Akers has been dead for decades, this new one too. This case is as cold as they come." She shivered and rubbed her arms to emphasize the point.

"Well, except the guy I interviewed about this yesterday died last night."

The three others looked at Derwood. "You didn't mention that," said Marty.

"I was getting to it."

Blanchard put her hands up. "Hold on a minute. Why don't we get out of the rain and talk about it? Has everybody had breakfast?" None of them had.

"Why don't we meet down in Southern Pines at Mac's and grab some eggs? I need to run by the station to grab a few things."

"Yea, me too," said Sinsley. "Plus, I got to change into some dry clothes. Again."

"Sue, I rode with you, but if Derwood here doesn't mind running me by my place for a quick clean up, we can meet you in forty-five minutes?" said Maggie, smiling again.

"Oh boy, here we go," said Sue. She looked at Derwood. "Good luck." She turned and left.

"What are you driving?" asked Maggie as she started off down the gravel toward the parked vehicles. "Let's get out of the rain and cleaned up. I could use an omelet."

Chapter 11

DERWOOD AND MAGGIE walked side by side to the pickup, shoulders touching under the large umbrella.

"So, you're the DA?"

"That's right."

"Huh. I feel like I'm in a TV show. What does a DA really do, anyway?"

"Mostly we run around jet-setting with movie stars and seeking headlines, but sometimes we help solve dastardly capers and bring justice to the wicked." Her eyes twinkled. "We protect the good people of the county and ensure justice is swift and blind."

She pulled off her cap and rubbed her damp hair. It smelled of flowers. Delicate, sweet, tropical. Probably the shampoo. Her tone became more serious. "Our website says: 'The mission of the District Attorney's Office is to seek justice by ensuring that victims' rights and the public's safety are our number one priority through the fair, equal, vigorous and efficient enforcement of the criminal laws.' That's what we try to do, believe it or not. Not much jet setting and not many headlines."

"Is there a lot of crime here?" Derwood asked, genuinely curious. The local citizenry was armed, and many carried concealed weapons. He'd never been the victim of a crime against his person. Maybe people could sense danger and knew to leave him alone. Not all criminals are stupid.

"We have our fair share. Mostly drug- and alcohol-related, or property crime. Burglary, breaking and entering, that kind of thing. Some robbery and assault, too. More murders than you would think, for a rural county, but most of those are gang related or drug related. Even our little slice of paradise has been infiltrated by drug gangs out of Raleigh and Charlotte. We don't get much really juicy stuff. Although that might be changing now." She looked over her shoulder toward the damp grave in the back of the dam.

"And as DA, you do what exactly?" Derwood prompted.

"I oversee the prosecutor's office. Determine who goes to trial, consider plea bargains, ensure everyone gets paid, that kind of thing."

"How long have you been doing that?"

"Not long," she laughed. "Can you tell?"

"Not really. But I wouldn't know what to look for."

"Well, not long. Just a few weeks, actually. The election was last spring, and that was my first time running." She shrugged. "We won."

"That simple, huh?" he asked.

"That simple. I took office a few weeks ago." She looked at him, eyes serious again. "But I've been a prosecutor for a while. I was an assistant DA for ten years. Seven of those were in Charlotte, and there is a lot more action in Charlotte. I've been around the block a few times. Moved back here about three years ago."

"Moved back, huh? You must be from here."

"Yup. Local girl. Pinecrest High School. Chapel Hill for college, then Chapel Hill for law school."

"Carolina all the way."

"That's me. Tarheel through and through. What about you? How'd you get here?"

"I got lucky," he said, dodging her question. "Lately, I've had some time on my hands, felt like I needed to be productive. Sheriff was willing to take a chance on me, and here I am, just standing in the rain, holding this umbrella for you."

"I'm surprised. Susie never was a risk taker."

"Maybe she doesn't think I'm that much of a risk."

She looked him up and down, his loose and casual clothes unimpressive. "Well, maybe she doesn't. Either way, I can't think of a better use of your time." She winked as she climbed into the pickup.

"Me neither," he said to himself.

Derwood drove to downtown Southern Pines, where Maggie kept a loft apartment above Swank, an eclectic coffee shop and used clothing store. The loft was a two-room affair accessed through a door in an alley off Broad Street, the main avenue through downtown. The door led to a narrow wooden stair, which creaked upward to the aged but bright and clean space above. The floor was old polished hardwood, and the ceilings were high. Large windows looked out over Broad Street in front and the alley behind. A fire escape led from the back window down to a parking lot. Exposed brick covered one wall. A large abstract print hung in the center of the brick, framed by boxwood topiary trees. There was no television. The space was aged but airy, bright, and clean with elegant modern décor.

Maggie led Derwood inside and pointed to the small kitchenette. "There's still some coffee in the pot. Grab a cup and heat some up if you want. I won't be a minute."

If she thought it unusual to have a strange man in her apartment, she did not mention it. Derwood wondered if that was a southern thing. She was not the only woman who invited him inside in the last few days, but she was the most attractive. Hitchcock had done the same. Maybe it was the badge.

Maggie was as good as her word, and ten minutes later was back in the living room with clean clothes and washed hair. She scrubbed a towel over her short hair. Once more the light scent of flowers drifted to Derwood's nose.

"God, I love short hair," she said. "Before I made the break and cut it all off, it took forever to dry. This is much better. You ready to go?"

"Ready when you are."

"Good. We can walk from here. Mac's is just a couple blocks down."

A LARGE BEARDED MAN walked out the door of the restaurant just as they arrived to walk in. He wore a purple shirt with the hospital logo stitched on the front. He did not seem to notice them, did not hold the door or slow his walk. He marched steadily out and up the street, as if he knew that everyone would get out of his way. He wore earphones and his eyes were dull pools that held no flicker of intelligence. As he walked, he slowed frequently to pick up refuse on the sidewalk and in the gutter. The huge man looked familiar to Derwood, although he did not get a good look.

"I swear I've seen that guy before," he said.

"Oh, sure. That's Billy. He gets around. He's, you know, not quite right? But he's always picking up garbage and tidying things up. He's big and he's strong, but he's harmless. He has been around here forever. Everybody knows Billy."

"Does he work at the hospital? I think I saw him a couple days ago, taking out the garbage."

"I think so. He used to work at city hall, but he was laid off with the budget cuts last year. He does a good job, never complains, and does not ask for much. He's the perfect employee, really."

"Huh," said Derwood.

"He is conscientious that way. Kept city hall spotless for years before he was laid off. It's a shame. He could use the county benefits. Health, retirement, that stuff. Hopefully he has the same at the hospital. He does a good job, never causes any trouble. Honestly, we need more like him."

A light clicked on in Derwood's mind. "Did you know his mother knew Fred Akers? Served on the board of directors at Woodlake at the time of the murder."

"Small world," said Maggie as she held the restaurant door open for Derwood.

Martin Sinsley and Sue Blanchard were already sitting across from one another, in a booth with two cups of coffee on the table between. Derwood slid in next to Marty, Maggie next to her sister.

"You know, there'd be more room if you two switched," said Marty. The men's side of the booth was a lot more crowded than the women's side.

"Yeah, but then I'd have to sit next to you, Marty, and I just took a shower," said Maggie.

"Ah jeez, Maggie," said Sue. "I can't take you anywhere." She looked at Derwood. "Sounds like you've been busy. Why don't you fill us in on where you've been and what you've been doing?"

"Some of this you know already," Derwood said. "Soldier disappears twenty years ago, then his body washes out of the dam last week. Marty tells me he was from my old unit, and we start poking around."

Maggie raised her eyebrows. Everybody around these parts knew there was only one 'Unit' with a 'capital U' at Fort Bragg. Derwood hadn't told her where he had worked in the Army.

Sinsley said, "Akers was not the only one to disappear from Woodlake. A couple years later an entire family went missing. Amanda and Jason Hinrichs, and their son JJ. The boy was 8 years old."

"Right," said Derwood. "So, Marty is looking for more bodies, and I keep poking around. I talked to Fred Aker's widow. She is convinced he was murdered. Local politics, she says."

"What local politics?" asked Sue.

"There was a dispute about lake use back in the day. One faction wanted to keep Lake Surf closed to motorboats, to preserve a certain kind of quiet lake experience. Another group wanted to bring in motorboats and turn the lake into a water sports playground. Fred Akers was one of those. He was running for the board of directors, and his vote would be the swing vote that would finally push the issue over the top, and open the lake to every kind of motorboat. Jill Akers thinks the quiet lake faction killed him."

"And two years later, Amanda Hinrichs was running for the Woodlake Board when she and her family disappeared," Sinsley said.

"Was she motorboat faction?" asked Maggie.

"Yup," said Sinsley.

"Huh. Ok," said Maggie and Derwood continued.

"Next I talked to a woman named Deloris Hitchcock. She's been around Woodlake a long time. The conversation went sideways, and she sort of kicked me out. Didn't learn much. Yesterday, I went over to Pinelands Estate to talk to a man named Willem Smits. He is another Woodlake old timer. He wasn't very helpful either. He is in a wheelchair, senile, pretty confused. When I asked him about Fred Akers, he went nuts. Started hollering and I basically got kicked out of there, too."

"People don't seem to like you very much, Derwood," said Maggie, smiling again. She smiled a lot. It was distracting.

"Yeah, it's my charming personality. Anyway, Willem Smits died last night."

"OK," said the sheriff. "Somebody killed Akers to keep him off the Woodlake Board of Directors. Two years after that, another prospective Woodlake board member goes missing, with her family. You guys are asking questions, and Smits ends up dead. Sounds like somebody wanted to keep him quiet."

"Yeah, that's not looking too good," said Maggie. "Dead bodies everywhere. But if the one from this morning is Hinricks, where is the rest of the family?"

"That damn dam needs to be excavated, entirely," said the sheriff. "Marty, let's make it happen."

"What about the rest of us?" asked Derwood.

"I'm going to Pinelands," said Maggie. "Smits' death cannot be coincidence. Somebody over there knows something. Somebody knew you'd been there asking questions. Maybe you scared somebody." Maggie had entered full DA mode. Confident. Directive.

"If somebody helped Willem Smits along his way into the Big Sleep last night, it could get dangerous," said Derwood.

"Well now that I'm working with you, I feel safer than a nun's virginity," said Maggie, eyes twinkling, smile lopsided.

"Oh, lord," said the sheriff.

Chapter 12

DERWOOD WALKED MAGGIE back to her loft, and they drove to Pinelands Estate. Derwood smiled at the receptionist behind the counter, the same woman as yesterday, and from his earlier visit this morning. She was a short overweight middle-aged woman with a round face, dull eyes set wide apart and thin brown hair. He greeted her kindly and introduced Maggie.

"This is District Attorney Margaret Kidd. She may have a few questions for you."

"Okay," said the receptionist uneasily.

Maggie intuited that this woman was most likely to respond to kindness and friendliness. She smiled. "Hi! Call me Maggie. I'm the District Attorney. What's your name?"

"Jennifer."

"It's nice to meet you, Jennifer. Don't worry, you're not in any trouble." She spoke gently, soothingly. The woman seemed intimidated by authority. "I just need to ask a few questions. Okay?"

Jennifer agreed.

"How long have you worked here?"

"About three years."

"Do you like it?"

"The people are nice, and they treat me good. Yeah, I like it fine."

"That's good. Were you here yesterday?"

"Yes."

"Do you remember signing this man in yesterday afternoon?" Maggie nodded at Derwood.

"Yeah."

"What time was that?"

"Maybe four-thirty."

"When did he leave?"

"A little after five o'clock, maybe? He wasn't here that long."

"Did you tell anyone about his visit?"

"No?" Jennifer said it as a question, uncertainty plain on her face.

"Are you asking me or telling me, Jennifer?" Maggie said, as gently as she could. "Listen, Jennifer. We're not here to make trouble for you. We just need to understand a few things. You said Willem Smits died in his sleep last night, right?"

The woman nodded.

"There are a lot of things going on, and we need to find out whether these things are connected." Maggie spoke as if explaining to a child, without seeming to condescend. It was a talent Derwood completely lacked. She went on. "It's okay if you told somebody about his visit. You didn't do anything wrong. But we need to know, because it might be important."

The woman shook her head, obviously worried. "I didn't tell anybody. Why would I?" She sounded defensive.

Maggie hardened her voice, just a little. "Jennifer, several people have been killed. Possibly, Mr. Smits was murdered here last night. You don't want to get in the way of a murder investigation, so let me ask you again. Did you call anyone?"

Vigorous head shaking, wide eyes. 'No, I swear. I really didn't."

Maggie eased off the pressure with a placating hand gesture. "Okay, Jennifer. I believe you." Gentle smile. "Do you keep track of all visitors? Does everyone sign in?"

"Yeah, everyone is supposed to sign in this book here." Jennifer's eyes were still wide, and she gave Maggie her full attention as she patted the sign-in log on the reception counter.

"Can I have a look?"

"Yeah, sure."

The woman slid the book over the counter and Maggie spun the log around. It was open to today's date. She flipped pages back and forth a few times, examining entries for the past week. There was only one visitor for Willem Smits, Derwood Flynn the day before. He had not signed out in his own hand.

"Jennifer, is this your writing?" Maggie pointed to the sign-out block in the log, where Derwood had been timed out of Pinelands.

"Well, he didn't stop by to sign himself out." Defensive again. "We are supposed to note when visitors leave, if they don't sign themselves out."

"That's no problem, I'm glad you signed him out. It helps pin down the time more precisely." Reassuring. "Mr. Smits has not had any other visitors recently, huh?"

The receptionist looked more at ease now. "He doesn't get many. I can't remember the last time someone came to see him. Thank goodness for Sarah."

"Sarah?" asked Maggie.

The receptionist smiled, her face now open and bright. "Oh, everybody knows Sarah. She's a saint. She comes to visit almost every day. She sits and talks to the residents. Mr. Smits is her favorite. She was with him yesterday."

Derwood remembered the young woman he had met briefly the day before. "The young redheaded woman?" he asked.

"That's her. She's here almost every day. Sits with people, like in the old times, when family or friends would just come and sit and talk, you know? It's sweet. People don't do enough of that anymore. Not like it used to be. Anyway, Sarah comes about every day to sit with one resident or another. She almost always makes time for Mr. Smits, though. Reads to him, I think." A dark thought crossed her face. "Oh," she brought her hand to her mouth. "She's going to be upset when she hears he's gone."

"Is she a relative?" asked Maggie, wondering why the young woman should have a particular interest in Willem Smits.

"Not that I know of," said Jennifer. She rubbed her hand through her thin hair. "But I don't really know. She's been coming a long time. Everybody knows Sarah, and she knows everybody around here." Now the woman's face showed traces of pride. "Sarah's going to be a doctor. She'll be a good one, too. She cares about people."

"She doesn't sign in to your book?" asked Maggie.

"Sarah?" The receptionist laughed. "No, she don't sign in. She's practically on staff."

"Maybe we can talk to her," said Maggie.

"Sure, but she's not here right now. She don't come until after school. She's in college over at Sandhills. She's going to UNC next year. Going to be a doctor," the receptionist repeated, warming with vicarious pride at the thought.

"Okay, Jennifer. Well, look, we are going to need to take this sign-in register and go through it in more detail, and we are going to need to get all the books going back the last few years. Do you keep them here?"

Now the woman hesitated. "I guess, but I think I should call my supervisor."

She did, and the supervisor came. After some discussion, Derwood and Maggie found themselves in the office of the Pinelands Estate executive director, Sheila Cuthbert. She was a no-nonsense woman of late middle age, efficient and pleasant. When Maggie said she needed copies of all the sign-in registers for the last five years, Cuthbert was happy to comply.

She gave them a list of all employees and contractors who might have had access to Pinelands. Of course she knew the saintly young woman who visited the residents on the memory unit. Everybody knew Sarah Smalls. All the staff knew about the story of her parents dying in a car crash, her grandfather taking her in, then leaving her alone to the mercies of foster care. Sarah had become a role model to many of the staff, even those older than she was. Somehow, she had pulled herself out of foster care, gotten an apartment, a car, and was putting herself through college. It was proof that hard work mattered, and good things really did come to people with a kind heart. Proof that the American Dream was still alive. Sarah was twenty years old now, and a student at Sandhills Community College, on track to transfer to the University of North Carolina next fall. She planned to go to medical school. Everyone agreed the girl was a saint.

Cuthbert was also willing to give up copies of all the surveillance camera footage of the property, and to arrange meetings with any staff members Maggie thought it necessary to interview. They started with the day nurse who found Willem Smits dead in his bed this morning.

"I hadn't worked for a few days. I was visiting my sister in Wilmington," said the nurse as she settled in. "This morning at sign-out rounds, there was nothing unusual. Mr. Smits had been his normal self the last few days. But when I went to check on him, he wasn't breathing. He was just dead." Her placid face was undisturbed, her voice calm and even.

"You don't seem very upset," said Maggie.

"Look around, Ms. Kidd. By the time our clients get to this floor, there is usually only one way out. It is not that uncommon for us to find one like that. Dead, I mean. A lot of families don't want their loved one dying in a hospital, so we do our best to keep clients here, keep everyone comfortable."

She paused and gazed at the ceiling. "Funny thing, though, you can usually see it coming." She looked back at Maggie. "We call it actively dying. It's a hospice thing. We have a lot of hospice patients here. You can usually tell when a client is done living. But not Mr.

Smits. He wasn't done. His mind was going, but he had some time left in him yet. I guess you never know."

They thanked her and left.

"We need to talk to the night nurse," said Maggie.

"I was thinking we need to talk to Sarah Smalls," said Derwood.

They were able to reach the night nurse by phone, a man named Steve. He was due back at Pinelands at seven for the night shift, but had not yet gone to bed for the day. They caught up with him at his gym, where he was lifting weights. Derwood normally tried to stay as far away from the gym as possible. Doctors' orders, he told himself, but he was willing to make an exception for Maggie Kidd.

Steve told them that Smits was more agitated than usual yesterday evening. He thought it was a consequence of Derwood's visit. Sarah Smalls had told the day nurse about the visit, and between them they calmed Smits down, but by evening he was agitated again. He took a regular dose of quetiapine 50mg each evening as a sleeping pill. Last night Steve had given a double dose on account of the agitation. But that shouldn't have caused any harm, and the dose could be verified by checking the locked dispensary at the nurses station. The double dose worked and eventually Smits went to sleep. Sarah stayed late to read to him as he dozed off. Steve said that was not her regular habit, but she did it from time to time. She was a saint.

"What time did Sarah leave?" asked Maggie.

Steve thought for a moment. "After evening meds. I'd say eight-thirty, nine o'clock. Somewhere in there."

"Was Smits alive when she left?" Maggie asked.

"Yeah, sure, of course. I checked on him during my late rounds. Between ten and eleven o'clock. Sleeping like a baby."

From the gym, Derwood and Maggie drove back to Pinelands to talk to more staff and continue to look around. Maggie busied herself checking through the records at the nurses station and verifying Steve's story. She made a thorough inspection of Smits' room.

Derwood had little to add, so he wandered around the unit, peeking in drawers and doors. Smits' room was at the end of the hall, in sight of the nurses station, but next to an exit door at the end of the hall.

The door at the end of the hallway led to a stairwell. A nurse said it was rarely used. It was a fire escape, and it was kept unlocked for reasons of safety and because the families of clients insisted upon it. The staff did not feel that ward security was important. Why would anyone sneak into a memory unit? No, the door was not alarmed. No, nobody ever used that stairway. Sure, he could open it.

Derwood exited into a lit and decently clean stairwell. The stairs were polished concrete with metal anti-slip nosing in place. Round metal rails hung hip high from block concrete walls, and the lighting was a wall-mounted bare bulb but nonetheless bright. He followed the stairs down. At the bottom floor were two doorways, one leading to a hallway and one leading outside. The inside door was locked from this direction. Derwood reached for the outside door and caught his foot on the upturned edge of a floor mat there. He reached to straighten the mat and noticed it was damp. The surrounding floor was dry, but there were traces of water dripped from the door to the mat, and faint streaks of moisture and debris on the mat. Someone had used the mat to wipe their feet. No surprise. It was a doormat, after all. But the nurse upstairs said no one used this stairway. If that was true, why was the floormat wet?

He opened the outside door and surveyed the scene. The door opened onto a broad expanse of well-manicured lawn, leading to a tree line near the perimeter wall. He stepped out and let the door close behind him. It clicked into place and he verified that this exterior door was indeed kept locked. He saw no trace of forced entry at the strike plate.

He looked around carefully, trying not to disturb anything, but he saw nothing else he thought might be relevant. He went back inside the front door of the building and took the elevator to the top floor. Derwood avoided stairs when he could. He found Maggie still inspecting the dead man's room.

"How's it going? Did you find anything yet?" he asked.

"No. It's hard to believe Smits' death is a coincidence, but coincidences do happen, right?"

"Maybe, but not with somebody sneaking in through locked doors."

Now it was Derwood's turn to smile as he led her down the stairs and showed her his discovery of the damp mat. After consultation with Cuthbert and her staff verified that the door was never used, Maggie felt she had enough to call her sister.

The case was growing. Derwood could see that Maggie was thrilled. As they walked out, she said, "I have worked other crimes, other murders even. But this feels different. Now I'm the District Attorney, and I'm finally in charge." Her eyes twinkled and she smiled broadly. "Feels like my first murder!"

Chapter 13

BY MIDAFTERNOON, SHERRIFF Blanchard concluded that the Moore County Sheriff's Department did not have the resources to manage the investigation alone. She called the North Carolina State Bureau of Investigation. Blanchard would maintain primary jurisdiction, but additional resources from the state would be placed at her disposal to provide manpower and expertise as needed, and to supplement the state crime scene team Sinsley had called in earlier.

Smits' body had been moved that morning. Space at Pinelands was at a premium, and management wanted his room turned over to a new resident by the next day. Sheriff Blanchard had other ideas. She declared Smits' room, the entire memory unit, and the stairwell fire escape an active crime scene. Soon the first technicians from the state crime lab arrived, and the funeral home was notified to postpone the embalming until after an autopsy.

Not long after that, Pinelands director Cuthbert called Maggie to say that Sarah Smalls had arrived for her daily visit. Maggie and Derwood found the young woman in a chair in the lobby. Cuthbert was sitting with her. A box of tissues sat on the table next to a lamp, and the young woman dabbed at crying eyes. Cuthbert rose to meet Maggie halfway across the lobby.

"What have you told her?" asked Maggie quietly.

"Just that Smits died last night. Nothing about murder. I was waiting for you," said Cuthbert. "She might take it hard. Mr. Smits was her favorite."

"So I heard."

Maggie sat next to Sarah Smalls and introduced herself. Sarah's damp eyes looked frightened, concerned.

"Willem Smits died last night in his sleep. You were with him yesterday afternoon." Maggie spoke softly, gently.

Sarah nodded. She dropped her head. In a small voice she said, "I think it's my fault." Maggie waited, but the girl said nothing more.

"You visit him often."

After a moment Sarah looked up. "Five days a week."

"That's a lot."

"Five days a week, every week since I was seventeen years old. That's three years. A little over three years, actually." Her eyes were drier now, her voice stronger. "Hard to believe, right?"

"Are you family?"

"No. I don't think so."

"You don't think so?"

"That's right," said Sarah, voice a little stronger still. "I don't think so."

"Why have you been coming here five days a week for three years?"

"No choice," said Sarah, faintly harsh.

"What do you mean?"

"Look Ms..." she paused.

"Kidd."

"Ms. Kidd. It's like this. I don't have any family, okay? They're all dead, or else they ran away." She no longer hid the harshness in her voice.

"It happened when I was a just a kid. My parents died in a car crash. I went to live with my grandad, my mom's dad. Mom was his pride and joy. His wife left him, and once he left the army my mom was all he had. Then one day he got a call, the one every parent dreads, and she was gone. Just like that. I guess he just couldn't take it." She nearly spat the last words, took a deep calming breath. She continued more gently.

"Her death tore him all up, and he started drinking more and more. When I was twelve, he left. Just ran off one day. Social Services got involved, and I went into foster care." She paused in memory and rubbed her face with both hands as she regrouped.

"Fun times. When I was sixteen, a lawyer said Gramps had left me a trust fund. It wasn't a fortune, but there was enough for me to live on my own with a little apartment and a car. Enough for college, maybe. By then I was ready to do just about anything to get out of the foster system. I took the money. I filed a petition for emancipation, and the judge liked it. I was free. I've been on my own ever since.

"Things were good for a while, but about a year later I had a visitor. He said he was a lawyer. He wore a suit. This time there were strings attached."

"What kind of strings?" asked Maggie.

"In order to keep receiving the trust money, I had to come over here and visit Mr. Smits every day, Monday through Friday. That's why I started 'volunteering' here." Air quotes. "At first I had to."

Cuthbert stared at Sarah with her mouth open like a guppy. The younger woman looked defensive, but she did not flinch from Cuthbert's gaze. Instead she reached out and took the director's hand.

"Mrs. Cuthbert, that's why I started coming here. It's not why I stayed. I love this place. Pinelands has given me a home, a purpose. I know what I'm supposed to do, who I'm supposed to be. You've given me that gift." Sarah's green eyes brimmed with fresh tears. "Thank you for that."

Cuthbert was now on the verge of crying herself. "Oh, sweet child," she breathed.

Derwood looked from the older woman to the younger in this moment of emotion. Was he supposed to feel moved? He glanced at

Maggie for a cue, and she seemed equally uninterested in the special moment. She broke it by asking the question that was also at the front in Derwood's mind.

"Who set up the trust fund?"

Sarah turned back to Maggie, but Cuthbert did not release the younger woman's hand. She patted it instead, her maternal instinct now fully engaged.

"I don't know. The law firm, I guess. Every month they send a letter in the mail to remind me."

"Do they visit?"

"No, just the letter. It's from Cranston Law Group, PLLC. P.O. Box 11288, Raleigh, North Carolina." She closed her eyes as she recited the address from memory.

"But Sarah, that's—"

"Ridiculous?" Sarah's eyes snapped open, meeting Maggie's. "You think I don't know that? I was sixteen years old when this started, and believe me, it's a lot better than being a foster kid. What was I supposed to do? Ask my social worker?"

"There's more, though. I have to file a monthly report on Mr. Smits. Particularly on any visitors he gets. Since there are never any visitors, it's never been an issue. But every letter is a reminder. If anyone comes around asking questions about anything from the past, about Woodlake, I am supposed to call a certain phone number. It's been in every letter for three years." Her eyes grew moist once more.

Derwood was having trouble following the girl's emotions. She was up and down like a roller coaster, shy and bold, gentle and harsh. Maybe it was her youth. He kept his mouth shut.

"Sarah, did you call that number yesterday after Deputy Flynn was here?"

Sarah's lips quivered as she pressed them tightly together. The moisture in her eyes finally spilled over and ran down her cheeks as tears. She did not trust herself to speak. She nodded. Maggie picked up the box of tissues and offered it to Sarah, who took it and wiped her eyes.

"It's okay, sweetheart," said Sheila Cuthbert. "It's okay. You didn't do anything wrong." After a few moments of Cuthbert's matronly ministrations, Sarah gathered herself.

"Sarah, what was you grandfather's name?" asked Maggie.

"James. James DeVaney. Everybody called him Jim."

Maggie looked at Derwood, who nodded almost imperceptibly. Jim DeVaney was on the list Sinsley had given him. He had been on the Woodlake board back in Akers' day. Motorboat faction.

As they left Sarah Smalls to the mercies of Sheila Cuthbert, Derwood turned to Maggie. "We need to talk to Cranston Law."

"We do," she said, brow furrowed in thought. "We do. And, I bet I know where to find Jim Devaney. Something tells me he never ran out on his granddaughter. I bet he never left Woodlake."

NEITHER DERWOOD NOR Maggie had yet had supper, and they agreed to dine together. They retired to Café Elegance, Pinehurst's answer to haute cuisine. The restaurant served classical French fare to rave reviews from the local clientele. The restaurant was full, but the maître d' recognized the district attorney and procured a table without delay. Derwood did not understand how he could recognize her, new as she was to her post, but the maître d' was paid for just such diplomacy. Maggie was flattered and did not refuse the privilege.

Dinner consisted of blanquette de veau with lightly blanched green beans served with a red Bordeaux wine. Paris-Brest complemented the meal as dessert. They talked longer and later than was wise, given the exigencies of the murder case before them, and yet Derwood wanted to keep her talking.

Something in her manner captivated him. He was long divorced, and had not thought of romance for years. He had Lizzy to worry about, and he was focused on that. The distracting news of her pregnancy rushed back into his mind. He had not really processed it yet, but he knew his teenage daughter would need his full attention. He had no room in his life for romance.

Still, another bottle of Bordeaux arrived halfway through dinner, and by the time they were done, it was a contest of who should drive home. Derwood, being much larger, took the responsibility. He drove home with great care, confident that he was on the right side of the middle line and probably the law, too. Arriving on Broad Street outside the alley that led to Maggie's loft, he parked and walked her to her door.

"Well, Derwood, that was an interesting day." She put both palms on his broad chest. "I cannot wait to see what tomorrow brings." She pushed him away with twinkling eyes.

She did not invite him in, and he was relieved. She seemed tipsy from the wine. Best part ways. They wished one another good night. Neither noticed the luxury sedan that pulled away from the curb on Broad Street after Maggie went inside.

Chapter 14

MORNING CAME EARLY and bright. Rays of sunlight snuck past the dark shades in Derwood's bedroom and found his eyelids as surely as a lodestone finds iron. Another morning, same ritual. Sluggishness. Brain fog. Coffee. Porch. And another phone call from Martin Sinsley.

"It's early, Marty," groaned Derwood.

"For you maybe. Not my fault you can't sleep."

"You are not helping," said Derwood

"Remind me to care. Look, we got ID on the second body."

"Yeah. It's Jim DeVaney," said Derwood through a yawn, the kind that threatened to dislocate his mandible. The phone transmitted Sinsley's irritation.

"Dammit, Derwood! That's twice. How the hell did you know that?"

"We talked to his granddaughter yesterday." He filled Sinsley in on the revelations from the afternoon at Pinelands, but he left out the details of dinner at Café Elegance with Margaret Kidd.

"Huh. If DeVaney was murdered, then who set up the trust? Who was watching Smits? And why?"

"Best I can figure is that Smits knew something about the murder of Fred Akers, but that does not explain why the killer left

Smits alive so long. Why not just do him sooner? No accounting for crazy," said Derwood.

"I'm not sure our killer is crazy, Derwood," said Sinsley. "There is a lot of method here. And a hell of a lot of premeditation. Like twenty years' worth. That's a slow burn."

Derwood could hear Sinsley fiddling with something that sounded like car keys jangling. "Today we're digging up the rest of the dam, draining the rest of Lake Surf. Come on over and have a look. See what us professional detectives do while you amateurs are sleeping in."

Derwood met Lizzy at Greenbow's for breakfast on her way to school. Kate had been spying on Lizzy ever since she found her at Derwood's several days before, and she had taken the step of tracking Lizzy's location on the teenager's cell phone. She was determined to keep her away from her father. To protect her daughter, she said. Lizzy was equally determined not to let that happen.

"Is your mother still mad?" asked Derwood.

"She's always mad. If it's not one thing, it's another."

Derwood smiled. "Yeah. I remember that. But it's because she loves you, and she's trying to protect you."

"That's what she says. She says you are dangerous. You are the one I need to be protected from."

"She said that, did she? Did she tell you why?"

"Not really. She just said you hurt people. I mean, you were in the army, right? Isn't that what you are supposed to do? Hurt bad people?"

Derwood chuckled. "Maybe. Not exactly. I guess. I don't know."

"She says you hurt a friend of hers." She looked at him. "Did you?"

He paused a moment. It was not like that. Early in their marriage Kate had bought in to the myth of invulnerability and power that surrounded Derwood and his fellow soldiers. Some of them thought they could do anything, that there were no limits. Kate had swallowed that idea hook, line and sinker. She thought she was special, that rules did not apply to her. She began to experiment with relationships outside their marriage, and when he found out about her dalliances, she pushed him to do the same. He was not interested.

Rather than back off in contrition and regret, she doubled down after the birth of their baby girl. She became more brazen about it, and declared that they now had an open marriage. Derwood did not agree. As a final effort to save their crumbling relationship, he did the only thing he knew how, and one of Kate's unlucky partners ended up in the hospital with a broken arm and shattered knee. Derwood barely knew the man, but had seen him around the neighborhood. After the incident, Kate left with the baby. Her anger had simmered since, but now that Derwood was back in their daughter's life, it threatened to boil over.

"Yes, I hurt someone."

Lizzy ate in silence for a few minutes. The waitress stopped by and refilled their drinks.

"Did he deserve it?"

"Yes."

She looked up at him and nodded.

"Okay," she said. "Then that's that. I trust you."

After a few more minutes of silence, she asked about the case. When he mentioned the young woman at Pinelands, Lizzy grew more interested.

"Sarah Smalls. Is she the redhead? The pretty one?"

"She has red hair," Derwood said.

"Yeah, I know who she is. She was at Pinecrest. She graduated two years ago."

"Do you know her?"

"Only a little. We had one class together. She always seemed a little strange."

"What do you mean?"

"Well, she's just..." She struggle to find the right word. "Just empty, I guess. Like she's just putting on a show, faking all the time, you know. Selfish. Like she wants to be liked, but she doesn't really care about other people. Like she pretends to and she wants people to think she does, but she doesn't, not really."

"Sounds like you know her pretty well."

"Ah, not really. I'm sure she's great. But you hear things, you know? Everybody has a rep. Especially in high school. It kinda sucks, actually."

"Do you think she is capable of murder?" Derwood asked.

Lizzy spit her pancake out in surprise and looked up sharply.

"Sheesh, Dad! I don't know. I hope not." She wiped her mouth. "Why do you ask?"

"Well, the old man she sits with at Pinelands rest home died, and we think he was murdered."

"And you think Sarah might have done it?"

"She was around. There are some suspicious circumstances." He shrugged. "Who knows? Somebody did."

An hour later, Derwood met Marty on Woodlake Dam. The work of the earth-moving equipment had progressed considerably since Derwood had last been there. The great rectangle was beginning to resemble more of a mudhole than a lake. Rising from the pit that was once a lake wafted the stench of stagnant water, wet pond grasses, and rotting fish. Thousands littered the exposed mud along the shores of the receding lake. The remaining area of deep water just in front of the dam occasionally wiggled and writhed as the surviving fish were concentrated into a decreasing volume of water.

Derwood stared at the largest remaining part of the lake, a sizable pool in front of the dam. What once had been home to watersports and weekend dreams was now a fetid expanse of mud and muddy water, full of desperate fish. As he stared, a shape resolved itself in his imagination. He stared patiently and long. In the background, crime scene technicians continued to work the dam, and he could hear Sinsley giving occasional directions. After a time as the water level continued to slowly recede, he grew more confident that something was submerged in the deepest remaining part of Lake Surf. He called Sinsley over and pointed into the muddy water.

"Marty, what is that, there?"

"A shithole, Derwood. That's a shithole. It's the dwindling hopes and dreams of a thousand yuppies."

"Funny. Ha-ha. I mean that shape. Is there some kind of submerged drain or structure?"

Sinsley looked more closely. It took him less time than it had taken Derwood, and his expression went from skeptical to curious. "Not sure. I don't think so. The spillway drain is there."

He pointed to a concrete pillar with a caged top which now protruded far above the surface of the remaining water. The spillway drain had been overwhelmed during the hurricane, unable to keep up with the volume of water pouring into the lake. It too had been the victim of inconsistent maintenance, but at its best it would have been unable to cope with the influx of water. Now it stood like a tall thin gray concrete grave marker consecrating the remains of Lake Surf.

"Maybe it's something left over from construction," said Sinsley. "A concrete block or something."

"Marty, isn't the dam is made of dirt?"

"Yeah, but there is some fill, too. Gravel, stone, debris, etc. It's not all just dirt and sand."

"Huh. Do you suppose they were putting in used Buicks, Marty? That looks like a car."

Sinsley stared harder. "Yeah, you might be right. I'm getting a bad feeling about this."

The remaining water was only a few feet deep, so it would have been ludicrous to call in divers. Derwood imagined them swimming around in just a few feet of muddy water, scuba tanks poking out of the water as they maneuvered in the muck. Better to wait for the reservoir to drain completely.

After a few hours, the rusted top of an old four-door sedan slowly poked into view above the surface. No telling whether it really was a Buick.

Work atop the dam slowed as everyone present paused to gawk and speculate about the car in the lake. At Sinsley's prompting, the crime scene techs got back to clearing areas of ground, and the earthmoving equipment followed behind to root out the dam. By midday, the area which had been the spillway was excavated to natural ground level, and the dam was fully breached. Even so, a natural depression in the lake bottom ensured that excavation of the spillway did not completely drain the water. Near the center of the dam remained a few feet of water in what had been the deepest part of Lake Surf. There in the remaining pool rested the rusted sedan, the muddy water lapping gently at the vehicle, flush with the bottom of the windows. The old car was submerged upright as if it had been parked and the owner simply forgot about it.

The automobile body was intact, and the windows were all rolled up tightly. The roof was rusted through in places. Mud, algae and grime covered much of the exposed surface of the vehicle and crept into the crevices around the doors, effectively sealing the passenger compartment. Through the holes rusted through the roof, dirty water sloshed gently inside the car. The water could not readily drain out through cracks and seams in the dash or around the doors, sealed as they were by muck and detritus from the lake, and the interior of the car held water above the level of the surrounding lake. It was like an old redneck bathtub. Derwood idly wondered whether the car was set on blocks, as it would be in yards throughout half the county, or whether the chassis was just nestled into the mud at the bottom of the lake. He hoped for blocks. The windows were smeared with mud, grime and algae. The interior was obscured.

Sinsley scavenged a kayak from a local homeowner and paddled out to have a closer look at the derelict. He invited Derwood to go, but Derwood just shook his head. "Doctor's orders," he said. Sinsley rolled his eyes.

Sinsley climbed into the kayak and paddled to the driver's side and plunged his hand beneath the water to find the door handle, but the door was stuck. He could see nothing through the opaque windows of the sedan. Derwood stood on the dam and waved in encouragement.

Paddling around the car, Sinsley discovered all the doors were welded shut by rust and grime. Sitting atop the kayak, he had no leverage and could apply little strength. He probed downward with his paddle and confirmed that the water was only around waist deep. He looked at Derwood, who smiled and waved and gave him a double thumbs-up sign. Grimacing, he lifted his legs over the side of the kayak and slid into the water.

His shoes sank fully into the slime, but the lake bottom firmed up after about six inches of muck. He positioned himself and reached for the handle of the rear passenger side door, just below the water line. The door was stiff but showed reluctant willingness to work with him, and after bracing one foot on the body of the car for maximum leverage, Marty wrenched the door open. The rusted hinges shrieked in time to his repeated tugs and the water inside poured through the opening.

As the water drained from the passenger compartment, Sinsley could see the interior matted with freshwater eelgrass. The windows and surfaces were covered in filamentous green algae. A rich wet grassy earth odor from the car mingled with the olfactory atmosphere of the lakebed. In the backseat of the car, a lumpy mass acted like a trellis to give structure to the plant growth. Marty imagined the eelgrass had waved its drifting fronds in the gentle bath of the lake, but now that the water had drained away, the grass draped like stringy wet green hair from the mass. A seatbelt was in place holding it in the backseat against an impact that would never come.

Sinsley felt bile rise in his throat as he reached into the backseat and brushed aside the grass. It parted just like hair, too. Beneath the tangled mat of grass, Marty could see the hollow eye of a human skull staring coyly back at him from beneath the matt of weed. Green algae covered the bones with an alien skin.

"Ah, no. No, no. Ah hell, no." He paddled the kayak away from the wreckage, but could not find air. His eyes burned. He must have gotten something in them. He pulled at his collar but had no tie to loosen. He looked around, but could not control the acid in his throat. Before he could get to shore, Martin Sinsley vomited his breakfast into the muddy waters of Lake Surf. He had just found JJ Hinrichs.

The car turned out to have three bodies in total, two in the front seat and the body of the child in the rear. All three bodies were covered in lake slime, algae, and aquatic plants, and all were badly decayed. Details would have to wait for autopsy, and everyone knew the water would have washed away any evidence of the crime. Grim determination took over the workers on the dam. They doubled their efforts and ordered bright lights against the darkness of night, still many hours away. They would work nonstop until the entire area was excavated. They owed it to the Hinrichs family.

Derwood walked back to his pickp. Akers. DeVaney. Amanda, Jason and JJ Hinrichs. Smits. Six dead, all of them from the Woodlake community. Could Amanda and Jason Hinrichs have been involved in the neighborhood swinging culture? If Jill Akers had killed her husband, could her rage have extended to an entire family? Could the boy have been collateral damage? And why Jim DeVaney?

Jill's assertion that neighborhood politics had something to do with the murders seemed more and more plausible. Four of the victims were tied to the Woodlake board of directors during the powerboat controversy. But why kill Smits, and why now? Obviously, because he was hiding something. He probably knew the identity of the killer.

Deloris was surely too old to get to Smits now. Sarah was too young to have been involved with Akers and Amanda Hinrichs. DeVaney was her grandfather. Maybe there were hidden issues? It wasn't exactly a stable home situation. Maybe she had some motive to kill Devaney, but the idea of a teenage girl planting her grandfather in the back of Woodlake Dam was too awful even for Derwood to contemplate. Sarah could have done for Smits easily enough, but why now, when his death was sure to be scrutinized? Too many questions. There was a killer on the loose, and Derwood was woefully short on answers.

Chapter 15

DELORIS HITCHCOCK HAD been told that she should not drive, that she was too old. Maybe her reflexes had slowed and her vision was no longer as good as it once was, but she knew she could still drive safely. Nonetheless, this trip to the Seven Lakes Hardware was chauffeured. William drove the late model luxury sedan leisurely into the parking lot and opened the rear door for his mother. The only thing missing was livery and a small driver's cap.

"Wait in the car, dear," said Deloris. "I will not be long."

"Yes, Mother."

She walked in to the store and turned towards the hardware section. Deloris had a screw loose. One of the cabinets in her kitchen rattled and squeaked every time she opened or closed it, and it had become intolerable. Just the sort of disturbance that grated on her nerves and interrupted her serenity. She was in search of replacement parts and lubricating oil.

She found the proper section and began to search in earnest through the dozens of bins full of tiny screws of different sizes lining one side of the aisle, when she heard a once familiar voice from the past.

"Hello, Deloris."

She turned to find Jill Akers standing in the aisle with a shopping basket in hand. "Jill! How are you, darling? It has been a long time." She moved to buss the younger woman's cheek but Jill pulled back. Deloris patted her lightly on the hand instead.

"Yes, it's been a long time," said Jill cooly.

Deloris had always admired the younger woman's looks. Jill's youthful beauty had matured into middle aged fullness. Unfortunately, she had lost her subtlety. Where once she possessed the charm and looks to stop men in their tracks without even trying, now she tried too hard. She wore a little too much makeup, and her tight yoga pants showed curves to the waist without any covering. It was a look that had come into fashion amongst teens and twenty-somethings. Deloris thought it looked desperate on middle aged women like Jill Akers.

"I am sure you've heard about the bodies in the dam," said Jill.

"Yes, of course. I was upset to hear about Fred, and I know you must be devastated. I am so sorry, my dear." What else could she say?

"It's okay, thank you. It was a long time ago." Jill looked uncomfortable.

"Did you hear they found James too?" Deloris asked.

"James?"

"DeVaney. James DeVaney."

Jill's eyes widened slightly at that. She probably knew him as Jim, like most people had, but Deloris did not use nicknames.

"I thought he ran off. Left that poor girl Sarah to fend for herself."

"Yes, well, apparently not."

Jill fidgeted for a moment, adjusting the items in her shopping basket. Yellow rubber kitchen gloves and disinfectant and thick silver duct tape. "Did the police come talk with you?"

"They did. A sheriff's deputy. You?"

"Yes. Again," said Jill. "I wish they would just leave me alone."

"They are just doing their job, darling. This will pass. Everything passes." Deloris paused. "What did you tell them?"

Jill paused a moment. "I told them the truth, Deloris. About everything."

The old woman smiled. "Oh, really? Which truth? That your husband was sleeping around? That you were a jealous wife?"

"Stop the charade, Deloris. It's tired. I'm tired. It was a long time ago. The better question is, what did you tell them?"

"Me? What do you mean?"

Jill looked at her. Deloris was old, but she still stood tall and straight, and she still had long thick hair and a natural beauty that belied her age. Surgery helped.

"Well, Darling," Jill said with sarcasm, "you certainly knew a lot of the men in the neighborhood back when people were going missing."

"Are you going to start that again?"

"Oh, come off it, Deloris. Everybody knows you were sleeping with my husband."

Deloris sighed. "Just stop! That is ridiculous. I could not stand the man! And he was too young for me. Too inexperienced."

Jill scoffed. "That didn't stop you. You're like a black widow!"

"That is the pot calling the kettle black, darling. Of course, you always were a hypocrite. I was not the one sleeping with James. You never could keep your skirt down and your panties up. Look at you now, dressed like that at your age." She tsk'd and shook her head.

"Shut up, Deloris!"

Deloris tittered in delight. "Is the stress getting to you? Why so uptight?" She paused. "Oh! I remember! They just pulled your husband's body out of the dam. I bet you thought he would never be found. I must say it was a good hiding place. Nobody wants to dig up the dam. Too bad for hurricanes, huh? You should have been more creative with where you put him."

Jill shook her head. "You really are crazy, you know that? You know who else they found? They found Amanda Hinrichs this morning, too. She was still there, right where you put her all those years ago. Was it really necessary to kill her family, Deloris? The little boy? Your time has finally come. They're going to get you this time, you old bitch."

"Oh, please, darling. I am seventy years old. My time passed long ago. But what do you imagine? Do you see me as a fifty-year-old woman running around killing a bunch of younger, stronger men?"

"The way you manipulate?" Jill spat. "Why not? You probably just got someone to do it for you. Like that other guy you used to hang around with. The Dutch guy. Smits! Or that crazy son of yours!"

"Willem Smits was a florist, for goodness sakes! And leave William out of this! He is a good boy. He can barely take out the garbage by himself, much less hide a bunch of bodies. You better get your affairs in order, because they are coming for you!"

Jill paused as she looked Deloris in the eye. "Well, we'll see. It's been real nice seeing you again, Deloris." Sarcasm dripped from her tongue.

"Oh, you too, Darling. I did not realize how I have missed out little chats. Please, do not be a stranger."

"Remember one thing, Deloris. What goes around, comes around."

"It certainly does, Jill. It certainly does." The two women stared at one another for a moment before Jill Akers broke eye contact and walked away.

Chapter 16

THE FILES MAGGIE KIDD took from Pinelands Estate indicated that Willem Smits' bills were paid by Cranston Law Group, PLLC, P.O. Box 11288 Raleigh, North Carolina, the same firm that sent Sarah Smalls letters and managed her trust. Maggie called Sarah on Friday morning, and met her at the local outpost of a wildly popular fast-food chicken restaurant. Maggie had never thought the restaurant was anything special, but most people could not get enough chicken sandwiches. She had to admit, the service was good.

Sarah brought all her copies of the letters for the past three years. There were thirty eight in all, and she had saved every one.

"This is everything," Sarah said as she handed a folder full of letters across the table to Maggie. "A letter every month."

The first letter had details of the trust arrangement, indicating that money would be deposited into a local bank on the first day of every month. An account had been set up in Sarah's name, and the letter had included a debit card and checkbook for her use.

A later letter changed the arrangement. It stipulated that she volunteer at Pinelands Estate and befriend the staff, with the aim of keeping an eye on Willem Smits. She was to report any visitors. She was to provide details of any contact monthly in writing to Cranston Law Group. If she ever heard any mention of Woodlake or the name of Fred Akers, she was to call a number given in the letter. In return, she would continue to receive monthly deposits into her account that would continue until she was twenty-five years old, at which time she would receive the not inconsiderable bulk of the trust fund as a lump sum transfer.

"Why do you suppose they wanted you to watch Smits?" asked Maggie.

"I don't know. I've wondered a lot. Old secrets, I guess?"

"Did he ever say anything to you? Give you any hint?"

She scoffed. "Uncle Will wasn't likely to say much. You never met him, did you?"

Maggie shook her head.

"Well, he wasn't going to say much. His mind was mostly gone."

"Mostly?"

"Yeah, mostly. He had his moments, these times where he'd remember something from the past, but he couldn't string two thoughts together most days. I don't think he even knew who or where he was, at the end. The only thing I ever saw was when your partner came to talk to him the other day, and he freaked out. Seemed like he must have remembered something. Your partner mentioned the name."

"Fred Akers."

"That's right, Fred Akers. Who's he?"

Maggie told her about the bodies in the dam. "Can you tell me anything else, Sarah?"

Sarah said she had upheld her end of the bargain, and Cranston Law Group had upheld theirs. She had never met anyone from the law firm except the man in the suit. Other than the monthly letters, there had been no further contact. On the afternoon of Derwood's visit to Pinelands, she had called for the first time the number listed in every letter.

The number had gone to voicemail. She left a message, and not long after she received a call back. She could not tell if it was the man in the suit. She described Derwood's meeting with Smits. The man thanked her and hung up. That was all.

"What was it like for you?"

"What was what like?"

"Sarah, you are an attractive young woman. You should be going out with friends, dating, whatever. This," she gestured to the pile of letters on the table, seeking the right words. "This can't be what you want."

Sarah smiled. "No, but it pays the bills, and it gets me where I need to go."

Maggie nodded. "And what happens now?"

"I hope I get to keep the money."

"That's all you want?"

"That's all I want."

"Did you kill Willem Smits?"

Sarah did not look away, but stared hard into Maggie's eye.

"No."

"You had motive, and opportunity."

"I suppose so. But I didn't do it."

Maggie didn't reply, but just looked at the girl skeptically, hoping she might reveal more.

"Look, I didn't do it. Why would I?"

"To get control of the money and control of your time. It cannot have been pleasant, going to the old folks home every day."

"Yeah, okay, but why would I do it now? Right when the police got involved? If I were going to do it, I could have done it anytime, right? Why now, when people are watching? I might be young, but I'm not stupid."

Maggie continued to look at her, then nodded curtly.

"Okay," she said, "that makes sense. Who do you think did it?"

"Whoever set up my little situation. Whoever is behind the money, whoever set up the trust. Whoever answered the phone when I called the other day. That's who you should be asking."

Sarah had little more information to offer. Maggie paid for breakfast and left. Back at her office, she sought and received a warrant for access to the phone records and the P.O. Box listed in Sarah's letters. Her task was easier because she had cultivated relationships with the local judges, and they trusted her.

The phone number was held by a national phone company. There was a local brick and mortar office, though, and she drove over accompanied by a deputy sheriff and armed with her warrant. She delivered the warrant to the unhelpful clerk at the office, but before long she realized that she would need to speak with someone higher up the food chain, probably in Raleigh.

She could get there in time for lunch. Thinking back to the dinner the night before made her smile, so she called Derwood. He answered on the first ring and seemed pleased by the invitation to join her on the drive. Maggie drove her Toyota Prius.

On the drive, Derwood texted Lizzie.

How you doing?

Meh.

Meh?

Upset stomach.

Oh boy. Need anything?

No. It'll be fine.

OK. Call me if you need. Talk later. Heart emoji.

Derwood put his phone away and filled Maggie in on the events of the morning and the disturbing discoveries at Woodlake Dam. When she learned that the car had been discovered in the lake, and that it held three bodies, almost certainly the Hinrichs family, her first response was, "How the hell did the car get in the lake?"

Derwood had been asking himself the same question. "The face of the dam is fairly steep. Maybe someone just drove the car in, and it floated enough to drift out before it sank. Or maybe it just rolled down the upstream face of the dam until the lake bed levelled out."

Maggie looked doubtful. "Could it have been there before the lake filled, way back when the dam was first built?"

"Not with three dead bodies, it couldn't. Somebody would have seen something."

"Well," said Maggie, "right now it doesn't matter how it got there. The question is, who put it there?"

The drive to Raleigh always seemed like it would be longer than it actually was. They made it in an hour, and after lunch the pair drove over to the regional offices of the phone company. When Maggie flashed her credentials and the warrant, good throughout the state of North Carolina, they were granted access beyond the nearly impenetrable barriers of the anteroom. Eventually they found someone at the phone company with decision-making authority who was helpful. Derwood could not believe it. All his adult life, he had never even heard of anyone at a phone company who actually would render assistance.

The helpful phone company official pulled the records from Sarah's cell phone and showed Maggie the number she had called that afternoon from Pinelands. It was registered to Stick-in-the-Eye Investigations. Sarah's outgoing call had been brief, consistent with her report that she left a message. Not long after placing her call, a call had come in to Sarah's cell phone from an office on the corner of Martin and South Blount in Raleigh. The office phone number was also registered to Stick-in-the-Eye Investigations.

Next, they drove over to the post office on Fayetteville Street, not far from where the phone call had originated. As expected, P.O. Box 11288 was housed in that office. Unlike phone company employees, postal workers were nearly always helpful. The resident assistant post master was happy to help, once he saw Maggie's credentials and the official warrant. The P.O. Box was indeed registered to Stick-in-the-Eye Investigations.

Maggie slid the Prius into an open space on Martin Street, a block down from South Blount. Stick-in-the-Eye Investigations was a storefront with a creaky metal sign above the door. The window was blacked out for privacy. A sign on the door indicated that interested parties should enter without knocking.

The office was tidy and clean. The walls were faded faux wood paneling. Bland landscape prints hung on the walls. The off-white drop ceiling had a long-dried water stain in the corner. The furniture was more modern, like something bought from IKEA, but not recently. The spare pastel chairs, tables and lamps all clashed. At least it was tidy and clean.

An open door led into a second room, where a tall man rose from behind a desk. He met them at the door between the rooms. The plain black T-shirt was tight over a muscular chest, and the fabric stretched at his biceps. Tattooed forearms led to large hands. His hair was an indeterminate shade of gray, cut short and balding on top. His face was weathered, and his eyes had seen things they wanted to forget. Derwood recognized the look.

"Good afternoon, I'm Daniel De Luca, Stick-in-the-Eye Investigations," said the man as he extended his hand. He looked at and spoke directly to Derwood.

Derwood took the proffered hand an introduced himself, but it was Maggie who announced, "Good afternoon, Mr. De Luca. We are from Moore County. I'm District Attorney Margaret Kidd, and this is Deputy Derwood Flynn. He is my investigative assistant." Derwood felt more official with every introduction. "Your name came up in an investigation. We need to ask you a few questions." She was getting good at saying that.

"Well, Stick-in-the-Eye is always happy to help the law." He led them into the back office, where they sat in two dated chairs that faced a neat desk. The office décor was more of the same, and the back wall was lined with file cabinets. "How can I help?"

"Do you know Sarah Smalls?"

De Luca pursed his lips and looked over Maggie's head at the wall behind her. "I am not sure I do. The name sounds familiar, but... no, I can't place it. Who is she?"

"She is the young woman in Southern Pines who's been receiving monthly correspondence from your address for the past four years." Maggie smiled sweetly as she spoke.

"Huh," said De Luca.

"Do you have a secretary?"

De Luca laughed. "Ms. Kidd, does it look like I have a secretary?"

"No. No it does not. And since you don't, I imagine you handle all of your own correspondence." The smile faded as Maggie looked him in the eye. De Luca shrugged.

"Do you do any work for Cranston Law Group?" asked Maggie.

"I do all kinds of work for all kinds of people, Ms. Kidd." He paused and rubbed his chin as if thinking deeply. Derwood rolled his eyes as the man finally added, "Cranston. That name is familiar too, but honestly I do not know why."

"What is it you do exactly, Mr. De Luca?"

"We are private investigators. We investigate." He waved a dismissive hand. "Mostly what you'd expect. Domestic disputes. Marital infidelity, mostly. We spend a lot of time following husbands or wives around town snapping photos of discreet rendezvous, hunting illicit love nests. Some insurance fraud investigation, too. Trying to catch people who claim disability out on the golf course, you know, or maybe carrying heavy groceries or out working in their yard. You would be surprised how many people try to game the system." He smiled.

"Do you do any work for law firms?"

"Oh, sure. Lots. Most of our clients come to us through law firms. Actually, most of the time the law firm is the client. They just pass our bill on to their client, with additional billable hours attached for legal consultation. You're the DA; you know how lawyers are."

"Where do you receive your mail, Mr. De Luca?"

"The mailbox," said De Luca, deadpan.

"Funny." Maggie did not smile. "Which mailbox, Mr. De Luca?"

"At the post office, Ms. Kidd. Couple blocks down."

"Ah. You use a post office box."

"That's right."

"What is the box number?"

"Really? Did you even google me? All this is on our website. Maybe you need a new 'investigative assistant,' Ms. Kidd." He glanced at Derwood, who stared back without moving or speaking. Derwood felt his dislike of De Luca growing. "It's P.O. Box 11280."

De Luca opened a file cabinet and pulled out a blank letterhead. The letterhead read "Stick-in-the-Eye Investigations, P.O. Box 11280, Raleigh, NC." Beneath in italics was written "Don't get mad; get even."

"Nice," said Maggie.

"Yeah, I like it too," said De Luca lightly. "This can be a dirty business. But somebody's got to do it."

"What's funny, though," said Maggie, "is that the post office has a different box registered in your name. Stick-in-the-Eye."

"Is that so?"

"Yes, that's so. And that other box, P.O. Box 11288, is the return address for Cranston Law Group. Sarah Smalls has corresponded with Cranston Law Group for years, using your P.O. Box. How do you explain that?"

"Not my place to explain it," said De Luca. "Probably, you should get your assistant here to investigate."

"Two days ago, a phone registered in your name received a phone call from Sarah Smalls. A short time later another phone also registered in your name called her back. The second call originated from this office. Did you call her on that phone, Mr. De Luca?" She pointed to an old-fashioned phone on the desk, the kind with square push buttons and a cord.

De Luca was silent, caught in his lie. Maggie looked at him. He looked at Maggie. Derwood looked from one to the other. Suddenly, the phone on the desk rang. The sound was startling, breaking the tension. It was an old sound, from Derwood's childhood, the trilling of a mechanical gong vibrating between tiny bells in the plastic housing of the phone. De Luca picked up the receiver, put it to his ear.

"Yeah. Yeah. No. Now? OK. Be there in five minutes."

He hung up the receiver. "Look, Ms. Kidd. I'd love to stay and chat, but duty calls. You'll have to excuse me."

"We are not finished, Mr. De Luca."

"Yeah, well, saved by the bell, huh?" He pointed to the exit as he gathered his things. "Call my secretary to make an appointment." De Luca laughed as he locked the door behind them and hurried down the street.

Maggie called after him, "Willem Smits died last night, after you talked to Sarah Smalls. We think he was murdered."

The private detective stopped but did not look back. After a moment, he continued on around a corner and out of sight.

Chapter 17

DERWOOD AND MAGGIE walked back to her car. The evening was pleasant, the air warm and laced with the sounds of the city. Raleigh was not a dense city like New York or Chicago, but compared to the countryside of Moore County, it was a metropolis. A faint smoky scent of barbecue from a local pit joint hung in the air and mixed with the diesel exhaust and rumble of a passing city bus. They climbed in the vehicle, and Maggie drove south, headed for Southern Pines.

"Here is what I think," Derwood began. "I think Smits knew something about—"

Maggie interrupted him. "Do we have to talk about murder right now? Let's start with something more basic. I don't know the first thing about you, really."

"That's not true. You know my name is Derwood. You know that I'm a friend of Marty Sinsley. You know I used to be in the army. You know I am now a sworn officer of the law. You know a lot about me."

"You know what I mean," she smiled. He felt it again, the transformative effect of her smile. It hit him somewhere behind and maybe a little below his belly button, right where the butterflies lived. What in the world? Was he in middle school? He told himself to get a grip.

But all he said was, "What do you want to know?"

"Where are you from? How'd you get to Moore County? What do you do for work? What do you do for play? Where do you live? That sort of thing. Normal people stuff. Not death and murder and psycho stuff."

"Well, let's see." He thought about it for a minute, then said as he enumerated on his fingers, "Nebraska. Army. Retired. Not much. Seven Lakes." Guarded with his past, as always.

She rolled her eyes. "Very funny." She punched him lightly on the shoulder as she pulled the car onto the freeway. "But I'm serious. I told you my story. A lot of it anyway. Now tell me yours."

"There's not that much to tell," Derwood yielded with a chuckle. "I am from Nowhere, Nebraska." His voice capitalized Nowhere.

"Is that a real town?"

"Might as well be. The actual town is called Manosa, and it is as close to nowhere as you can get. High plains, just across the border from Colorado. I grew up there. Just a bunch of open land, low hills. Ranches for cattle and crops. Not a lot of people. Cold as hell in the winter, hot as hell in the summer, and always dry and dusty. Dust bowl country. Railroad runs right through town. When I was a kid, I always wanted to hop a train and get out of there. Didn't matter where it was headed, just anywhere but Nowhere. But trains don't stop in the middle of Nowhere. Don't even slow down."

"Sounds small."

"Yeah. My high school graduating class had thirty-six people, and we were the biggest class in a decade."

"So, you joined the Army?" Maggie asked.

"Yup. Easiest way out of town. Either that or be a cowboy or a ranch hand. Not a lot of opportunity in Manosa."

"No college?"

"Nah. Not for me. I was tired of waiting around. I wanted to do something more than I wanted to be something, if you know what I mean. I'd had enough sitting around waiting. So, I joined the Army. Did my time."

"You make it sound like a prison sentence," said Maggie.

"Do I? Nah, that's not what I mean. It was great. Glad I did it. Got to travel the world, meet interesting people…"

"And kill them," they said in unison. They both laughed. It felt good to laugh with her. Derwood had not smiled or laughed much in the last few years, but Maggie Kidd smiled a lot and laughed easily and often.

"Something like that. Anyway, I was in the Army and ended up stationed at Fort Bragg. A lot of the guys from my old Unit migrate over to Moore County. Better schools, safer communities, higher quality of life, that sort of thing."

"Do you have anyone? In your life, I mean?" She kept her eyes on the road.

He hesitated. He was unsure what was happening here, but he knew enough not to hold back. "Yeah, as a matter of fact, I do."

She glanced at him, surprised, then back to the road.

"I have a daughter, Lizzy. Her mom, we had a thing a long time ago. It didn't work out. But Lizzy, she's great. I wasn't around much until recently. I'm trying to get to know her better. To be the right kind of man, the right kind of father."

"Better late than never?" she said.

"Something like that."

The drone of the road seemed louder in the awkward silence that opened between them. Then Derwood said, "Anyway, that's how I ended up here."

"Well, I'm glad you did," said Maggie as she turned to look him full in the eye. The butterflies started buzzing in his belly again.

"Yeah?" he asked, meeting her gaze. He wondered briefly if it was a good idea to be hurtling down U.S. 1 at eighty miles per hour making googly eyes, but he decided to just go with it. Fearless Derwood Flynn.

"Yeah." She turned back to the highway. "Now that I'm the DA, I need a thug. And here you are." She said it with a light tone and that smile. He could not tell whether she was serious or just pulling his leg. Maybe both? She continued. "You were about to tell me your theory of the case."

"Right," said Derwood. He shooed off the butterflies and gathered his thoughts. "Smits lived in the same community as Akers, and Devaney, and Hinrichs. All three of them were part of the powerboat faction at Lake Surf. Willem Smits played for the other team, the status-quo bunch."

"The 'no-powerboat' faction," said Maggie.

"Right," nodded Derwood. "And they know they're going to lose the vote, and lose their peaceful lake experience. Somebody decides that the best way to protect their turf is murder. Smits knows all about it. Maybe he did it, maybe not. But he knows all about it, and somebody else knows too.

"Smits gets old, his mind starts to go. Alzheimer's maybe. He ends up at Pinelands. For some reason, whoever else knows about the killing does not want to kill Smits. Who knows why? So instead they come up with this surveillance scheme. They get a person on the inside to keep an eye on Smits."

"Sarah Smalls," said Maggie.

"Right. Things are fine for a long time, years maybe. But then Miranda blows through, and—"

"That rainy bitch," said Maggie. Derwood thought he saw the hint of an upturned lip at the corner of her mouth, but he went on.

"Right. The hurricane washes Fred Akers out of the dam, and people start asking questions. I go talk to Smits. Sarah Smalls follows orders and calls De Luca. Later that same night, Smits is killed to shut him up. De Luca has to be involved. He took Sarah's call. Cranston Law Group, too. They set up the surveillance."

"What about Sarah?" asked Maggie. "Did she kill Smits?"

"I can't see it. You got a look at her. Do you think she is a killer?"

"Looks can be deceiving. I mean, just look at you. Here you are, a big teddy bear, but didn't you, uh, do things? You know, in the army?"

Derwood muttered something under his breath.

"The point is, looks can be deceiving," Maggie went on. "That girl is tougher than she looks. She's had a rough go. She's not an innocent schoolgirl," said Maggie.

"Maybe, but she would have been in diapers when Akers was killed, if she was even born yet. Same for DeVaney and the Hinrichs. She'd have been way too young."

"She could have killed Smits. She had motive."

"The money? Yeah, maybe, but she left Pinelands hours before he died. The night nurse confirmed that."

Maggie nodded. "But he also said she stayed late to read him to sleep. Maybe she poisoned him, you know, with some delayed poison that killed him a few hours later. She was reading Agatha Christie to him, after all. Wasn't she always writing about poisons and stuff like that?"

"Maybe you've been watching too much TV," said Derwood.

"What about Steve, the night nurse?" said Maggie. "He was the last one to see Smits alive."

Just then Wagner blasted forth from Derwood's phone. Maggie looked at him curiously as he took it out.

"What?" said Derwood defensively. "So, I like opera."

Maggie just shrugged.

Caller ID said Martin Sinsley. "Hey, Marty. Yeah. We're on our way back from Raleigh. Yeah. Hold on, let me put you on speaker." Derwood activated the speaker phone. Sinsley's voice came out of the small speaker, thin but intelligible.

"Got a bit more on Smits. The guy had money. He was a flower merchant, of all things. A damn florist! Importing tulips from

Holland. Made a fortune! Retired young, moved down here from New York. You believe that? A damn florist!"

"Maybe you're in the wrong line of work, Marty," said Derwood. "I can see you in a flower shop. It's never too late to follow your dreams."

"Yeah, screw you Derwood. And, y'all are not going to believe this, but the coroner up at the state lab thinks Smits was poisoned."

Maggie smirked at Derwood and wiggled in her seat. Her dimples shone. Now Derwood shrugged.

"Lead poisoning. Apparently, you can see it on the gum line. She thinks that's why he was losing his mind. Not just senile dementia, but chronic lead poisoning. She said it's not that easy to accidentally poison yourself with lead these days. It's too high profile, too many safety precautions in place. Coroner thinks somebody's been slipping him lead for years."

The car hummed along near eighty, and Maggie nearly had to shout to be heard through the speakerphone. "Was that the cause of death?"

"Probably not. Coroner's not sure yet. She's still running some tests. His body shows no signs of a struggle." He spoke in short sentences, as people do when there is a doubtful phone connection. "She thinks he died of asphyxiation. He wasn't strangled, no bruises or marks on the neck. No bruising on the face, no cloth fibers or anything unusual in the pharynx. Nobody smothered him. But he couldn't breathe.

"Coroner says there are some medical drugs that will basically paralyze people for a while, then wear off. She says she's seen it before. Says it's more common than you'd think. Anyway, more to follow. Talk later." Sinsley severed the connection.

"Huh," said Maggie.

Derwood had read that ever since Michael Jackson died in 2009 of propofol overdose, poisoning with medicines or medical drugs had been on the rise. There are hundreds of cases per year these days. There was usually a medical connection, if an investigator could find it.

"If she finds a needle mark from an injection site, she might be able to isolate the specific drug that was used. Killers always think they're smarter than they really are. They assume these drugs leave no trace, but all it takes is a quick internet search to find out that's not true."

"Have you heard of this before?" asked Derwood.

"Once, when I was in Charlotte," said Maggie. "Anesthesiologist injected his wife with a paralyzing agent, the kind used in surgery. He wanted to collect her life insurance money and run off with his nurse. He didn't get far." She laughed to herself, then continued.

"It's actually a pretty good way to go," she said. "Once you get past the fear when you realize you can't breathe, it's over pretty quickly. Sort of like drowning. Seems awful when you think about it, but it's fast and any pain is short-lived. Or that's what they tell me." She laughed uncomfortably. "Beats a slow death by cancer any day.

"So maybe we're looking for someone with medical training who was at Lake Surf around the year 2000, who is still around, and who was against powerboats on the lake. That narrows it down some."

"Steve the night nurse has medical training," said Derwood. "And opportunity."

"Sarah Smalls wants to be a doctor," said Maggie.

"And they know each other," said Derwood.

"But neither was old enough to be involved with the Akers thing," said Maggie. "Or DeVaney, or the Hinricks."

"Yeah. What about the lead poisoning?" asked Derwood. "That used to be a thing, right? Kids eating paint in old houses. Leaded gasoline, that sort of thing. You don't hear much about it these days."

"I read once that lead poisoning was the reason Rome collapsed. They used lead pipes for indoor plumbing. They all got stupid, or went nuts," said Maggie.

"Huh. I never heard that. Is that what lead poisoning does?"

"Yup. Makes you stupid, or crazy, or both."

"Huh. Does it affect memory?" asked Derwood.

Maggie glanced over at him. "What are you thinking?"

"Well, Smits was losing his mind, losing his memory. Somebody was trying to keep him from talking. His body showed evidence of lead poisoning. What if somebody was playing a long game, trying to shut him up in a more subtle way, without actual murder. Trying to, you know, disrupt his memory or something."

Maggie looked at him with new respect on her face. "Derwood, that is either the smartest or the dumbest thing I've heard all day. Would that even work? Plus, why not just kill him? It would be a lot safer."

"Beats me," Derwood said. "Hey, are you getting hungry? All this talk of killing is making me hungry."

"Talking about killing doesn't bother you?"

Derwood shook his head. "Nah. Some people need killing."

They decided to dine that night at the Bell Tree Tavern on Broad Street. Maggie parked near her loft, and they walked over. The tavern sported a mahogany bar with brass rails, and about a dozen televisions hung around the place, but tonight's entertainment was live music. A jazz quartet occupied the small raised dais in the back corner and pumped out a steady stream of rhythm. A few sophisticated items on the menu augmented the more standard bar fare. The place was not known for its menu. It was more of an atmospheric kind of place.

The establishment was crowded on a Friday night, but the owner behind the bar recognized Maggie and prepared a table along the left-side wall, made of brick that looked a hundred years old. The other patrons still waiting for a table scowled at the pair as they went to their seats. Derwood could get used to this kind of treatment. As hoped, the beer was cold, the food was tolerable, and the music was steady. Derwood and Maggie ate and drank and talked long into the evening.

Later Derwood walked Maggie home. In her alley, at the door to the stairs leading to her loft, she fumbled in her purse for her keys. She found them and put them in the lock. She turned and looked up at Derwood. He could hear the sounds of cars passing the mouth of the alley, and Thursday night was always lively, for a small town. Couples walked, and revelers laughed into the warm night as they headed to or from the bars and restaurants lining Broad Street.

"Another interesting day, Derwood Flynn. I like having my own personal thug. Do you want to come up for coffee or a nightcap?" She smiled. The butterflies swarmed in Derwood's guts. He really was acting like a middle schooler. He had to get a grip. But maybe that could wait until tomorrow.

"What are you trying to do here, Ms. Kidd? Steal my heart? Don't you know I am a sworn officer of the law? That could get you arrested."

"Did you really just say that?" Maggie rolled her eyes. "Excuse me while I puke in the alley." She mimed gagging, then stood and pretended to wipe her face clean. "I was thinking we could put our heads together and see if we could come up with a viable list of suspects. Then tomorrow, we go poke them. See what we find."

"Ah," said Derwood, a little embarrassed. Had he misread the situation and her intent? She smiled at him again. More butterflies. Stop it, Flynn, he told himself.

"But..." she said coyly as she eyed him.

"Good night, Maggie. Best if I head on home. There are some things I still need to do tonight. I've got to talk to an old friend."

Her smile faded and she suddenly seemed unsure, hesitant.

"I'll see you in the morning, okay?" he said. "You're right. We need to go through our suspect list. Tomorrow. Good night." He squeezed her hand and walked out of the alley as she stood watching him go with her key in the door.

Derwood was not lying. He did have to meet an old friend, his friend from Kentucky. When he got home, his friend was in the liquor cabinet where he always kept it. He poured himself a glass on the rocks. If he had to dream, he wanted to do it while he was awake. Just as he raised the glass to his lips, his phone droned. When he saw the caller ID, he put the glass down immediately.

"Lizzy, sweetheart, it's late. Everything okay?"

She sobbed into the phone. "No, Daddy. Something's wrong. It's bad. Help me, please!"

Chapter 18

THURSDAY

"THANK YOU FOR PICKING me up, Brandi."

"It's what sisters do. You need the help."

William laughed at that. "Me? What about you?"

Brandi was idiosyncratic. Deloris called her obsessive-compulsive, but despite years of effort, she had not been able to break her daughter of the need for symmetry. Brandi required order.

Deloris did not like that outside forces exerted control over her children, but William thought he understood it. Maybe symmetry for Brandi was like music for him. It brought order and purpose to an otherwise senseless world.

The drive from Brandi's apartment in the city to their mother's house in Woodlake took about an hour. William had spent the night at Brandi's place, as he sometimes did. They drove together south on U.S. Highway 1 in her subcompact, headed for a lunch date with Mother. There had been no need to ask when lunch would be served. It was always at the stroke of noon.

"If you slow down a little, we will miss the bell," said William.

"You really are trying to make her mad," said Brandi in her pseudo-iambic speech.

"She's just going to want to talk about the bodies, and I don't like that. It makes me sad."

"I know, dear brother. I know. But what can a person do?" She nearly stumbled over the last statement. It had no meter.

"I don't want to be around Mother anymore. I don't like the things she makes me do."

"When do you work today, William?"

"Three to eleven at the hospital tonight. Why?"

"There is more yet to do," Brandi mumbled to herself. "Things are not even."

"Huh?"

"Never mind. We'll put it right," she said. "And we're going to cure you of Mother's training, William. Be still and close your eyes."

Recently, Brandi had been working with him whenever she could. She called it counter-conditioning, talking William down, guiding him through the effect of the Wagner. The process was slow. He had to overcome years of ingrained obedience to Mother. It was difficult and frightening, but William could feel it working. The Wagner still had an immediate and powerful effect on him, but he was increasingly able to fight it off.

She reached for her phone and pulled up the Wagner. The music came richly, rolling out of the surprisingly robust sound system of the subcompact. As the horns sounded, William winced. He ground his teeth through the rising register, and by the second horn blast he was trembling.

"Stop it. Make it stop!"

Brandi turned the music off.

"It's not that bad," she said. "I think people judge Wagner more harshly than he deserves. Probably because the company he kept. Or how his music was used."

"I hate it," growled William, barely moving his lips.

"Of course you do, dear brother. But it is useful. Let's do it again."

He sighed and closed his eyes as she activated the music again.

William's relationship with his mother was complicated. She always told him he was a difficult child, and they had worked together for years to establish effective behavior and boundaries. She had nearly given up on him before she discovered the music. He could not remember when it started, but he knew well enough the effect.

When he was young, he was disconnected. He found the world and the people in it dull and uninteresting. But when Deloris hit upon playing music for him, something changed. He could see the music as it floated in the air. It sharpened his focus and gave him purpose. He could not get enough.

Once Deloris realized music was the stimulus she had long sought, she began his training in earnest. She recorded it all in leather-bound notebooks. There had been many early failures, but the music brought success. She was subtle. To William, the sessions felt more like games than experiments. Eventually, all he wanted was the sweet sound of the music. He would do anything to get it. Deloris shifted reinforcement schedules, just as she had been taught. Her professors at college would be proud.

At first she tried to correspond with the man she considered her mentor, but Professor Skinner barely remembered the young woman who had worked in his lab. Deloris' habit of seduction had not worked on him. She was on her own as she worked to mold William into a projection of her own will. But she kept records. Meticulous scientific journals of daily successes and failures, and she recorded her progress. She continued to pen letters to Professor Skinner, but as her experiments grew in sophistication and yielded greater success, she stopped sending the letters. Part of the reason was discouragement that the great man did not respond to her letters, and part was a growing realization that her work might be viewed unfavorably by small minds. That was okay. Pioneers often worked alone. She was no different. But she kept the letters, and she imagined receiving letters from the professor in return. The letters celebrated her success as, over time, William was nearly perfectly conditioned to obey her directives. He was like one of Pavlov's dogs.

That had begun to change as Brandi grew up. Independent from the first, she had chafed under Deloris' authority, and she had gradually inserted herself as a buffer between them. In an odd twist, the younger sibling was protector of the older.

THEY ARRIVED AT THEIR mother's house shortly before noon and in time to be greeted by the bell. Once they were at table, Deloris opened conversation as always.

"I am sure you have both heard the local news. Bodies are just popping out of the ground like flowers." She smiled to herself. Inside joke. "We need to discuss options for containment."

"Mother dearest, do not act surprised," said Brandi, speaking slowly. "The Good Book says, 'Whatever one sows, that will he also reap.'" She smiled, delighted with herself. Ever even.

"She is doing it again, Mother," said William. "I don't like it when she does that."

"Forget that now, son. We need to focus on the situation. We need control before things get out of hand. Our exposure extends to the lawyer. William, here is what you are going to do..."

Brandi interrupted. "What about the woman? The district attorney on the television? We need more women. We are uneven, Mother." Brandi smiled sweetly.

William fidgeted in his seat.

Deloris stared at her daughter. The speech pattern had been going on for years, but this was something new.

"No, darling. She is too dangerous. Mother will take care of everything."

Brandi turned her lower lip down into an exaggerated pout. "You are no fun."

"Leave her alone, Brandi. Do you understand?"

"Yes, Mother." She winked at William as she looked away. "A girl can dream, can't she?"

William slapped the table. "Stop it, Brandi! Stop doing that!" His face was red and his eyes squinted in anger.

"Control yourself, son," said Deloris calmly.

He rose from the table abruptly, and his chair toppled backward onto the floor. He turned to Deloris, both hands planted on the table, looming over her. This too was new.

"You did this. You can make her stop!"

"Sit down, son," Deloris continued, recognizing the need for de-escalation. She did not raise her voice. "Control yourself."

"You did this to both of us! You can undo it!"

The large man still leaned over the table, looming over the old woman in her seat. Their eyes were locked in an animalistic struggle for dominance, and despite the physical difference between them, the huge man slowly began to draw away. Deloris stood slowly to her feet and grabbed her phone. She activated the music, and the horns of the *Götterdämmerung* filled the house, piped through hidden speakers. She stood to her full height and pushed her son away from the table, hand on his chest as she forced him back. He backed up until his calves hit the edge of a chair in the living room, and it took but a light shove from Deloris to fold onto the chair in a seated position.

"You will do as I say, when I say," Deloris snarled. "You do not get to think for yourself, you do not get to have opinions. And you do not get to judge your sister." Malice dripped from her tongue. "She cannot help the way she is, just as you cannot. If it were not for me, where would you be? You would be in a group home medicated with tranquilizers and staring at the wall. And your sister would be in an asylum, or worse. So control yourself, William, now." She loomed over him as he sat on the couch. "Do you understand?"

She stared hard into his eyes, her gaze heavy with disgust. He trembled and dropped his head.

"Yes, Mother," he mumbled.

She let the music play a minute longer, until order had been restored, and the Hitchcock home was tranquil once more.

ALONE LATER THAT EVENING, Deloris sat in the dark. William had the three to eleven swing shift at the hospital, and Brandi had gone who knows where. The children were becoming a problem, particularly William. It had taken years of work to complete his conditioning, but her grip was loosening. She needed to modify the regimen. Perhaps she had been lax. Things had been going smoothly recently. He had even earned a reputation in the community as a reliable worker. She still felt pride at the thought. But maybe his little successes outside the home had emboldened him. Or maybe her reinforcement schedule had been too inconsistent. Whatever the reason, her grip was slipping. She sighed. She would not allow that.

Chapter 19

LIZZY SAT IN HER BEDROOM, finishing an essay she was writing for one of her classes. She had found over the last year that writing came easily to her, but she was distracted tonight. All day, a nagging ache had increased in her gut. Now, it throbbed painfully. She had taken another pregnancy test, and it was still positive. She kept hoping for a negative, but no luck. At least she could pretend this was not happening. She was a good kid, a hard worker. Normal. But soon everyone would know the truth. She was in trouble.

Her belly throbbed with pain and nausea. She stood and paced, but that did little to relieve her pain and even less for her anxiety. She glanced at her phone. 11:00. Down the hall, her mother was probably already asleep. She was early to bed, and although she often stayed up to read, she was never up this late. Lizzy, on the other hand, was a night owl.

She had not told anyone about the pregnancy, except her dad. She had not told the baby daddy, and she had certainly not told her mother. She was not sure how either would react. She did not really care. The guy was just a friend from band at school. It's not like they had an undying love. They were really just friends experimenting, and things had gotten out of hand. He was not going to make an honest woman of her. It had been fun at the time but awkward since, and she did not want to deal with his reaction. Her mother was a different story. She would freak out, and Lizzy could not deal with that.

She paced the floor and looked at the walls, but they had no answers. Suddenly, she felt her insides rip. The throbbing became sudden searing pain, and she gasped and fell to the floor. She felt like someone was stabbing her in the lower right side of her belly. The peak intensity lasted only a few minutes, but it was enough to make her weep. After a little while, she recovered enough sense to pick up her phone.

Her dad answered on the first ring. "Lizzy, sweetheart, it's late. Everything okay?"

"No, Daddy. Something's wrong. It's bad. Help me, please!"

"Are you home?"

"Yes."

"Where is your mother?"

"I want you, Daddy. Please help me."

"I'll be there as soon as I can."

A few minutes later he pulled up to the house where Lizzy lived with her mother. She had made it out to the driveway and clutched her abdomen as she limped to the pickup. She was in her pajamas, fuzzy and pink and covered in balloons. She looked pale and clammy in the dim light. Derwood helped her in the truck.

"What's the matter, honey?"

"I don't know. That little ache got a lot worse tonight. Something's wrong." She was still tearful but under better control than when she had called. Derwood pulled out and drove to the hospital.

"Where is your mother?"

"I didn't wake her up. She doesn't know anything. That's why I called you."

"Lizzy, she needs to know. She's your mom."

"You know how she is. She'll freak out! She will either want me to join a convent or get an abortion. I'm not ready for her judgment or her advice. Please, just let's drop it for now."

They were jostled by a small pothole and Lizzy shrieked.

"Ahh! Take it easy! These bumps are killing me!"

Derwood ignored her pain and pressed the accelerator.

"It's going to be alright, sweetheart. Hang in there."

They drove the rest of the way to the hospital in silence, broken only by Lizzy's occasional moans of pain.

At the emergency department, check-in was quick but the waiting room was full. Lizzy felt lightheaded, and her forehead had a sheen of sweat. One look at Lizzy, and the triage nurse brought her right in. Her initial blood pressure was low, and her heart rate was climbing. She was taken to a bed in the hallway minutes after entering. A young woman doctor was at the bedside right away.

"What's wrong tonight? How can we help?"

Lizzy described her symptoms as a nurse worked to put an IV in the back of her hand. Lizzy barely noticed the pinch in her hand over the fire in her belly. When the doctor asked about her monthly cycle, Lizzy hesitated, but Derwood did not.

"She's pregnant," he said.

"How far along?" asked the doctor.

"I don't know," Lizzy sobbed.

The doctor and the nurse exchanged concerned glances, and the doctor hurried off for a moment, then returned with a portable ultrasound machine, the kind on wheels. "We need to get her into a room right now," she told the nurse.

"They are all full," said the nurse. She darted across the hall to a linen rack and grabbed a blanket, thrust one end at Derwood.

"Hold this."

He held one corner and the nurse held the other. The blanket hung between them, a makeshift curtain hiding Lizzy from the bored gaze of the drunk lying on a stretcher across the hall.

Behind the blanket, the doctor raised Lizzy's shirt and squeezed cold jelly onto her belly, then gently maneuvered the ultrasound probe. She studied the tiny gray screen.

"Honey," she said, "did the bumps hurt in the car when you drove here tonight?"

Lizzy nodded, biting back tears.

To Derwood, standing at the bedside holding his daughter's hand, the screen looked like a snowstorm in a winter forest at night, but the doctor pointed to a black stripe on the screen.

"See that?" she said. "That's probably blood. She probably has a tubal pregnancy, and it is probably ruptured. She is bleeding into her belly.

"We need another nurse here, now!" The doctor did not exactly shout, but her voice carried.

"Two large-bore IV's. Draw blood for everything. Type and screen. Hang normal saline. This one's going to the OR."

Moments later, two nurses appeared at the bedside, and Lizzy had another IV, this time in the opposite arm from the first. Two bags of IV fluid were hanging above her, and the doctor was on the phone with the on-call specialist.

Just then, a large man in a purple shirt with the hospital logo rounded the nurses' station, pushing a large plastic cart, and slowly rumbled through the wide hallway. The cart stopped a foot from the small crowd of nurses at Lizzy's bedside. Billy wore his earphones and stood smiling, mouthing words and bobbing his head in time to music only he could hear.

After a moment, one of the nurses turned to the man and smiled in recognition. "Hi, Billy," she said. The man blinked and looked at her with dull eyes.

"You got to go around, sweetie. We can't move this time."

"Okay," muttered Billy, but he stood there a moment more before Derwood gently pulled the front of the cart toward a new path. Once the way was clear, Billy pushed the cart around Lizzy's gurney and on down the hall. As he passed, he glanced once toward the young woman under the sheet on the gurney. Derwood caught the faint strain of piano leaking from the headphones.

"I need a man like that," said one of the nurses. "The strong, silent type."

"Yeah," said the other. "Helpful, and he does what he's told."

An hour after that, the gynecologist was at the bedside. He was an older man, but Lizzy was beyond caring. She was lightheaded from blood loss and groggy from pain medicine.

The specialist told Derwood, "She has a ruptured tubal pregnancy. These things can bleed, a lot. We have to take her to the operating room. It's the only way. Are you able to sign the consent?"

Derwood did not have custody. He was Lizzy's father, and he could give emergency consent, but it was time to call her mom. Past time, really. He pulled out his phone as he signed the consent form.

"Let her talk to her mother before you take her away."

A groggy voice answered on the third ring. "Hello?"

"Kate, it's me."

They did not speak often, but she recognized his voice immediately. "Derwood. What's wrong? What time is it?"

"It's late. Listen. Lizzy is in the hospital. I'm here with her. She is sick, but the doctor says she'll be okay," Derwood lied. "She has to have surgery."

"What? What do you mean? She's in her bed, here, in her room!"

"She's not, Kate. She called me a couple of hours ago. She was sick. I brought her here, to the ER. I'm with her now. Here she is."

He handed the phone to Lizzy, who even in her near stupor looked daggers at him, but she took the phone.

"Hi, Mom," she said. She tried to sound strong, but her voice betrayed her.

"Honey, what's wrong? Where are you? What's going on?"

"I'm scared, Mom. I'm at the ER."

The doctor tapped his watch, and Lizzy said, "I love you, Mom."

She handed the phone back to Derwood as a nurse started to wheel her gurney out of the room.

Her mother's voice came out of the speaker, "Lizzy! Elizabeth!"

Lizzy grabbed Derwood by the arm and said, "Don't you say a word to her about this."

"Lizzy, I gotta tell her something."

"Make something up." Her fingernails dug into his arm. "Don't you say a word about this. That goes for all of you!" She swept her gaze around to include the doctor and the nurse at the bedside. Then she was gone, wheeled to the OR.

Derwood put the phone to his ear.

"Listen, Kate. She called me a couple of hours ago. Asked me to come over. By the time I got there, she was outside in the driveway and—"

"Dammit, Derwood! What did you do to her? Did you hurt her?"

"Calm down, Kate."

"What did you do, you son of a bitch?" Kate screamed into the phone. "I'm calling the police, then I'm coming down there and I'm gonna kick your ass!"

"Kate," said Derwood insistently. "You need to calm down."

"Go to hell, Derwood! I knew this was going to happen! I told her to stay away from you!"

A SHORT TIME LATER, Derwood sat quietly in the waiting room, leafing through some throw-away magazine designed to sell homes in the area. Funny how pervasive those are. Because that's what's on everyone's minds in hospital waiting rooms: where can I find my next house? Kate came rushing in, and Derwood stood up.

"What the hell, Derwood? Where is my daughter?" They were alone in the waiting room, and Kate did not hold back.

"Calm down, Kate."

"Stop telling me to calm down, you asshole!" Kate shouted. "You kidnap my daughter, then call me in the middle of the night and tell me she is in the hospital about to go into surgery? What the hell did you do? Did you hit her? Did you break out some of your "I'm-a-tough-guy" jujitsu or whatever you call that secret soldier bullshit on her?"

"No, Kate."

She stared at him, jaw clenched and eyes tight. "Where is she? Where the hell is she?"

"She's in surgery, Kate."

Kate grabbed her hair with both hands, like she might pull it out. Her face flicked through a range of emotions: anger, fear, concern. After a bit, she regained control.

"What's wrong with her?" said Kate through clenched teeth.

"The doctor said it might be her appendix," Derwood lied.

"How did you find out? Why did she call you?"

"She just called me out of the blue a couple of hours ago. I don't know why. She asked me to come get her."

"Why did she call you? Why didn't she wake me up?" Anger took her again. "Why didn't you wake me up?" She poked him in the chest, hard.

"I don't know, Kate. She asked me for help. What was I supposed to do?"

Kate huffed in frustration and turned away.

Thirty minutes later, a nurse came out to inform them that the operation was over, and Lizzy was going to recovery. Not long after, the doctor came out and spoke with them.

"She's stable now. There was a lot of blood loss. It had ruptured, but we got everything under control. We had to remove the—"

Derwood interrupted. "The appendix? Her appendix had to come out. Thank God we got here when we did."

The doctor and Derwood shared a moment of eye contact, and the doctor nodded. "It was a close call. She had a lot of bleeding, and we had to give her several units of blood in the OR, but everything is under control now. She'll feel weak and have some pain for the next few weeks, but she will be back to normal in a month or two."

"Can we see her?" asked Kate.

"In a little while," said the doctor. "Let her wake up first. She will be going to a hospital room after recovery, probably in an hour or two. You can meet her there."

The hospital room was small, but it had a window. There was one recliner, which Kate took as Derwood hunted the hall for another chair. Ninety minutes later, they wheeled Lizzy in on a big hospital gurney. She was awake, although pale and groggy. She held a tiny plastic cup of ice water.

"Hi Mom," she made a small wave.

"Oh honey! I'm so happy to see you!" Kate forgot her anger and confusion for a moment as she rushed to the bedside to hug her daughter.

"Easy, Mom!" Lizzy gasped, as Kate inadvertently put pressure on the recent abdominal incisions.

"Be gentle," said the nurse. "She is going to be fragile for a few weeks."

Once the nurse had her settled, Kate started in with the questions.

"Lizzy, what happened? I thought you said you just had a little stomach bug. Why didn't you call me? I was just down the hall."

"I don't know, Mom. I was scared. I didn't want to bother you. I didn't know this was going to happen."

Derwood excused himself to get coffee, so mother and daughter could talk in private. Kate and Lizzy talked until nearly dawn, and when Derwood returned, he heard quiet laughter filtering into the hall from the room as he approached. When he arrived, both were smiling.

"Everything okay in here?" he asked.

"It's fine," said Lizzy.

"Lizzy's fine," said Kate. "You're still an asshole." She went to the hospital cafeteria to get some breakfast.

"What did you tell her?" asked Lizzy.

"That you had appendicitis. They removed it. The doctor played along, too. Didn't lie, exactly, but he did not say anything about, you know."

"Yeah. That's what I said, too. Thanks, Dad."

"You gotta tell her, Lizzy."

"No, Dad, I don't. And neither do you. And neither do any of these people." She waved her hand in a gesture to encompass the entire hospital.

"It's none of her business, and I don't want her to know."

Derwood sighed and collapsed into the recliner. It had been a long night, without sleep, and he was grateful to be off his feet, if only for a little while until Kate returned. Outside the window, the sky was still dark, but dawn was near. He closed his eyes. Only for a little while.

Chapter 20

THURSDAY NIGHT

THE TWO FIGURES STOOD outside on a street, silhouettes in the dim light. There were no streetlights. When local residents had asked for them as a crime deterrent, the town council had said they would destroy the ambiance of the night sky. Local residents did not believe it. Just another excuse not to spend money on the poorer side of town.

"I don't want to do this," said William Hitchcock as he stood next to the smaller figure in the dark.

"I know you don't. But you have to."

"Don't make me, please," he begged, shaking his head.

"It's the only way."

"No, it isn't. I don't want to."

"And I do not want to do this," she said as she pulled up the Wagner on her phone. "Do not make me."

The large man recoiled and his shoulders slumped. "Okay. Okay. I'll do it."

He put his headphones on. Not Wagner of course, he hated Wager. He chose Beethoven's Piano Sonata No. 8, in C Minor. It was fitting; he felt emotional, and there would be suffering. He vowed to make it quick.

Her door was locked, of course, and there were neighbors. Best not to disturb them. There were no lights on in the apartment. She must be asleep by now. That would be best. Less pathos that way, he thought. Cleaner. Easier. On the balcony before her door, he paused the music while he worked.

The crowbar fit easily into the loose door, and steady gentle pressure was enough to force the door fitting from the jamb. The latch bolt cleared the strike plate with little effort. The deadbolt was harder, but the short-throw bolt was old, the wood soft, and the screws shallow. His patience was rewarded as the door gave with more steady gentle pressure. His entry made little sound.

He crept inside and closed the door behind him. The room was dim, but the green glow of the clock on the microwave oven was enough for his night-adjusted eyes. All was nearly silent, save for the sound of ocean waves emanating from the bedroom. He smiled sadly to himself. The nocturnal noisemaker. Perhaps if she had been better able to sleep, she would not need such support. No matter. Soon she would sleep forever.

He silently crept to the bedroom door and turned the handle. It too remained silent, and he pushed the door open. The young woman lay alone on the double bed, a dark figure in a dark room, washed only by the soft light from her phone at the bedside. Bedside deadside. The sound of the sea poured lightly from the phone and caressed her dark shape. He could see her hair piled on the pillow, color indistinct, a darker mass against the pillow in the dim light, but he knew her hair color. The woman outside had called her a redhead. Redhead deadhead. He could not make out the time on her phone.

She lay wrapped in covers, sheets twisted about her body, a body-length pillow gripped to her like a living companion to keep loneliness at bay. Another pillow lay unused, knocked to the floor. Or perhaps tossed there. As he watched, she grunted lightly in sleep and turned, twisting the cover even more about her body. A restless sleeper. No matter. It was time.

He activated the Beethoven and approached the bed. He picked up the pillow from the floor and said good bye to the girl in the sheets. He took his time. The sonata could not be forced. The opening was played "grave" – he smiled at the irony- and he felt it, very slow. Solemn. He moved slowly, the pillow clutched in his hand, a two-fisted baton as he conducted the pianist in his head. He had to wait, or the tempo would be wrong. The notes and chords climbed and escalated. Grave and he breathed deeply. Incalzando and he swayed. He trembled at allegretto.

Finally two minutes in, he felt it, the soaring allegro notes crashing in his head and he threw himself atop the sleeping figure in bed and forced the pillow over her head.

She woke instantly but too late. The music rang loudly into his ears, and he could not hear her muffled screams beneath the pillow. The bed was soft, softer than his. Softer than he liked. He had to press the pillow hard.

He was glad he had waited. Patience was a virtue. The writhing woman on the bed was his metronome, and they moved in time to the rushing notes, straining to leap into the air. Glorious! He threw his head back as he bore down on the pillow.

They danced together, he and the woman. In her struggle, in the magic of the music, they bonded. As the piano resounded in his brain, he felt her. He understood her. He had not expected it, this connection. As she writhed beneath him, bodies separated only by the twisted covers and soft pillow, each enclosed in sound -his a blanket of melody and hers the buzzing silence of terror and approaching death- he connected with her. He felt at last the joy of truly knowing someone. The light of understanding. The notes swirled and soared with his soul. Until they did not anymore. Toward the end of the movement, her movement had stopped also. Her death came at the end. All that was left was the slow chords and final burst of "Pathetique."

The ten-minute piece had been long enough. He was satisfied. He stood slowly, and lifted the dead girl, his new friend – his soulmate! – and held her gently in his arms. Her limp body was warm and smelled of lavender. He laid her gently on the floor at the end of the bed, limbs composed just so. He arranged her hair gently and smiled at her for a moment.

As he left the apartment and they drove home, he felt a greater understanding for his sister, too. Maybe she was right. Maybe this was what she sought. Maybe symmetry mattered after all. Wholeness. Evenness. He felt a deep calm, and knew he was complete.

Chapter 21

FRIDAY MORNING

DAWN LINGERED BEYOND the eastern horizon when Derwood's phone rang. He had dozed off minutes before. The tone climbed into the high register before it pulled him from the depths of slumber, and although his body tried to stay asleep, he could not overcome years of conditioning. When he was awake, he was awake. The blasting horns that followed a beat of silence over a minute into the ringtone finally shattered the last remnant of sleep. He rolled over in the reclined chair next to Lizzy's hospital bed and grabbed the phone without looking at the caller ID.

"Marty, you are killing me. This better be good," he growled.

"Sarah Smalls is dead," said Sinsley.

Twenty minutes later, Derwood pulled into a parking lot off a residential street in West Southern Pines, downhill from the Broad Street business district, across the train tracks that bisected downtown.

In ages past, it was considered the ethnic part of town. Even now it felt segregated. Nearly everyone living in West Southern Pines was black. The Latinos, legal and otherwise, seemed to prefer more rural parts of Moore County. But Sarah Smalls, a young red-headed white girl with light freckles and green eyes, had lived there too. She moved there because she could afford it. She stayed because she liked her neighbors. They were kind to her, protective. She was welcomed when she arrived, and she felt at home there.

Sarah lived on the second story of a two-story apartment complex, the kind with a fenced-in swimming pool in the parking lot. Next to the pool was a picnic table and one of those heavy-duty black iron grills with the heavy grate that you can lift off the grill with a spring iron heat-proof handle. The pool area was empty when Derwood pulled in the lot. It was still early, the sun just peeking over the eastern horizon. The day promised to be warm, but the morning held a late summer chill.

Derwood saw three sheriff's vehicles already on site, parked crookedly around the lot. There were open spaces, but the cops parked askew anyway. Maybe it made them feel important. I did not have time to park correctly, it said.

He recognized Maggie's Toyota parked neatly in a space next to the sheriff's vehicles. Sinsley must have called her, too. Her flat was only a half-mile away. Derwood wondered how long it had taken her to get out of her flat. He had barely had time to wash his face.

As he parked, Maggie approached from a knot of bystanders, neighbors and residents of the complex. She held two insulated coffee containers. She looked well put together, not like someone who had been rousted out of bed before dawn to investigate a murder scene. Not like someone who had been up all night and caught a short nap in a hospital chair. When she got to Derwood's car, she held out one of the coffee containers to him. An angel of mercy.

"I wasn't sure you had time for coffee, so I brought you a cup."

"I think I'm in love," said Derwood.

Maggie did not smile. Instead, she jerked her head for him to follow.

"Neighbor called it in," said Maggie. "She and Sarah were supposed to meet for breakfast. When Sarah did not answer the door, she let herself in, found the body."

She led him across the asphalt parking lot and up a set of metal and concrete stairs, along a concrete balcony with metal railing to the door of Apartment 15, near the center of the building on the upper level. She paused briefly and muttered something under her breath. Then she opened the door and entered.

Sue Blanchard and Martin Sinsley were inside, along with another deputy Derwood did not recognize. Sheriff Blanchard pressed her phone to her ear and shouted, "I don't care what time it is! Get them over here now!" She hung up the phone and turned to Marty. "Crime scene techs are on the way." She turned away and continued to meticulously examine the scene. Sinsley stood nearby making notes in a small book he kept in his pocket.

The apartment was a two-room model. The front door opened to a room with a small kitchen and a table that could seat two but had only one chair. An old couch fronted a small television, but the dominant feature of the room were the bookcases lining the wall. They were full of paperbacks and old reference texts.

Blanchard led them into the bedroom. The walls were hung with pictures of European cities, impersonal, the kind you might see on the walls of a coffee shop in an upscale suburban neighborhood. A door led out the back to a fire escape. The shade was drawn. A double bed occupied the center of the room against a side wall. The sheets were ruffled and the cover lay askew. A lamp was knocked to the floor, the only sign of struggle.

Sarah lay on her back, face toward the ceiling in the space between the foot of the bed and the door leading to the bathroom. The bed did not have a footboard. The spot on which she lay was narrow, three or four feet, but wide enough to accommodate her slender form reposed in death. Her pillow was next to her on the carpet. The carpet itself bore stains of long use, but it was lined with vacuum marks as if someone had vacuumed the room not long before.

The body was ugly. Derwood shared with death the easy familiarity of long acquaintance. He knew death in many forms. Some deaths were beautiful, a loving grandparent at the end of a long life well lived, at home surrounded by children and grandchildren. A death to be embraced.

Sudden unexpected death that stole upon a person unawares and interrupted plans and ambition, like a thief in the night, was more difficult to bear. A car crash. A sudden heart attack in a middle-aged father. A young mother succumbs to cancer. The natural order of things, even though heartbreaking.

Some were righteous. Some people needed to die. Derwood had visited many of them in the night and served as the instrument of justice.

But sometimes, death was just ugly. Sudden and violent, visited on the defenseless and innocent. It left a stain on human consciousness. These should not be. They were steeped in wrongness.

Sarah Smalls wore fuzzy pink pajamas covered in balloons, the same style Lizzy wore. Her bare feet pointed out at angles to each side, and her arms lay at her sides. She looked... arranged. The pajama top had fallen upward off her exposed belly, where the flesh looked like polished marble. Livor mortis had begun on her flank nearest the floor, skin faintly mottled reddish purple, and her limbs were stiff from rigor mortis. Her face appeared pale, bloodless and tight. Gone was the blush of youth and the rose from her cheeks. Her hair was still red. In a flash, Derwood saw his daughter Lizzy lying there.

He turned away and walked out of the apartment. He saw Sarah's red hair in his mind, and a red film descended over his vision, tinting everything. The streetlights outside had red halos and the moon in the sky above had a reddish tinge. A blood red harvest moon. Sarah

Smalls spoke to him then, in her death. He saw her stiff body and red hair. She spoke to him as plainly as if she had been standing next to him.

Harvest time has come, said the image of Sarah Smalls. He was not crazy. Some might say damaged, but not crazy. The vision was not real. The girl lay dead in her apartment, and he did not imagine that her spirit really spoke to him. But the mental image was clear, and Derwood knew his role. He was what he had always been, even if he had suppressed it for a while. Harvest time had come, and he was the reaper.

Chapter 22

THE BALCONY OUTSIDE Sarah Smalls' tiny apartment faced east. From the second story Derwood looked out toward the horizon, where the bright stripe of the rising sun washed away the pallor of dawn. Time for him to go. He had work to do.

Derwood had not known the girl. He met her only twice, and she had not seemed to like him much. But he had a daughter not much younger than Sarah, and he'd read Dave Grossman's controversial essay "On Sheep, Wolves, and Sheepdogs." The author had written "If you have no capacity for violence, then you are a healthy productive citizen, a sheep. If you have a capacity for violence and no empathy for your fellow citizens, then you have defined an aggressive sociopath, a wolf. But what if you have a capacity for violence, and a deep love for your fellow citizens? What do you have then? A sheepdog, a warrior, someone who is walking the hero's path. Someone who can walk into the heart of darkness, into the universal human phobia, and walk out unscathed."

Derwood did not hold with metaphors or psychobabble. Others might call him a hero, especially if they knew the particulars of his past, but he did not consider himself heroic. Heroes jumped on hand grenades. Heroes rushed into burning buildings to save helpless people. Heroes stepped outside their ordinary routine to help others when they could not help themselves. Soldiers being soldiers did not make them heroes. He did not feel the need to justify himself or his actions. He only knew that the world was a complex place, and there were assholes who needed killing. He had work to do.

Tonight, he would search Daniel De Luca's office in Raleigh. Lack of attribution would be key. De Luca might put two and two together to conclude that he or Maggie had been there, but the man probably had other enemies higher on his suspect list. As long as his vehicle was not identified, he left no evidence and there was no witness – living or digital – there could be no attribution.

The army had all manner of sophisticated devices including rapid data transfer technology that could suck all the data off a computer hard drive in minutes, high-definition digital cameras that recorded everything in sight for later detailed analysis, and communications jamming gear that would block cell phones and radio. Derwood did not have most of that. But he had experience, and he was motivated.

A glance at a map showed a convenient apartment complex about a quarter mile from De Luca's office. The apartments were adjacent to a small park, a greenway with a paved path and trees and water. The greenway fed into another old city park across from the office. He could cover the quarter mile from the apartments to the office on foot, and the parks offered ample exit points. The area might be deserted at night, but it could be occupied by the homeless or the junkies, or others seeking anonymity in the dark. Nonetheless, the park should provide ample darkness and cover to meet his needs.

If De Luca's office was alarmed, police response time could be as short as three to five minutes. Raleigh police had been criticized over the last few years for slow response times to armed robbery and murder, and they had reduced those delays, but an office alarm in the middle of the night remained a low priority. Most property alarms were false alarms, and if the police rushed willy-nilly to every one, they would be unable to respond to personal crimes in progress. More likely, the police would arrive the next morning to take a report.

Derwood never depended on being lucky. He took advantage when luck came his way, but luck was unreliable. He would be in and out of De Luca's office within three minutes.

He would take as little of his personal gear as possible, to avoid hairs, fibers, or other forensic evidence pointing back to him. He had to take a weapon and night-vision gear, but everything else he could pick up with cash at a big box store on the way. He stopped by the bank for cash on the way home to gather his gear.

He had been a day sleeper for months at a time on deployment. When his team had hunted the nighttime deserts in Asia, he slept in a climate-controlled, insulated and soundproof cargo container. The Unit put serious effort into keeping its operators prepared, and that meant effective sleep. They could endure prolonged and profound hardships when necessary, but the men were more operationally effective when well rested. Derwood knew the value of sleep, though his strategies to improve his sleep had only been marginally effective.

At home, he locked the doors and drew the shades. He hung a thick blanket from the stout curtain rod above the sliding glass door to his bedroom to block out light, and he put a towel beneath the door to the hallway. He turned the air-conditioner up, and he turned his phone to airplane mode and called up the white noise feature. The house was cool and dark, even in the daylight sun. The bedroom was near black, and the white noise blotted out all exterior sound. Derwood set an alarm and lay down to sleep.

He thought of Sarah Smalls, the remainder of her life ripped from her.

In the desert, he had never had trouble sleeping. The sense of purpose he felt had allowed him to switch his mind on and off as needed. He did not dwell on the past or the future. He existed in the moment, and he responded to the needs of the moment. Once the planning was done, once all contingencies had been considered, there was no point in going over things again and again. He had learned to trust himself, and he trusted that his plan was sound.

A door opened in his mind, a door that he had shut when he left operational status in the Unit and vowed to keep shut. There was no place in polite society for what lay behind the door. But the spirit of Sarah Smalls had knocked on the door, and Derwood opened it. He stepped through, turned off his mind and slept.

THE ALARM SANG HIM awake as intended at four o'clock in the afternoon. Derwood shaved and took a long shower, then dressed in a tight-fitting jogging outfit with a light jacket. He checked his phone and saw a missed call from Martin Sinsley, and a couple of text messages from Margaret Kidd.

Sinsley's message was short.

Call me.

Maggie's first text asked, *Where'd you go?* The second echoed Sinsley's message, *Call me.*

He called Lizzy, and she immediately answered.

"You left in a hurry this morning. Is everything okay?" She sounded better.

"Something came up. There are things I have to do now. How are you?"

"Fine, I guess. Mom's driving me crazy, and my stomach hurts, but I'm okay. They sent me home after breakfast. The doctor said I should start walking as much as I can, and I get to eat anything I want. But I'm not hungry, and I don't wanna walk. Can I come stay with you? Mom won't leave me alone."

"Not today, sweetheart. I'm sorry. There's some things I have to do. I'll call you tomorrow."

He turned the cell phone off and put it on his nightstand. Cells phones had built-in tracking technology. Better to leave it home. Pick up a prepaid phone instead.

On the way to Raleigh, he stopped at a huge box store just off the highway and bought new clothing, dark jogging suit and hat similar to what he wore now but without any possible link to Derwood Flynn. He bought two backpacks, the kind a student would use to carry books, and he bought a small but versatile assortment of hand tools. Crowbar, hammer, wire cutters, pliers, screwdrivers. He bought sanitary wipes, Lysol, gloves and duct tape. He bought a prepaid cellphone with a camera feature. At the register, he self-consciously felt like he was buying a kidnap kit. He avoided eye contact and paid with cash. There were security cameras about. He kept his head down and his hat pulled low.

He drove north until he found an isolated side road. He pulled off and diligently cleaned and wiped all the tools, to remove any fingerprints. He would not touch them again without gloves.

He got to Raleigh around seven in the evening and parked in the lot of the Woodborough Apartments, about four blocks from De Luca's office on the corner of Martin and South Blount. He wore both backpacks, one empty and flat to his back, the other packed with his clothing and equipment, laid directly over the first. The fit was awkward but workable.

He walked the streets as twilight fell. He put a small stone in his shoe to force a limp and shuffling gait. Although no expert, he had seen the kind of gait recognition technology available to intelligence services and certain government agencies. The Chinese had pioneered the technology and been widely criticized for it by the U.S. press, but the U.S. government applied the technology with gusto, albeit with more secrecy and discretion. Hypocrisy knows no bounds. If he were picked up by a stray camera, maybe the old stone in the shoe trick would lessen the odds of recognition. He kept his head down to avoid any unseen cameras in storefronts or ATMs.

The lights were still on in De Luca's office, visible through the blackout on the window, but it was impossible to tell if anyone was there. He walked an expanding grid along the streets surrounding the office, taking in the storefronts, windows, alleys, fire escapes, traffic signals and patterns. He lay the living map before him atop the mental image he carried from his study of the maps earlier in the day. He imagined multiple different escape routes, and when he clearly understood the environment, he went back to the park across from the office. He settled into a wooded copse near the street just across the intersection from De Luca's office. The park received frequent visitors throughout the evening. He watched and waited as night deepened.

About nine, he saw the lights go out in De Luca's office, and the man himself appeared, locked the door behind him and walked down the street and around the corner into the night. Derwood remained motionless, sitting with his back against a tree in the blackest shadows of the small grove. He was invisible in the night.

At eleven o'clock, he stretched in place. By one, the stream of passers-by and evening diners and revelers had dwindled, and the streets were quiet. At two, he rose from his nest. He had sat nearly motionless for over five hours, and it took a moment to get his blood flowing. He moved from the copse of trees, walked a circuit around the park, then around the block. He saw desultory foot traffic here and there, but nothing and no one to interrupt his plans.

He approached De Luca's office from the parking lot that led to the rear door. With a gloved hand he removed the crowbar from the backpack. The crowbar would leave marks on the door, but there were not that many ways to break and enter, and simple was usually best. He activated the timer on his wristwatch. Three minutes. He slipped the crowbar into the crack at the strike plate. The door neither protested nor groaned, and he was inside.

He flicked on his headlamp and quickly inspected the edges of the door. He saw no contact plates or wires to indicate an alarm. That might give him another few minutes. The door opened directly into De Luca's back office, and the file cabinets sat against the wall as before with the computer on the desk. Derwood moved to the front room, where a quick scan proved that he was alone.

He opened the file cabinet. Say what you like about De Luca, the man was organized. There filed under "C" was Cranston. Derwood shoved the thin file into his pack. He found no file for DeVaney, but the "S" cabinet had a thick file for Smalls. He shoved the file in the pack and checked his watch. Ninety seconds gone. He paused to listen but heard nothing.

He considered the computer on the desk. The device was off. He could easily disconnect the monitor and grab the console. It might even fit into the backpack, but what then? It would be easy to attach another monitor and reboot the computer, but it was undoubtedly password protected, and he no longer had access to the intelligence arm of the Unit, so good at hacking and exploiting data from computers. If he took the computer, De Luca would know instantly that someone had been in the office, but if he left it in place it was just possible that his clandestine entry would go unnoticed. If De Luca did not use his back door. Or check his files. Derwood did not think he could access the data on the hard drive anyway, certainly not quickly enough to suit his purposes. He checked his watch in time to see the digital display tick to zero and heard the timer start beeping.

A final glance around and he saw an inbox on the left side of the desk, with a corresponding outbox on the other side. He quickly shuffled through the papers and saw a bill for electricity service at address on Bedford Avenue in Raleigh. The service was in Daniel De

Luca's name. Derwood quickly pulled out the prepaid cellphone and snapped a photo of the bill.

Time was up, and he needed to get out. In the front room the glow from the streetlights was visible through the shaded window. He listened but heard no sound. He opened the front door and quickly glanced up and down the empty street. The park beckoned across the intersection, and he pulled the door to behind him and hurried across.

There was no sign of pursuit, so Derwood headed carefully but quickly back to his pickup. He drove away, careful to obey the speed limit and traffic laws. In fifteen minutes, he was miles away.

Chapter 23

FRIDAY OVERNIGHT

DERWOOD PULLED INTO an all-night gas station. The station had a large rain roof over the pumps, and bold fluorescent lighting lit the night.

De Luca had put together a thick file on Sarah Smalls. Cranston Law Group engaged De Luca several years ago to handle correspondence and act as a cutout should she ever need to call. The file began with biographical information like her age and birthdate. Her parents were indeed killed in a car crash, and she went to live with her grandfather, James DeVaney. When DeVaney disappeared, she entered the foster system.

There were records of each foster home and periodic reports from the social worker in charge of her case. Not all of the information was benign. Sarah had seen hard times and suffered physical and emotional abuse. The social worker had done his best to protect her, removing her from one home immediately. Charges were filed, but De Luca had not recorded the outcome.

There were copies of all the letters to and from Sarah herself over the last few years, filed in chronological order, regular as a metronome. There was no variation, and nothing had occurred to upset the pattern until the last page of the file. The page had handwritten notes on lined yellow legal paper and was dated Wednesday, two days before. Sarah had called to report Derwood's visit, and De Luca had called Mike at Cranston Law Group Wednesday evening.

The file on Cranston Law group was similarly arranged, beginning with background information. Cranston Law Group proved to be a misleading name. There was no group, just a man named Michael Cranston.

Cranston appeared to be a case study in "sleazy lawyer." He graduated college without incident and enrolled at the School of Law at the University of North Carolina, but he was kicked out for an honor code violation.

You cannot keep a good man down, and Cranston applied immediately to the Queen City School of Law, a private for-profit institution in Charlotte. He was accepted, but tuition was steep. He resorted to identity theft and credit card fraud to pay his bills.

At Queen City, he learned that not all law professors and indeed not all law schools had the same code of conduct. He was able to skate through his coursework using a combination of smarts and "borrowed" work.

A couple of years passed without incident, at least with nothing reported in De Luca's file. Cranston successfully completed the program at Queen City Law and eventually passed the bar, although according to De Luca's file, it took him three tries. He tried to find work with reputable law firms all over the state, but no one would take a chance on a third-rate lawyer who graduated from a disreputable law school and barely passed the bar. Cranston hung his own shingle out of a dingy office in South Raleigh.

His first success came in a murder case where a man named Stanley Hernandez drove his car off the road and killed another man named Oscar Argueta. The incident occurred at a county park where a group of immigrants had gathered to play soccer on a Sunday afternoon. Everyone was from the same town in El Salvador, and the prosecution claimed Hernandez and Argueta were rivals reaching all the way back to the streets of San Salvador.

The tire tracks swerved through the park, and a picnic table had been destroyed. The speed limit on the local streets was thirty miles an hour, and the prosecution claimed it would be impossible to lose control of the car, drive across the park, swerve across the soccer field and crash through a picnic table before finally hitting and killing a man, all by accident.

The eyewitness testimony in statements taken by the cops on scene provided damning evidence. Unfortunately for the prosecution, none of the witnesses could quite remember details at the trial. The inconsistencies in the state's evidence led the judge to declare a mistrial.

Caseloads being what they were and the incident involving a minority, and an immigrant at that, the Wake County District Attorney had decided not to press the case further. After all, there was an election coming up, and immigrants were not popular.

Since that case, Cranston had been noticed by others in the Raleigh area, and had a steady stream of business. He became a successful defense attorney, but over the last few years he had largely abandoned the practice of criminal defense. He now worked for a range of private clients who preferred discretion to public notice and did not mind an attorney willing to bend the rules.

It was Cranston who first contacted De Luca regarding the Sarah Smalls affair. De Luca had a modest service he labelled private investigation, but which in reality had evolved into a multispecialty boutique service. One of De Luca's specialties was to act as a screen for clients who preferred anonymity, and he was known in the Raleigh underworld for his discretion. De Luca was not the trusting sort, and he investigated Cranston as thoroughly as he could.

He accumulated a few names of clients that Cranston represented, and he was able to discover that Cranston Law was the manager of the Sarah Smalls Trust. He never discovered who funded the trust. Derwood found no indication in the files of a link between Smalls and Smits.

Cranston did not practice out of an office. He used cutouts like De Luca and Stick-in-the-Eye as points of contact. He preferred P.O. boxes for mailing addresses, and used De Luca and others like him to run interference and provide another layer of insulation between the affairs of his clients and outside scrutiny. Derwood decided it was time for a visit.

Chapter 24

DERWOOD PUT THE FILES down and assembled the pieces in his mind. Willem Smits is a successful flower merchant, and retires to Lake Surf seeking a peaceful lake experience, and that is what he gets for many years. But times change, and not all the new residents at Woodlake share his vision. Enter Fred Akers, a recently retired special forces operator seeking fun and sun on the lake. He runs for the Woodlake board and someone bashes him over the head and buries his body. Smits is involved, somehow. A few years later, more murders. The Hinrichs. DeVaney. Was Smits involved again? But then who murdered Smits?

DeVaney is grandfather to Sarah Smalls, and when he disappears, she goes into foster care. Sometime later Smits starts to lose his mind and ends up in a rest home. His body shows evidence of lead poisoning. Sarah Smalls is rescued from the foster care system to watch Smits. Why? Why not just kill him? Given the body count, what is one more?

All is quiet for a while, until a hurricane destroys the dam at Woodlake and uncovers the body of Fred Akers. An old investigation reopens, and Derwood questions Willem Smits. Suddenly, it is not enough to watch him and trust his silence. Perhaps Smits' mind is too far gone. Perhaps the killers think he will say things he shouldn't. Smits is the next murder victim.

But Smits' death does not go unnoticed and the investigation intensifies. Sarah Smalls is questioned, then she is struck down shortly after. Why? What did she know? Whoever set her to watch

Smits had to be involved. Did she know the identity of her mysterious benefactor?

Michael Cranston would know. A shady lawyer, a known cheat. His firm set up the trust for Sarah Smalls, and oversaw the affairs of Willem Smits. Michael Cranston was the nexus around which the events of the last few days swirled.

Derwood would talk to the lawyer, and De Luca would know where to find him. He glanced at his wristwatch. 3:05. He had time yet, and darkness, so Derwood drove. When he arrived near De Luca's address, he cruised along the deserted streets to get a feel for the neighborhood. Typical suburbia. Mature trees in well-kept yards, children's toys lying in driveways, and flags hanging from poles mounted on front porches.

He parked a few blocks from De Luca's house and approached on foot. The house was a typical 1970's split level, a variation that existed in every city across the country from Seattle to South Florida. He knew the floor plan instinctively. Every American child growing up in suburbia in the latter half of the twentieth century would have spent time in such a house. Steps led up to the front door, which opened into a living room, perhaps with a dining room combo. There might be a separate den and kitchen, depending on whether the home had been remodeled. It was impossible to tell from the outside.

Half-stairs would lead up to a hallway fronted on either side by bedrooms, perhaps with the master bedroom the last door on the hallway. Another half-stair would lead down to a laundry room, possibly a storage or rec room, maybe more bedrooms, and the inevitable attached two-car garage. An American architectural classic.

Derwood preferred more time for reconnaissance, but he did not hesitate. He approached the front door and listened. Silence and darkness inside. He pulled out the prybar and jimmied the front door. Noise upon entry was unavoidable, and the crack when

Derwood forced the door resounded through the quiet neighborhood. Derwood rushed into the house with night-vision goggles in place. He glanced around and saw no one in the green glow. He took the stairs two at a time and sprinted down the short hallway. He arrived at the master bedroom door six seconds after breaching the front door. After the noise of entry, there was no time for stealth.

Derwood understood sleep inertia. The transition from sleep to wakefulness was not instantaneous. A normal human waking from a dead sleep might take as long as thirty minutes to reach a fully functional state. Even a pilot or trained operator waking from a controlled rest catnap would not come awake at peak capacity. If Derwood had picked the right bedroom and De Luca was asleep, there should be at least a few moments of disorientation accompanying the shattering of the doorjamb.

Derwood grabbed the handle and thrust open the door. As he entered, he glimpsed a figure just sitting up in the bead and reaching for something on the far side. Without pausing he dodged, threw himself to the floor. He landed in a roll and tucked his legs as his momentum carried him through a complete forward roll. The night-vision goggles dislodged and clunked to the floor. In one fluid motion, he completed the roll and pushed down hard with both legs, springing up and toward the figure on the bed.

The shadow now had something in its right hand, wheeling around back toward Derwood, but the shadow was too slow, and the full weight of Derwood's flying body struck the figure. He was not gentle. He led with his right elbow, smashing into the temple and ear of the shadow on the bed. There was a sickening crack and snap of the head, but Derwood carried on, left hand reaching and finding the shadow's right wrist. The shadow on the bed was stunned and did not have the will to resist. It fell back on the bed. Derwood wrested a pistol from its right hand and turned it to the forehead of the figure.

"Hello, Daniel," he whispered. "Let's talk."

He straddled the supine figure in the dark, knees on forearms, pinning them to the mattress, the mount position used by mixed martial artists. De Luca did not struggle, dissuaded by the cold steel barrel dimpling his forehead.

"No one needs to die tonight, Daniel, including you, but I don't mind killing. I want you to tell the truth."

De Luca nodded.

"Is there anyone else in the house?" Derwood continued in a whisper. He liked the effect. He thought it added an element of uncertainty and fear. It also allowed him to hear whether anyone else was stirring in the house.

"No," said De Luca. "I live alone."

"I hope so, Daniel. We would not want any collateral damage. Sarah Smalls is dead, Daniel, and you are to blame. I've come for restitution."

In the darkness, Derwood could sense the body posture change, some of the tension and fight draining out like a plug was pulled. "You got the wrong guy, man," De Luca said.

"Maybe. We'll get to that. Right now I want you to tell me what's going on. Everything."

"I don't know anything, man."

Derwood pressed the pistol into De Luca's forehead with his right hand. With his left, he quickly reached across to his belt and drew a tactical knife. Without a word, he swung the knife down and to the left, behind his torso, plunging the blade into the lateral aspect of the right thigh of the man pinned to the bed.

The angle was bad, and Derwood knew the wound was shallow, but the shock was real. De Luca howled and bucked from the pain. Derwood wiped the blade on the bedsheets and quickly sheathed it.

"I do not think that is true, Daniel. I want you to tell the truth. No one needs to die here, including you. Do you understand?"

De Luca whimpered and nodded.

"Tell me everything you know about Sarah Small and Willem Smits."

"Okay, okay. Give me a minute. Uh..." he stammered as he gathered his thoughts. "Okay, um, it was a few years ago, I got a visitor, a client. Man named Cranston. Michael Cranston. He's a lawyer. He said there was a fellow at a nursing home down in Southern Pines. Place called Pinelands Estate. Guy's name was Willem Smits. He wanted me to coordinate surveillance on this guy. But he had a very specific plan. He said there was a girl, that's Sarah Smalls. She was in foster care, and he had set up a trust fund for her. For her to get the trust money, she had to keep an eye on Smits. He had this letter typed up that explained everything, and he wanted me to be the intermediary, to contact the girl and be the go-between."

"Why you?"

"I don't know, man, it's what I do."

"Explain."

"Plenty of people want business done, but don't want to do it personally, so I help them out. As a point of contact. Check the mail, man the phone, you know. That kind of thing. That's all."

"Okay. Cranston hires you to set up surveillance on Smits. What then?"

"Nothing then. That's it. I just set it up. Started sending monthly letters to the girl. She needed the money. What else was she going to do? She had to go along with it. Every month I send a letter, and she sends a letter back. Nothing else ever happened until a couple of days ago. See, there was an emergency phone line, too. I monitor it, but nothing until a couple days ago. Then the girl calls to say Smits had a visitor. The girl tells me, and I tell Cranston. He comes to my office, I step out, he calls her back. That's it. That's all that happened."

"Why did Cranston want you to watch Smits?" Derwood dug in the pistol muzzle until De Luca flinched.

"Now, take it easy, man! Cranston works for some nasty people. If they find out I am talking to you, they'll kill me."

"I am the one you'd better worry about, Daniel, not them. I don't mind killing. But as long as you behave, nobody will ever know I was here. Why did Cranston want Smits watched?"

"I don't know, man. I swear. I think somebody just wanted to keep an eye on him, make sure he didn't talk to anybody."

"Who?"

"I don't know, man. Really. Cranston might be connected. Smits too, maybe. But that's all I know."

"What are they afraid of?"

"I don't know. I swear." De Luca nearly sobbed. "I don't know."

"Why not just kill him?"

"I don't know, man. I just check the mail and the phone."

"Okay, Daniel, why Sarah Smalls? How does she fit in?"

"I don't know. I don't know anything. I checked her out, but I don't know the connection to Smits, except that her grandfather used to live in Woodlake, same as Smits. His name is Jim DeVaney. He and Smits used to serve on the board of directors at Woodlake, at the same time. They would have known each other. But DeVaney disappeared years ago. Hit the bottle after his daughter died, then he hit the road. He took the kid in for a while, but eventually liked the booze better and abandoned her. The girl ended up in foster care. Maybe Smits and DeVaney had some sort of relationship."

Derwood saw no tell. Either De Luca was a very good liar, or he was telling the truth. The man did not know DeVaney was dead.

"Tell me about Michael Cranston."

"Man, my leg hurts, I'm bleeding."

"That's true. You are. Keep talking."

"He's a lawyer. Shady as hell. He runs rackets with identity theft. Credit card fraud, trust fraud, fake powers of attorney, that kind of thing. He's the one you need to talk to."

"Where can I find him?"

De Luca gave the address.

"Pay attention, Daniel." Derwood reached around his back to the other man's leg where he had stabbed him minutes before. He formed his left fist into a thumb strike position and jabbed the wounded man's leg at the spot of the stab wound. De Luca let out a satisfying howl.

Once he had quieted, Derwood whispered, "I do not mind hurting you, and I do not mind killing. Do you understand that?"

De Luca nodded.

"I am going to get up now and leave you alone. What you do then is your own business, but I have two rules. First, if you ever approach me or my business, I will kill you. Second, if anyone ever hears of our conversation tonight or of my visit here, I will kill you. Do you understand, Daniel?"

De Luca nodded.

"It is very important that you understand, Daniel. I want you to live."

De Luca nodded.

"One more thing, Daniel. You might want to lay low for a while. Whoever came for Sarah Smalls might see you as the next link in the chain. Good night, Daniel."

Derwood used the barrel of the pistol pressed into the other man's forehead as leverage to push himself up from the bed. Grabbing the night-vision goggles and replacing them on his head, Derwood backed out the door into the hallway and hurried out of the house.

Chapter 25

THE ADDRESS DE LUCA provided led to a house only a few miles away. When Derwood pulled up the address on his tablet and examined the surroundings, he nearly laughed out loud. Lots of privacy. Perfect.

The house was in a well-to-do neighborhood, at the end of the road with a large private yard tucked hard against a forest. The backyard bordered over two hundred acres of managed forest riddled with walking trails, set up as a teaching and research forest for NC State University. The forest provided an ideal avenue of approach to the back yard.

Derwood parked at a park and ride lot, conveniently located adjacent to the forest. Grabbing his equipment, he walked across the road and plunged into the dark wood. His watch showed 3:30. He allotted himself thirty minutes to approach the back of Cranston's home, and as he walked, he plotted his egress. Early on Saturday morning no one would use the park and ride lot, but he still wanted to be long gone by sunrise, around seven o'clock. Dawn would begin lighting the sky closer to six. Plenty of people would rise earlier than that, and some might even walk the forest trails at dawn, but as long as darkness held, he was safe from prying eyes.

The trails through the wood were worn, well-marked and easy to follow, with less undergrowth than he had expected. Walking was easy and comfortable. The hiker's lamp cast a dim glow on the trail as it wound along a small creek. Consulting his tablet again, he followed a smaller spur west and then north less than a half mile until the marked trail ended at a clearing. The wonders of wireless. Using the tablet and wireless connectivity beat overland orienteering with a map and compass, a skill he had mastered early in his army days.

Cranston's house lay only a few hundred feet from the clearing through the woods to the northeast. He could see the glow of lights spilling into the backyard. He moved off the trail and slowly walked through the forest. The night was quiet. It was too late for the summer cicadas and too early for the waking birds. He hoped Cranston did not have a dog.

As he approached, he switched off the head lamp. The interior lights filtering through the windows and glass doors on the back of the house provided ample illumination for his night adjusted eyes. He was pleased to see there was no fence, and even happier to see no sign of a dog. He paused well inside the edge of the forest to watch the scene. His watch read 4:00. He was on schedule.

He edged onto the lawn. The house and yard bordered directly onto the forest, which would be full of wildlife. There would be deer in the woods, and they would come out at nighttime and forage through the forest and neighboring yards and gardens. If there were any motion sensors, they would be activated all night long, night after night. The inhabitants would be weary of continual false alarms.

Derwood moved slowly across the backyard to the porch, but no lights came on, no horn sounded. There was no indication of an alarm. He crouched on the porch where he could see into the house. A television flickered in the main room, and a man sat sprawled on the couch facing the TV. A moment later, a woman walked into the room carrying two snifters of amber liquid. She handed one to the man and settled on the couch next to him, keeping the other for herself. The woman was not particularly beautiful, but she was distractingly naked. Whoever the man on the couch was, he was not alone.

Derwood would have to deal with the woman. He preferred to keep his operations simple and avoided collateral damage when possible. In many cases hunting terrorists in Asian deserts, his commanders had judged that women were an acceptable form of collateral damage, because they supported their men in their pursuit of evil. The culture was male dominated, and perhaps the women were oppressed, but at least they were adults and theoretically capable of independent thought and action. That is what he told himself anyway, and he had found over the years that as long as he did not think too much about it, the lie worked to assuage his conscience.

But here in suburban North Carolina, he could hardly storm in and involve the woman in whatever violence the situation demanded. He would have to get her out.

A simple and efficient plan came to him. The woman, dressed as she was – or wasn't, actually- would be helpless as a threat, unless she was really good at concealing a cell phone – that thought gave him pause... where would she put it? He shook his head. Focus, Flynn. She would be unable to alert anyone until he had made his escape. He would simply crash the party and lock her in a bathroom. That should safely get her out of the way while he spoke with Michael Cranston.

Derwood came of military age under the rapid dominance doctrine, which held that overwhelming display of force would sap the enemy's will to fight, and his time at the Unit had done little to dissuade him of the doctrine's effectiveness. It might be overhyped, but the fact was that Shock and Awe worked. The difficulty lay in delivering the shock and instilling the awe. Easy to say, but resource intensive to actually carry out, and logistically challenging. As one man on a suburban back porch, shock and awe might be out of reach, but he still had surprise and fear. Derwood knew he had surprise on his side, and if he chose, an element of savagery inside him that the man on the couch was unlikely to match.

Derwood pulled out a black handheld device the size of a brick, although lighter. From the top protruded ten rubberized whip radio antennae. He switched the device on and set it on the back porch. While in the desert, he had commonly used cell phone jammers and other technology designed to disrupt enemy communication on the battlefield. On his return to the States, he was amazed to find the devices commercially available on the internet. The ads said they were good for teachers in the classroom, librarians, concert halls and theaters, and such. He hoped the device would work as well for his purposes. He did not intend to allow anyone inside to get to a cell phone, but better safe than sorry.

On the back porch sat a wrought iron patio table, the kind with an umbrella hole in the center. Fairly sturdy, not overly heavy, and weatherproof, wrought iron patio furniture never went out of style. Derwood calculated that the table would make a nice battering ram to lead through the glass doors into the room where the man and woman sat, now sipping from the snifters and watching television. The man had his hand draped lazily over her bare thigh very near the business section, while she snuggled next to him like a large overindulgent cat.

After a moment's consideration, Derwood picked up the table, pivoted and ran directly at the glass door, holding the table top in his strong hands. The large porch gave him a twenty-foot runway and at the last second, he raised the table legs first and crashed full force into the plate glass door.

When he was a child, Derwood had a friend who had run through a plate glass door and ended up with seventy-nine stiches before he left the emergency room. Since then manufacturers had changed their processes and glass doors were made with shatter-resistant tempered glass. They were designed to prevent shattering and lacerating foolish children who did not see the glass as they ran in for lemonade. The changes had been reasonably effective, but they were not designed to resist the full force of a charging man led by a wrought iron table fronted by four legs, each focusing the entire force in a tiny area on the glass. The effect was satisfying. The legs punched right through the glass, and spiderweb cracks instantly shot out all around. When the table top itself smacked into the remaining glass a fraction of a second later, it exploded inward in a crash. Following his momentum, Derwood launched the table fully into the room, but the action cost him his balance and for the second time that night, he ended up on the floor, this time in a pile of razor-sharp broken glass. He felt the sting of the shards through his gloves and the fabric of his shirt, but he did not stop to look. He continued into the room in a tumble and scrambled to his feet.

The man on the couch was quicker and more alert than Derwood had expected, and although surprised, his response was immediate. He rolled off the couch and reached for a table beside it. The man popped up clutching a revolver in his right hand and a cell phone in his left. He aimed the pistol.

There was no time to be clever. Derwood launched himself bodily at the man as the gun moved toward his center of mass. The man was quick, but surprise and preparation made Derwood quicker. His flying body struck the other man in the chest just as the man squeezed the trigger. The room exploded with a muffled boom as the pistol cracked, but the shot went just wide, and before the man could twist the barrel the final inch for another go, Derwood found the top of the weapon with his gloved left hand. He clutched the revolver and twisted, the palm of his hand firmly over the hammer such that even if the other man squeezed the trigger, the hammer could not travel back to generate the firing sequence. Those who loved revolvers loved them for their simplicity and reliability, but the design still relied on the hammer levering back and forward. Derwood's iron grip stopped that motion, and the pistol could not fire.

He simultaneously struck the man's face with his right elbow and wrenched the pistol and the man's wrist as they fell to the floor in a heap. Derwood let his momentum continue to carry him and landed hard on top of the other man, who let out an involuntary huff as his back struck the floor.

But the man was not done yet. He reacted as one who had been trained in martial arts, raising his knees and bucking his hips. Derwood's reliance on his own momentum came back to bite him as he flew heels over head right on over the man on the floor. He crashed to the floor and now the men lay on their backs, head to head, eyes to the ceiling. During the flip, both men lost their grip on the pistol, and it was now out of sight. The woman on the couch had curled into a fetal position. She whimpered softly.

With no time to think, both men scrambled to their feet. The man assumed a basic guard stance, feet shoulder width apart, torso slightly rotated, knees slightly flexed, arms up with hands loose and claw like in front. How many times had Derwood confronted this stance on the training mat at the Unit? He had lost count. No doubt the man was trained in martial arts, probably Krav Maga, the violent Israeli fighting style. A slight grin spread on his thin lips.

Pressed for time, his night growing longer by the second and uninterested in a fair fight, Derwood reached for his own pistol. Rather than wave it around threateningly, he pointed at the man's leading left leg and pulled the trigger. The crack of the revolver earlier had filled the room with sound, but it sounded like a popgun compared to the boom of Derwood's big automatic. In the silence echoing after the thunderous discharge, the man dropped like a stone.

Derwood had fired tens of thousands of rounds on the range and in the shoot house. He was an excellent shot, and he did not miss. The bullet had damaged Cranston's lateral thigh, but missed bone, nerve and major blood vessel. The man would limp for a few months, but he'd be fine. Of course, the man did not know that.

Derwood saw the woman still lying curled on the couch. She was not an immediate threat. The man on the floor moaned and clutched his thigh as Derwood put the gun to his forehead. He tried to control his heart rate and let the adrenaline surge pass. Long experience helped him calm down quickly, and he spoke in a harsh whisper:

"Who else is in the house?"

The man shook his head. "Nobody else."

Derwood shoved the barrel in the man's eye socket and twisted.

"Nobody. Nobody else. Just the girl."

"Who's she?"

"Just a rental. Nothing to me." He spoke through gritted teeth. "You shot me, asshole."

"Yeah? You shot first, asshole."

"You have no idea how screwed you are. You are in over your head, pal."

"Right," said Derwood. He grabbed a roll of duct tape from his pack and quickly secured Cranston by taping his wrists together behind his back, taping his ankles and knees together, and taping his mouth closed. He secured the scene by locating the wayward revolver, which had fallen under the couch in the struggle. Once Cranston was immobilized, he secured the hands of the call-girl, still curled up on the couch. He led her down the hall to a bathroom and shut her inside with instructions to lie still and quiet on the floor. She was scared half to death; she would obey.

Derwood quickly moved through the house and cleared each room. No one else was home. A minute outside on the lawn convinced him that the neighbors were far enough away that the gunshots had probably not been heard. It was time to talk to Cranston.

In the living room again, Derwood ripped the tape from the man's mouth. "We are going to have a little talk, you and me."

"You don't want to do this, buddy. I don't know who you are or what you think you're doing. This is not going to go the way you think. But I'll tell you what, if you leave right now, right now, I'll pretend none of this ever happened. No harm, no foul."

Derwood looked at him. After nearly a minute, he slowly shook his head.

Cranston said, "What the fuck do you even want?"

Derwood continued to stare at the other man, the way an arachnologist might stare at a particularly interesting spider before pinning it to a board, with a detached curiosity but without fear. Finally, he sighed and said, "I am trying to decide whether it is worth my time and trouble to talk to you, or whether I should just shoot you again. Honestly, I think it would make me feel better to just shoot you." He leaned over and tapped Cranston on the forehead. "Right there."

He pulled out the large automatic and put the barrel hard against the spot and placed his finger on the trigger. Cranston squirmed and turned his head. "Fuck! Fuck! Fuck you, man! I'm going to fucking kill you, you fucking asshole!"

"You don't want to talk?" asked Derwood, mildly impressed by the man's recalcitrance. "Okay. Be right back."

He went into the kitchen and rummaged around. A few minutes later he returned with a towel, a plastic garbage bag, a glass, and a pitcher of water. He muscled Cranston up off the floor and securely bound him to a kitchen chair with the duct tape. Handy stuff, duct tape. Derwood kept a roll in his truck. Never know when you might need it. He whistled quietly as he worked. The other man occasionally groaned from the pain in his thigh, but watched Derwood with increasing dread.

Once he had Cranston well secured, he poured himself a glass of water and set it on the table. "Sometimes I get thirsty when I work," he said. "Are you ready to talk yet, or do you need to toss out more threats?"

"What the fuck?" said Cranston.

Derwood shook his head sadly and put the black plastic garbage bag over the other man's head. He roughly pushed the chair backward and it tipped hard to the floor, where the back of Cranston's skull cracked on the hardwood floor with a snap. He moaned again. Derwood flattened the air out of the bag and snugged it around the man's neck, until soon he was writhing and gasping for air. The bag was impermeable, and it made a dark silhouette as Cranston's attempts to breathe sucked the bag against his face. When the struggles reached the height of desperation but before he lost strength, Derwood used his gloved hand to poke a hole in the bag over the man's mouth. Cranston sucked air greedily through the opening, his chest heaving with the effort.

Just when he appeared to be catching his breath, Derwood suddenly wrapped the towel tightly over his face, covering the bag with its small opening. He reached for the pitcher of water and began to splash it on the towel directly over Cranston's mouth.

When he was in the desert, Derwood occasionally used enhanced interrogation techniques on detainees. He was impressed by the speed with which some of the techniques overcame a man's reluctance to talk. He had never personally been waterboarded, although some men from the Unit had been, as part of a training exercise. It was in the same category as guys getting tear gassed or tazed, so as to know what to expect and how to deal with it, if it ever happened for real.

They all said the same thing. There is no way to deal with it. No point in trying. It sucks, then you pass out. The exercise had been advantageous, though, because it taught the men that waterboarding would not kill them. Probably. They would not drown, but some weak few might succumb to cardiac arrest from an adrenaline surge. Of course, the Unit did not have a weak few, but the rest of the world was full of them.

Derwood hoped that Cranston's heart would not give out, because the man was surely having an adrenaline surge, the way he was churning and bucking under the towel. He put remarkable strain on the duct tape binding his forehead and his neck veins bulged, and for a moment Derwood thought he might actually tear free, but the tape held.

As he had seen in the desert, it did not take long. Derwood had heard that the average CIA agent who volunteered to undergo the technique lasted only fourteen seconds before tapping out. He'd seen video of a Hollywood actor who had volunteered to be waterboarded for a piece in *Vanity Fair*. He had lasted fifteen seconds. Not bad. Better than the CIA.

Cranston was a tough bastard. He lasted nearly thirty seconds by Derwood's reckoning. But then his flailing and inarticulate howling slowed. Derwood quickly removed the towel and pulled the bag from over the nearly unconscious man's head. After a moment he began to cough and gag, sputtering water from his mouth and nose. Five minutes later he had recovered and was lying on his back taped to the chair, on the living room floor of his house staring at Derwood with hate in his eyes. Derwood knew of the reports of false information given by victims of enhanced interrogation. He knew of their propensity to lie, to say anything to get the torture to stop. But in Michael Cranston's eyes he saw only truth.

"Are you ready to have a conversation, Michael?"

Cranston closed his eyes and slowly nodded.

Chapter 26

"WHO IS WILLEM SMITS?" began Derwood. Cranston still lay on his back on the floor, hair wet from a mixture of tap water and sweat, his head in a pool of cool water.

"Holy shit! Is that what this is about? I should have known. I didn't hear anything about that fucking guy for years. Then I get a phone call out of the blue that some asshole went to visit him and stir up a bunch of trouble."

Derwood smiled. Realization entered Cranston's eyes. "Oh shit. It was you, wasn't it?"

Derwood kept on smiling, and said, "I ask. You answer."

"Bullshit. It was you," said Cranston.

Derwood reached for the towel and the pitcher, and Cranston's face grew immediately damp as sweat broke out on his upper lip. "No, man. No. Not necessary. You made your point. Willem Smits sold flowers."

"Yeah?"

"Yeah. Flowers. You believe that shit?" He was laughing nervously now, speech pressured. "Roses. Tulips. That kind of thing. Flowers, you know."

"How did you get involved with him?"

"He came to me for some legal work a few years ago now."

"Why you?"

"I don't know. We had some mutual friends, you know? Some guys we both knew. They referred him. He wanted discretion, which is my specialty."

"I thought all you lawyers were discreet. Attorney client privilege and all that."

"I guess some of us are more discreet that others. Can I get up now?"

"No."

"Come on, man. You shot me. You fucking... I don't even know what that other thing was. You fucking waterboarded me, asshole!"

"Are you ready for more?"

"No, man. No more."

"Then stop whining. Who were your mutual friends?"

"Ah man, come on, you do not want to know about those guys. They got nothing to do with this."

Derwood shook his head and sighed, reached for the towel and the pitcher.

"Just some guys from New York, man. Some guys Smits used to know. He sold them flowers, I guess, for funerals and stuff. Big spreads of roses, they said. Big spreads. I met a couple of them down here a few years ago. They had some work for me. That's it, man. Don't worry about those guys. You do not want to know, believe me."

Derwood decided to let it pass for the moment.

"What were you doing for him?"

"Minor work, really. He wanted me to set up a power-of-attorney and a trust."

"Go on."

"There's this girl, must be about twenty by now, but back then she was just a teenager. Rough life, parents dead, grandad abandoned her, you know. Smits, he wants me to set up a trust that will help her out. Wants to fund it using, you know, somebody else's money. Just to help her out, you know?"

"And you have some experience using other people's money?"

"Uh, maybe a little, you know. Nothing serious or anything. This other fellow, James Devaney, he is her grandfather, but he was a drunk and apparently ran off and ditched the kid. I guess Smits and the guy had been friends at one time, and he wants to help the kid out."

"Nice guy," said Derwood.

"Whatever. A while after DeVaney ran off, Smits asked me to, you know, make him power-of-attorney over DeVaney's assets. So he could set up this trust for the girl."

"Don't you need consents and signatures to do that?"

"Well, I mean, normally you would, but it's kind of a niche thing. If you know what I mean?"

"You mean it's illegal."

"Well, you know, maybe a little. But anyway, it's for a good cause, right? That was it. We set up a POA so Smits could get DeVaney's money and use it to create a trust for DeVaney's granddaughter. That's it, man."

"But there were strings attached, weren't there Michael?"

"No," said Cranston.

"What about setting the girl to watch Smits? Whose idea was that? Was that your mutual friends from New York?"

"Oh, no, not those guys. I told you before, it had nothing to do with those guys."

"So, who was it?" asked Derwood.

"That came later. At the beginning, it was just Smits setting up a way to help out an old friend's kid who'd had a tough shake. But somehow this woman found out about it. Or maybe she knew all along. Anyway, she knew a lot about it. I think she knew Smits and DeVaney both. Maybe the girl, too. They were all from the same neighborhood."

"Woodlake," said Derwood.

"Right. Woodlake. Anyhow, this woman just showed up one day. She obviously knew Smits. That's the only way she would have known to come to me, but Smits didn't know she came, see. She knew about the POA on DeVaney. She wanted me to add her name to the document."

"Did you?"

"Well, she brought her daughter. They were pretty persuasive, you know. They came a few times. They were persuasive. Her daughter in particular." Cranston grinned, wickedly he probably thought. Lying on his back duct taped to a chair in a pool of water on the floor, face glistening with sweat and moisture, Derwood just thought he looked desperate. A man trying to form some connection to his tormentor, seeking common ground. Derwood had seen it before. He smiled.

"I bet she was."

"Oh, you better believe it. But they didn't stop there, see. The older woman wanted another POA made up, this time on Smits. She wanted me to draft a document granting her full general power of attorney over Smits."

"How was Smits behaving around that time?" he asked.

"What do you mean?" said Cranston.

"Was he, how do you put it? Was he 'of sound mind'?"

"You mean was he crazy? Or senile?"

"That's what I mean," said Derwood.

"Nah, I wouldn't say that. Maybe a little scattered, but not senile."

"Did you draft the second power of attorney for her?"

"She was pretty damn persuasive, I have to say."

"Umm-hmm. Did Smits know?"

"No, of course not. Discreet, remember? Can I get up now?"

"No."

"Why did she want a POA on Smits?"

"She said he was losing his mind. Needed someone he trusted who could look after his affairs."

"Why did she want it kept secret from him?"

"I don't know, man. Like I said, I don't ask questions."

"So, Smits sets up a POA on DeVaney, and a trust for his granddaughter. Later, this woman sets up a POA on Smits so she can control his affairs."

"Yup," said Cranston.

"Who set up the surveillance on Smits?"

"She did. She has me revise the initial trust, using Smits' POA. Makes the trust payments contingent on the girl watching Smits. Has me set up this whole thing of letters and phones and all that."

"Why?"

"I don't know, man."

"Because you don't ask questions?"

"Bingo."

"So what happened Wednesday afternoon?" asked Derwood.

"Well, somebody went to visit Smits and started asking questions, and the girl did what she was supposed to do. She called Danny; Danny called me."

"And who did you call, Michael?"

"I called Brandi. Brandi Hitchcock."

"Hitchcock?" asked Derwood. "Brandi Hitchcock? Huh. Any relation to Deloris Hitchcock?"

"Yeah," Cranston laughed. "That's her mother. I don't know who is crazier, but they are damn persuasive, I'll tell you that. Particularly Brandi."

Derwood checked his watch. He had been here too long, but he had gotten what he came for. It was time to go. He picked up the towel and moved to place it back over the man's head. A satisfying look of terror leapt into the man's eyes, and Derwood smiled. He wrapped the towel tightly back over the man's head.

"I know you are tough, Michael. And I know you have some tough friends. But I am tougher. If you mention our little soiree tonight to anybody, I'm going to come back."

Beneath the towel, the man shook his head frantically side to side. He spoke with desperation as he said, "No, no, no. Nobody. I swear. Nobody. Don't do it!"

"Remember," said Derwood as he tilted the pitcher to splash a little water onto the towel over the man's eyes, "the United States government does not even classify this as torture. It can get much, much worse. If I hear from you, I'm coming back. If I see you, I'm coming back. If I even think about you, I'm coming back. Do you understand?"

Cranston nodded rapidly under the towel. He had had enough. He probably would not sleep soundly for months, if ever again. He would wake in the night in a cold sweat, short of breath and gasping for air, feeling like he was suffocating. He would dream of drowning. He had had enough. Derwood put the pitcher down next to him on the floor and made a quick sweep of the room.

He left through the shattered glass door and picked up the phone jammer. Out in the yard it was still full dark as he walked quickly into the forest. By the time he got to his pickup at the park & ride, the darkness began to give way to morning's first faint glow.

Chapter 27

SATURDAY MORNING

AS HE DROVE, THE SKY brightened, and his stomach began to rumble. He checked the time. Just after five-thirty a.m. Morning now. Five o'clock was the cutoff where you could say it was morning, no longer the middle of the night. Early, but perhaps not too early. He texted Maggie.

You awake?

A minute later his phone pinged.

Yes! Where have you been? Are you okay?

He typed back as he drove, ignoring the laws, road signs and public service announcements imploring him not to text and drive.

Fine. Breakfast?

Where?

Mac's. 8:45.

See you there.

Derwood pressed the pedal farther to the floor and headed home. On the way, he stopped for a coffee and a shower at an all-night truck stop. His clothes had served him well. There were tiny shards of glass captured in the clothing and in his hair, but his forearms and hands had avoided any damage. He bagged up the clothing. They would go in the dumpster outside. In the pay shower, he scrubbed the nights' exertions from his body. He had a few minor scratches on his face, but nothing deep, nothing telling.

Looking in the mirror, he judged the scratches could have come from walking through the woods. He hoped it was the woods. He did not want his DNA left on broken glass in Michael Cranston's living room, in case the man actually called the cops. A careful crime scene investigator might recover traces of DNA, and Derwood knew his was on file with the U.S. government. There was nothing to be done about that either way.

Showered and changed, he carefully inspected his pickup for shards of glass or any other residue that might link him to the night's activities. Once he was satisfied, he tossed the bag in the dumpster and drove home. One final stop, where he cleaned and wiped the gun, then tossed it into Deep River. He was due at breakfast.

He arrived at Mac's in Southern Pines at precisely at 8:45. Maggie was waiting for him in a booth with two cups of coffee on the table. Derwood noticed as he walked toward her that she was dressed in a V-neck T-shirt designed to emphasize some of her finer qualities, but he knew better than to stare. He slid in the booth on the bench opposite her. Eye contact, he told himself. Eye contact. Women always noticed the quick dart of a man's eyes downward. Discipline was everything.

"Where have you been?" she asked, exasperated. "I tried to call and text, but I couldn't get through. We were worried about you after you left Sarah's place." Her face bore a mixture of frustration and concern.

"I had some things I had to do, is all. It's fine. I'm fine. Don't worry about it."

"No, Derwood, it's not fine. The sheriff cannot have you freaking out at a crime scene and running away. I can't have that. Tell me what happened. What's going on?"

He sighed and put his hands flat on the table. "Maggie, do we have to do this now? We've got more important things to talk about.

I know what's going on here. Part of it, anyway. You need to hear what I have to say."

Confusion entered her eyes, but the frustration remained. She looked at him with tightly pursed lips and huffed through her nose. "Fine. Talk," she said through clenched teeth.

"Several years ago, after James DeVaney went missing and Sarah Smalls ended up in foster care, Willem Smits contacted an attorney named Michael Cranston to set up a trust for Sarah. Smits and DeVaney knew each other before DeVaney disappeared, and apparently Smits felt some obligation to the girl. He contacted Cranston, who deals in various forms of identity theft. One of his tricks is to create what appears to be a valid power of attorney on someone, without their knowledge or consent, and sell it or use it to rob them. Clear out their bank accounts, whatever."

Maggie's confusion and frustration were replaced with a thoughtful expression as her mind worked through the implication. "You could use that to do anything, really," she said. "Open accounts, close accounts, transfer funds, buy houses, take out loans, open credit cards, whatever."

"Exactly," said Derwood. "Smits gets Cranston to create a power of attorney for DeVaney, and use it to fund a trust for Sarah with DeVaney's money. DeVaney was dead and buried. Smits knew about that. He had to know. Why else would he call Cranston?"

"Maybe he just wanted to rob him?" Maggie asked hesitantly.

"No. He knew. He gets the POA on DeVaney, and uses it to set up the trust for Sarah. Sometime later, but not much later, Smits moves into Pinelands. Now, enter the Hitchcocks."

Maggie's eyebrows rose.

"Deloris Hitchcock finds out about the trust and the POA. Remember that she, Smits and DeVaney have a history," said Derwood.

"They all served on the Woodlake Board at the same time, around the time of Fred Akers' murder," said Maggie.

"Correct," said Derwood. "Deloris and Brandi Hitchcock go talk to Cranston."

"Brandi Hitchcock? Deloris' daughter?" said Maggie.

"Apparently, she can be very, uh, persuasive." Derwood used his fingers to put air quotes around the word "persuasive."

"The Hitchcocks convince Cranston to add Deloris to the POA on DeVaney, but Smits doesn't know anything about that. She uses the POA to modify the trust Smits created for Sarah, and insists Sarah keep watch on Smits at Pinelands."

Maggie's brow furrowed in concentration as she tried to keep track of the machinations. "Say that again," she said.

Derwood did.

"But they don't stop there. Cranston creates a new power of attorney, this time on Smits himself. Smits is going downhill fast." Derwood paused. "Maybe the lead poisoning. Anyway, they set up a power-of-attorney over his affairs. Thing is, Smits himself doesn't know anything about it. But he goes downhill and Cranston Law Group starts to, uh, handle his affairs.

"Now we have Smits in Pinelands with his mind gone, and Cranston Law is managing his affairs. We have Sarah Smalls' trust fund demanding that she keep an eye on Smits, and Cranston manages that as well. But Cranston is just a smokescreen for the Hitchcocks. Cranston uses De Luca as a cutout, someone he can hide behind. De Luca is smokescreen for Cranston."

Maggie nodded, confusion giving way to understanding. "The hurricane comes, and we find Fred Akers. You go to ask Smits about it. Sarah follows her instructions and calls De Luca. De Luca calls Cranston. Cranston calls Hitchcock. Smits is murdered that night, and Sarah Smalls the next."

Derwood nodded.

"But what about Akers?" said Maggie.

"I don't know what happened twenty years ago to Fred Akers, but as for the murders this week? That trail points right back to Deloris Hitchcock. Maybe her daughter, too. Or her weird son." Derwood paused as the waitress arrived and they ordered breakfast. As soon as she left, Maggie turned to Derwood. She looked at him, chewing her lower lip.

"Deloris is too old to overcome Sarah," said Derwood. "She had to have help."

"Hold on a minute," said Maggie. "Back up. How could you possibly know all that?"

She would not approve of his nocturnal activities, and he had gone to some effort to keep it out of view. The rules of law enforcement were restrictive, but his methods got results, and he was not going to apologize. A small part of him wanted to explain exactly what he had been up to, but all he said was, "Investigating. You know, trying to be helpful."

"Mmm-hmm. Is that what happened to your face?"

"No. Cut myself shaving."

"Mmm-hmm. Look, Derwood, I need to know where you've been and what you've been up to. You are a sheriff's deputy. That makes you part of a team. Where have you been the last twenty-four hours?"

"Leave it alone, Maggie," he said. She thought she wanted to know, but she really did not. If she knew, she would instantly be complicit. It could ruin her career. As it was, he was working for the sheriff, not the district attorney. If he were found out, it could bring down Sheriff Blanchard, but Maggie might escape unscathed.

"I know you were in the army, and I know you've seen things. It's hard to believe you would freak out at the sight of a dead body. So, I'm guessing you went back to Raleigh, didn't you? Maybe you decided that our friend De Luca had not been forthcoming enough.

Did you go try to persuade him, Derwood?" This time Maggie used air quotes around the word "persuade."

He smiled faintly. "It doesn't matter," he said.

"It does, Derwood. You can't just run around like a vigilante."

He ignored her. "I told you what I know. Now it's time for the next step."

"Ah, the next step. And what would that be?" she asked with sarcasm in her voice.

"I don't know," he said. He was tired, and he had politely asked her to leave it alone. "You're the damn DA. Go bring somebody in for questioning. I'd suggest Deloris Hitchcock, or maybe her daughter. The whole damn family. They're obviously tied up in this." He knew she would disapprove of his methods, but his information was sound. Was a little gratitude too much to ask?

"Have you ever heard of probable cause?" she hissed. "What would I bring them in for? What do you expect me to tell a judge? My thug went up to Raleigh and threatened a witness or two? Roughed them up? Got them to talk, or they'd get concrete shoes or some other bullshit?"

Derwood did not speak. The waitress delivered two plates. She refilled coffee and asked if they needed anything. They did not.

Maggie was forced to unclench her teeth to get the scrambled eggs between them. The effort did not make her happy. They ate in silence for a time, until Derwood sighed and spoke.

"I know we see this differently. But sometimes the fastest way into the back room is right through the front door. People are dying, Maggie. Sarah Smalls is dead. She was an easy target. Single woman, living alone."

He counted on his fingers.

"Akers." One. "DeVaney." Two. "Hinrichs." Three. Four. Five. "Smits." Six. "Smalls." Seven. Derwood paused, then put up an eighth finger. "These people killed an entire family, Maggie. An eight-year-old boy. They killed Sarah Smalls. A defenseless girl. Who do you think is going to be next?"

He stood and threw a twenty-dollar bill on the table. "Breakfast is on me. Have a nice day." Derwood turned and walked out of the diner. Maggie watched him go. He did not look back.

Chapter 28

MARGARET KIDD SAT AT the booth finishing her breakfast. The eggs were rich and creamy, just the way she liked them, and the coffee was sweet enough. She thought about Derwood Flynn. He had obviously been up all night.

Yesterday at Sarah Smalls' murder scene, he had been out of sorts. Not queasy or troubled by the fact of death, but deeply affected by that particular death. Before, when he learned that Willem Smits had been murdered, he seemed totally unaffected. Likewise with the others: Akers, DeVaney, even the Hinrichs family. The Hinrichs child. Why then, was he so disturbed by Sarah Smalls that he left the scene without a word and dropped out of sight for twenty-four hours?

She knew little of his past, only that he had been one of Fort Bragg's secret soldiers. She had grown up here, in the shadow of Bragg. Like all the locals, she had ideas of what went on behind the wire. The operators would not speak of it. Classified and all that. But everyone had their suspicions and everybody seemed to know somebody who worked there. She had dated a guy who claimed he worked there once, but she doubted it. He lacked that indescribably hard quality that lurked beneath the social veneer of many of those guys. But Flynn had it. She detected beneath his reserve a depth of emotion and intensity belied by his casual attitude and efforts to remain out of the mud and muck, to remain clean. Maggie suspected he had gotten plenty dirty in the past.

And now she worried that he had dredged up methods from his past that would cast dirt on her and her sister, on Martin Sinsley, and the entire law enforcement establishment of Moore County.

She doubted she could use the information Derwood had produced. Even the most conservative judges frowned on coercion. The days of forced confessions and backroom intimidation at the police station were long gone, even in the conservative South.

And what of her own feelings? She had sensed a connection between herself and Derwood. She knew he had sensed it, too. His clumsy attempts to hide his attraction had not worked. As a prominent woman in what remained a man's world, she had learned long ago how to read men. She could see what a man was thinking by the look on his face, the movements of his eyes, the pattern of his speech. She had learned to use her intuitive understanding of men to her advantage. Many people, men and women alike, considered any successful and powerful woman to be manipulative. She did not see it that way. She just used the advantages she found in life to forge her own way, no different than any other successful person.

But she felt genuine attraction to Derwood Flynn. He projected calm and good will, and she liked that. But beneath the surface she detected a lurking rage. He hid it down deep, but he carried a darkness within him beneath the easygoing exterior. Maggie saw the darkness. He had hidden scars from things he had seen and done. She now feared that she was yoked to that darkness, that he had brought home terrible things that happened in other places.

She snorted into her coffee. Stop the foolishness. Flynn did not bring any monsters home with him from the Army. The monsters had always been here. Just ask Jacob Hinrichs or Sarah Smalls. It was her job to root them out. If she could not approach a judge with Derwood's information, the least she could do was use it to ask her own questions. She wondered whether the answers would be the same for her in daylight as they had been for him in the dark.

She settled her bill and left a generous tip. Maggie had waited tables as an undergrad in Chapel Hill. It was one of the most underappreciated jobs anywhere. She always left generous tips.

Ever the southern girl, Maggie thought of last Sunday's service. The pastor had preached from Matthew 5:23. "So if you are offering your gift at the altar and there remember that your brother has something against you, leave your gift there before the altar and go. First be reconciled to your brother, and then come and offer your gift."

She resolved to call Derwood and make peace, but first she needed to reclaim the initiative. She needed information. She needed to talk to Daniel De Luca. Perhaps he could give her probable cause on Cranston, and then Cranston on the Hitchcocks. By following the links in the chain, she could build a case that would hold up in court.

The private investigator did not sound happy to hear from her, but he was willing to meet her at his office in early afternoon. She pointed the car north and drove back to Raleigh. When she got to De Luca's office, he met her at the door with a limp. He seemed relieved that she was alone.

He was not limping when she had seen him two days ago. "What happened to your leg?" she asked.

He glared at her and shrugged. "Tripped over a root jogging yesterday. It's fine. Didn't bring your goon today?"

"Not today. Sometimes you catch more flies with honey than with vinegar, and I thought maybe we could start over."

"Huh. Well, come in and have a seat," he said.

"Look, Mr. De Luca," she began. "We have a serious problem, and what I don't know is whether you are part of the problem or part of the solution. We've already got you connected to at least one death. The way I see it, you are at the very least an accessory to murder. In this state, that means a zealous district attorney can charge you with felony murder. Life in prison, without parole. Even the death penalty." She smiled sweetly, and put a little syrup into her voice. "But, I don't think that's necessary. I think you're in over your head. I think I can help you."

"Is that what you think?" he asked.

"It is. See, I think the person we are really after is your friend Mike. The lawyer. Michael Cranston. Or his clients, anyway. And I think you know that."

"You do, huh?"

"I do. If you help me, I think I can help you, too. We don't really need to make an issue of what you do here." She swept her hand around to indicate the city outside the office. "It's not even in my jurisdiction. It'll come up once we get this thing to court, but I see you as a witness for the prosecution, not the defense."

De Luca thought for a moment but finally spoke. "You see me wrong, lady. I don't want anything to do with this. I'm not testifying about anything, ever." He turned and opened his file cabinet. He rooted around a bit and came up empty. "Son of a bitch!" he spat. "That son of a bitch!"

Maggie suspected she knew the source of De Luca's irritation, but he was about seventy miles south doing who knows what on a Saturday afternoon. Her face showed nothing.

De Luca regained his composure before turning back toward her. He put his hands on his desk, palms upward and open, emptyhanded. "I must have misplaced some of my files. But maybe that's better anyway. I don't want you to hear this from me."

"Fair enough," she said.

"You want to talk to Cranston. He set everything up. The trust, the letters, the surveillance, the phone. All of it. I just run interference on stuff. I've worked with him before, but far as I know nobody's ever gotten hurt because of it. Not physically anyway. I don't want any part of that. That's all I know."

"What do you know about Cranston himself?"

"Not much. Just that he's a lawyer. Had some trouble at UNC, finished in Charlotte. Some shady business dealings, maybe on the wrong side of the law, but that's none of my business. Discretion is our business model. Fair fee for a fair service, that's all we provide here. I don't want anything to do with murder.

"I got a call from the Smalls girl a few nights ago. That's the first time ever. Somebody was asking the old man at Pinelands some questions. I passed on the message to Cranston. Next day, you and your goon show up and tell me the old man is dead. That's all I know."

"Well, I need to talk to Michael Cranston. Where does he live?"

De Luca gave her the address.

"Listen, lady. People are dying. I wouldn't go talk to Cranston alone. Call your goon."

Chapter 29

AFTER LEAVING MAC'S, Derwood drove straight home. He needed sleep, but he was satisfied with his night's work. He understood the connection between Hitchcock, Smits, Devaney and Smalls. Unfortunately, Maggie had not seemed grateful. What was the point of deputizing a man like Derwood Flynn if you didn't want aggressive and off-book tactics? He was no peace officer, and he did not like rules. Maybe he should not have gotten involved.

He had felt an unexpected attraction to her, from the moment they met on the Woodlake Dam. He felt like a fool then, tongue-tied and clumsy, while she mocked him. Derwood was not a romantic and did not believe in love at first sight, but he could not deny that meeting her had been powerful. He had spent months trying to blunt emotion and blur memory, but now his rekindled relationship with his daughter Lizzy and the very existence of Margaret Kidd threatened to destroy the walls he had built. For the first time in a long time he felt hope for the future. Someone needed him, and he had acted.

He felt no guilt or uncertainty about it. Instead, he thought of Sarah Smalls. She should not have died. Too young. She was hardly older than Lizzy.

And what about Maggie? The killer had to be watching her, and her sister too. Her official position might give her a sense of security, but a killer who would end JJ Hinrichs and Sarah Smalls, the latter in the middle of an investigation, would not be dissuaded by a badge or a title. The world was full of assholes, and there were assholes loose in Woodlake. Somebody had to put them in the ground.

HE WOKE IN MIDAFTERNOON to the blaring E-flat from his cell phone. Maggie was on the line, and wanted him to meet her in Raleigh. She wanted to interview Michael Cranston. Derwood considered begging off. She should be safe enough, on a Saturday afternoon in the city, when her sister and others knew her whereabouts. Then he remembered Cranston's supposed friends and the threats he made. He remembered Sarah.

Perhaps they could not officially use Derwood's information, but no judge would exclude information given voluntarily to a district attorney during a legal interview. Maybe Derwood could encourage Cranston to cooperate. He whistled as he drove to Raleigh.

They met at Cranston's home. Maggie was already there, with a local sheriff's deputy from Wake County. The deputy had jurisdiction here, which might be useful.

The house looked different in the light of day, and from the street rather than the back yard. Whereas the rear of the house was largely glass and stone, looking over the large backyard and the parkland and woods beyond, the front had few windows. Imposing stone and wood fronted the street and told strangers to mind their own business.

Maggie pressed the doorbell, and a woman opened the door. Derwood did not recognize her. Definitely not the prostitute he had seen last night. This woman was dressed in traditional nurse's garb, complete with white apron and hat. She looked like the kind of nurse one might order out of a catalogue of Russian brides, the snug uniform leaving little to the imagination, even though it was modest in length and buttoned to the neck. Derwood took comfort in the fact that she could not be concealing a weapon.

Maggie introduced them, and asked whether Mr. Cranston was home. He was, but was not taking visitors. He had been ill, and had spent the night and morning in the emergency room. He needed rest. The local deputy produced a warrant, secured that morning at Maggie's request. It was good to know people. The frowning nurse led the three visitors into the living room.

Derwood saw that the broken glass had been cleaned, but there had not been time to repair the window. The large hole he had made when he crashed through hours before was now covered, draped by a heavy blanket. Cranston sat on the couch where he had sat the night before when Derwood arrived, this time wearing a thick terrycloth robe belted at the waist, with his leg propped up on the coffee table in front of him. The television displayed an immaculate golf course, where pros who looked like teenagers were making millions.

When Maggie introduced them, Cranston's eyes lingered on Derwood. The visitor in the night had been masked and covered head to toe, and had spoken only in a whisper, but the eyes looked familiar. He could not be sure.

Maggie explained why they were there. She asked for his cooperation. Before Cranston could reply, Derwood quietly asked, "Michael, can I get you anything? You look uncomfortable. Would you like some water?" As he spoke his voice became progressively quieter, until he was speaking just above a whisper. Sweat broke out on Cranston's forehead.

He turned to the nurse, who was standing behind him with one hand on his shoulder. "Sasha, can you get me a drink, sweetheart."

They all watched Sasha sashay out of the room. "She is a nurse, you know," Cranston said as he followed her movements out of the room. "Amazing service, very helpful. She'll be with me a few weeks."

"Yeah, I bet," said Maggie. "What happened to your leg?"

Cranston looked at Derwood. "I cut it on that door." He nodded to the broken glass door. "Last night. Party. One too many, I guess. You know how it is. I spent all morning at the ER getting put back together. Sasha met me here when I got home. She's a real nurse," he said again, as if he could not believe it himself. "It's amazing some of the home health services you can get these days, if you know where to look."

"I hope the leg isn't too bad," said Derwood quietly.

"Nah, nothing vital. They tell me it will be fine in a few weeks," said Cranston.

"Lucky," said Derwood.

"Yeah," agreed Cranston. "Lucky."

"Let's talk, just the three of us," said Maggie.

Cranston kept his eyes on Derwood as he asked, "What do you want to talk about?"

"Lots of stuff," said Maggie. "But why don't we start with Sarah Smalls? Did it bother you when she died, Michael?"

"You don't know what you are talking about," said Cranston.

"Yeah, Michael, I do. Here is how it is going to be. You need to talk to me here and now. You're in a pickle, and maybe I can help you out. At the very least, you are an accessory to murder. In this state, that's as good as felony murder itself. When the jury sees the pictures of Sarah Smalls, you'll be going away for a long time. When they see JJ Hinrichs, you'll get the death penalty."

Cranston looked smug. "Lady, you think you're the first ladder climber that ever threatened me? I'm not an accessory to anything, and I think this conversation is over. Sasha!" He called out for the nurse, who slid back into the room with feline grace.

Derwood spoke, "Ms. Kidd, Deputy, would you excuse us for just a moment? I'd like to have a few words alone with Mr. Cranston here. Do you mind?"

Maggie glanced at Derwood, but she did not protest. The deputy followed her out. After a few minutes of muffled conversation, Derwood called them back in.

"I think he'll talk to you now." The man on the couch looked pale, a little clammy, but undamaged. The bandage on his leg was undisturbed. Derwood stood off to the side, watching without expression.

"Okay. Here are my rules. I'll tell you what I know, but you got to leave me out of it."

"I'll do what I can," said Maggie, "but I'm not covering up murder. Some of your involvement will come out. There's no way to hide the phone calls or the documents. I'll talk to the Wake County DA. We can come to an arrangement. As long as you tell the truth here and now, I'll leave you be, the best I can, for what's related to this and gone before. What you do from now on is up to you, and I'm not making promises about any other business."

"Do I get a lawyer?"

"Do you want a lawyer?" asked Derwood. He smiled faintly as he asked, looking in the other man's eyes.

"No, I guess not," said Cranston shakily. "Not right now."

And just like that, he began to tell the story. Smits had come to him requesting a power-of-attorney on DeVaney, so that he could set up a trust to help DeVaney's granddaughter Sarah Smalls. Cranston swore he did not know DeVaney was dead. He set it up to help the girl out, he said. Smits, who had been in good health, began a rapid decline and ended up in a rest home.

Brandi Hitchcock approached him with her persuasive wiles and convinced him to add her and Mother's names to the POA, and to set one up on Smits himself. That was when the trust arrangement changed and Sarah started her surveillance. Last Wednesday, the night of the phone call, Cranston followed the instructions given him by Brandi Hitchcock. When he got the call from De Luca, he hurried to Stick-in-the-Eye and called Sarah back for details, which he passed on to Brandi. He swore that he had nothing more to do with it. He didn't know anything would happen to Smits or Sarah Smalls. He said he regretted his involvement altogether.

"You need to track down Brandi Hitchcock. She's the one you want."

"Where can we find her?" asked Maggie.

"She works at Drake Health. She is a clinical pharmacist. I don't know where she lives."

IT ONLY TOOK ONE PHONE call to the local Sheriff's Department to find Brandi Hitchcock's address. They arrived at her apartment a few minutes later. She was home on this Saturday afternoon, and she opened when Maggie knocked on the door. She invited them inside.

She was a striking woman. Tall, thin in the waist but not the chest or hips, with high cheekbones and deep blue eyes, she spoke with a trace of her mother's patrician accent, but slowly, caressing each word as it left her lips.

"Come on in, please. Would you like tea?" She spoke with an odd cadence. "I can put on coffee if you prefer."

They declined. The apartment was large. The classical French décor was too ornate for Derwood's tastes. A writing desk beneath the window probably cost more than his pickup. The room was dominated by a large oil painting of a matronly woman. Derwood realized with surprise that the picture was of a younger Deloris Hitchcock. Although he had met her only once, the high cheekbones and bottomless eyes were unmistakable. It could just as easily have been a picture of Brandi Hitchcock herself. Mother and daughter could have been sisters, almost twins. Deloris Hitchcock had been a strikingly beautiful woman.

"We are not here for coffee or tea," said Maggie. "We are here to discuss the murders of Willem Smits and Sarah Smalls."

"I see," breathed Hitchcock. "I had not realized that they were dead. Just awful!" She did not look like she thought it was awful.

"I understand why you killed Smits," said Maggie. "But why Sarah? What did she know that could hurt you?"

"You really think I killed them?" she purred. "You cannot be serious."

Maggie shrugged. "Coroner says Smits was probably killed with a medical paralytic, and you are a pharmacist. Imagine that. We know Cranston called you the night he was killed. We know you were involved with Smalls."

"Who is this Cranston?" asked Hitchcock.

"We know you are from Woodlake. Did you kill the Hinrichs, too?"

"Sweetheart, you are coming on way too strong," said Hitchcock, with her slow drawl. "I appreciate your zeal, but I think I should call my lawyer. Do you think so?"

"Call whomever you like, and I'd also pack an overnight bag. You are coming with us."

"Oh, really? I do not think I will. I have other things to do this afternoon. But I would be happy to meet you later on this week. We can set up a time. Let me find my planner and see when would be most convenient."

"Uh, no," said Maggie. "I don't think you understand, Ms. Hitchcock. You are under arrest for the murders of Willem Smits and Sarah Smalls."

"Oh, Dear! Is that really necessary?"

"Deputy?" said Maggie, and the deputy read Hitchcock her rights. They allowed the woman to pack a small bag of clothes and essentials, but did not leave her side. She called her lawyer as promised, and they made their way to the car, where the deputy released her into Maggie and Derwood's custody. The jail in Carthage was only an hour and a half away.

Chapter 30

ON THE DRIVE BACK TO the jail in Moore County, euphemistically called the Public Safety Center, Maggie called her sister. Together they decided to let Brandi Hitchcock stew in jail overnight. She might be more cooperative in the morning. Sheriff Blanchard called Bill Seamons. She and Judge Seamons had been high school classmates and remained friends. The judge agreed not to meddle as long as charges were brought soon.

Brandi remained silent except to request a private cell at the detention center. Luckily for her the jail census was low. There were the usual suspects housed at the jail, awaiting trial but unable to make bail. Debtors prisons may have been abolished, but somehow poor folk still rotted behind bars awaiting their day in court. American justice.

The next stop would be Deloris' home at Woodlake. Brandi could not have been involved with Fred Akers twenty years ago. She was too young. Nor could they imagine how she might have been tied to DeVaney or the Hinrichs murders. But Deloris could have been. Maybe ratcheting up the pressure on Deloris would yield a confession, or provoke further action. They still had no direct evidence. When they arrived at Castleberry Court at Woodlake and rang the bell, full dark had arrived.

Deloris answered and regarded them for a moment. "Ah. Derwood Flynn, if memory serves. And who is your companion?"

"Good evening, Ms. Hitchcock. This is the district attorney, Margaret Kidd."

Deloris Hitchcock looked at the younger woman, taking in the details of her face, eyes, hair, and dress. "Indeed," she said. "I recognize you from your campaign literature. You look better in person, if I may say so, although the prints on your brochures and billboards were flattering."

"That's very kind of you, ma'am," said Maggie. She felt odd, exchanging pleasantries with this woman, suspected of mass murder.

"Strong women must stick together, my dear. It is still a man's world, and they will try to destroy you. Don't doubt if for a minute." Her face softened as she invited them inside. If she was bothered by their visit, she did not let it show. "Won't you come in?"

She led them into the same room Derwood had seen before. Night had fallen and there was no view out toward the lake. The darkness outside and the lights inside turned the large picture windows into mirrors reflecting the room back at them. On the table before the couch sat a snifter full of amber liquid.

"I was just enjoying a nightcap. I do enjoy a nip of brandy in the evening. Always have. Let me offer you some." She moved to pour from the decanter on a serving table near the wall.

"Thank you but not tonight. We are on duty," said Maggie.

"I should have guessed, I suppose. It is quite late for a social call. More's the pity."

"What are you drinking?" asked Derwood.

"This is Martell Cordon Bleu."

"Cognac," said Derwood. He was no stranger to spirits, although his tastes ran more to corn derivatives than the fruit of the vine.

"Indeed. A very fine cognac."

"But you called it brandy."

"Well, it's like a diminutive. A term of endearment. Not to put too fine a point on it, but this is my oldest friend." She held up the sifter and swirled the liquid around the glass. "We go way back, but

I would not want you to get the wrong impression. One per night, never more," she smiled.

Derwood did not see any of the telltale signs of the lifelong alcoholic etched in her features. Her face was not reddened, eyes were clear with no sign of icterus, the skin was not slack or spotted, no spider capillaries crawling towards her nose. He looked at his own reflection in the large picture window, but the window was too far away and the image was blurry. He turned back to the older woman.

"Did you name your daughter after the drink?" asked Maggie.

"Excuse me?" said Hitchcock.

"Brandy. Isn't your daughter named Brandi?"

"Well, it's only her middle name. Her given name is Agatha. But yes, I've always called her Brandi. She has brought me great comfort over the years. Now, Miss Kidd, why do you bring up my daughter?"

"We arrested her today. She is in custody right now."

"I see." She paused. "That is unfortunate. Why, pray tell, did you arrest her?" asked Deloris.

"We believe she conspired to murder two people this week. Actually, one of them is your old friend Willem Smits."

Deloris Hitchcock snorted, but she did not look surprised or upset. "Hmm. Old Rosie is finally dead? Who will send him flowers?"

Derwood and Maggie exchanged glances, curious.

"Old Rosie?" said Maggie.

"People used to call him Rosie, a long time ago. He is Dutch, you know. They like flowers. He was a florist, once, before he retired. I do not know where he got the nickname.

"I am not surprised he is dead. He has been fading, and the end had to come. It comes for us all. He has been in a nursing home for years. I suppose I will send flowers."

She cocked her head. "But what makes you think my daughter could possibly have been involved in his death? He was a sick old man."

"He was murdered," said Maggie. "Brandi had means, motive, and someone created the opportunity."

"Motive. Bah. What motive?"

"We think she was helping you cover up another set of murders, earlier. From years ago." Maggie watched the older woman as she said this. Was there a twitch of consternation on her face?

"You do?" tittered the older woman. "My, that is thrilling! Me, a murderer? I suppose you have me pegged as a cackling crazy old lady hidden behind a mask of civil decency?"

"Something like that, yes," said Maggie.

Hitchcock was thoughtful. "Well, that is very interesting. Have you been reading Agatha Christie, my dear? I do remember that Rosie loved her stories. You must have read several. Now you talk as though you are in one. Wonderful! Who did I kill?"

"It started with Fred Akers. Then James DeVaney. Then Amanda and Jason Hinrichs, and their eight-year-old son, JJ."

Hitchcock was silent, looking at them with a half-smile on her patrician lips.

"What I don't get, though," said Derwood, "is why you killed Sarah Smalls."

Hitchcock's smile slipped, and dark malice flashed behind her eyes. After a moment she said, "I think I have heard quite enough. William!"

Moments after her call the big man lumbered into the room. Derwood stood to face him, but the large man towered over him. He was not lithe, did not look fast or flexible, but he was huge, and looks could be deceiving. Derwood had underestimated the speed of big men before, to his sorrow, and he would not make that mistake again. He unobtrusively shifted his feet into a ready stance, hands loose at his sides. He wished he had brought a firearm. Luckily, the large man just stood still with his arms at his sides and an intensely vacant expression on his face.

"William, our guests are just leaving. Please escort them out."

Maggie stood and looked down at the old woman. "Okay, Mrs. Hitchcock. We will be going now. I just wanted to stop by to wish you a good night. By tomorrow morning, I expect we will be back. We'll bring handcuffs. If I were you, I would pack a bag tonight. A toothbrush. Maybe some of those Agatha Christie books you were talking about. They let you read in jail these days. Good night." They turned and walked out.

After they had gone, Deloris Hitchcock sat her son William down on the couch across from her. "Dear William," she said. "You've always been a good boy, and Mother loves you. You know that, don't you?"

The huge man shifted uncomfortably, eyes downcast at the floor. "What did you do, William? What happened to that girl?"

He neither spoke nor made eye contact, but began to shake his head slowly from side to side. Deloris could see a spell coming on him. It had always been thus, ever since she first got him out of foster care. His life before had been hard, a cycle of abuse and abandonment. She eventually kindled an attachment in the strange boy, to her. Only her. Over time she would learn that his behavior was consistent with an autism spectrum disorder, but back when she began his training, nobody talked about autism.

She conditioned the boy. It had taken time, attention and effort, but she succeeded. Ever a fan of Richard Wagner, the brilliant German composer, and the ideas of his philosopher friend Nietzsche, Deloris used the opening strains of *Götterdämmerung* as a stimulus to control William's spells. He responded with calm and eventually submission and obedience. She knew nothing of Brandi's recent deconditioning.

As William shook his head faster, Deloris reached for her phone. He saw the move and instantly calmed.

"Don't turn it on, Mother," he said, eyes downcast.

"What happened to the girl, William? She was not a part of this."

"She was, Mother. Brandi said so. You said so."

Deloris took a deep breath. "Go on, son. Tell me about it."

"Brandi came on Thursday, while you were out. She said the man at Pinelands was not enough. It was uneven. She said there had to be balance. I don't like it, how she talks. But she said everything has to be even and balanced. And calm and deliberate, just like you always say too, Mother."

"What has to be even and balanced, William?"

"Everything, Mother. Brandi said everything." His voice shook. "The words. The living, the dead. The men and the women. Even, not odd. She said there had been too many men. She said we had to even the scales. She said you wanted it that way. I knew you did, because she played the music. She's played it a lot."

Deloris felt a chill creeping through her. Brandi had always appreciated symmetry. There was a component of obsessive-compulsive disorder there, but Brandi had always controlled it. Had she decided more women had to die? There had to be balance?

"And the girl, William?"

"I did it like Brandi told me. I did not think I would like it, but I did."

"Oh my sweet boy." She hugged him gently and counted quickly. Brandi did not know the truth about Fred Akers. Her count would start with the Hinricks. Two males, if you counted the boy, plus DeVaney made three. Amanda Hinrichs made one woman. Sarah Smalls made two. Brandi needed one more.

Deloris had lost control of the situation. She had taught her children well, and now they were moving independently. Brandi had used the Wagner. It was not possible. The Wagner was hers! Fury rose within her, but she was icy calm. There was still time to rectify the situation. William was a killer, no doubt. Could he be a savior? She placed her hand gently on his cheeks.

"William, listen to me. Your sister is not telling you the truth. Symmetry does not matter. It means nothing. Submission and obedience, William. That's what matters."

The big man began to shake his head again, but this time he kept his eyes up, locked on his mother's face. "No, Mother," he said.

"Listen to me, William. I am your mother."

"No, Mother," he said. "You don't understand. Brandi said you wouldn't."

Deloris activated the Bluetooth feature on the phone to connect it to speakers in the corners of the room. When she activated the music, the horns blared.

William shook his head faster. "No, Mother, no."

The music climbed the scale as Deloris spoke louder. "Submit, obey!"

"You don't understand, Mother! She said you wouldn't!"

The music soared.

"Stop it, Mother! Stop it!

"Submit, boy! Obey!" screamed the old woman.

Something broke inside William then. A fragile construct, something that Deloris had pieced together over thirty years. She had slowly drawn together the fragile pieces of his childhood psyche and welded them together into a functional human being. But the seams shattered as the big man flew forward off the couch. He tumbled into his mother sitting in the chair opposite him as his large hands found her throat. The chair fell over backward, but he stayed atop her and squeezed. He was large, and strong, and he did not let go. He squeezed and cried and shouted.

"Stop it, Mother! Stop it!"

After a time, the music did stop. The Berlin Philharmonic recording that Deloris Hitchcock had on her phone was only four and a half hours long, after all.

Late in the night, when the music stopped, William came to his senses. His throat was raw from shouting, and his hands were cramped so badly he could barely release them from his mother's throat. Her bulging eyes looked at him, but he saw no judgment in them. Her lolling tongue did not speak, but he imagined his sister's voice. In his mind, he heard her say well done, William, my good and faithful servant. The scales are balanced.

The words gave him a deep sense of peace, but he knew there was more to do.

Chapter 31

DERWOOD SAT ON HIS back porch watching the stars. A gentle wind stirred wavelets on the lake, and they lapped irregularly against the bulkhead. He did not like Maggie threatening to return and arrest Deloris Hitchcock later. Getting the woman safely behind bars was the better move.

He worried for her safety, had even offered to stay to watch over her, but she discounted the risk. She said that with Brandi in jail and Deloris on notice, there was no danger. Besides, she would not live her life in fear. If the district attorney was afraid to walk the streets at night or stay home alone, she was not doing her job. Nonetheless, he thought she needed protection.

Derwood contemplated the night sky and the susurrating waves for a few more minutes. He thought about the whiskey cabinet, and he considered the form and texture of the investigation. They had been pulling threads, and now they had hit upon the main. A little more tugging and the entire thing would unravel. Brandi was in jail, and her mother would be next. They would play one against the other to break them both. He had seen it done in the desert many times. He wanted to stay sharp, so he left the whiskey cabinet closed. On his way into the bedroom, he picked up his mobile phone from the kitchen table where he had left it. He did not notice a missed call from Margaret Kidd.

LATE AT NIGHT, BROAD Street was deserted. Southern Pines was surprising for its nightlife, given its small size. Proximity to Fort Bragg and its thousands of young soldiers made it so, but in the small hours early Sunday morning, only a few hours before dawn, the bars and restaurants had closed, the last revelers had departed, and the streets were dark and silent. There was no one to see the large shadow creep into the alley leading to Maggie's apartment.

The moment he heard about Brandi's arrest, William Hitchcock had not needed instruction from Mother or his sister to make up his mind. Brandi had foreseen it. She predicted the death of the girl would force the police to action. She had prepared him. The only logical thing for him to do now was remove the threat. Margaret Kidd had arrested his sister and put her in a cage. Now she would help William get her out. He had to remember not to hurt Kidd, because they would not trade for a broken thing. Once he freed Brandi, she would know what to do. She always knew what to do.

He knew where the woman lived. He had watched her. He knew she lived alone. He entered the alley and paused at the door. He had everything he needed as he grabbed the knob. The door was locked of course, and he expected a deadbolt. There would not be a bar behind the door, though. There never was, not anymore. Barring doors had gone out of fashion.

He leaned his shoulder in and tested the door. Solidly locked, as expected, but not overly heavy. The door was wooden, fitted in the old building many years ago. It had held up well, but there was some play in the door. He backed across the alley and lunged at the door shoulder first. It splintered about the locks with a crack, but the sound was muffled by the alley and would not carry.

Margaret Kidd awoke in the night. She usually slept well, neither heavy nor light, untroubled by her conscience or the murky uncertainties of the future. What time was it? What caused her to wake? She listened and heard feet on her entry stairs. Suddenly something fired in her primordial brain: unknown sounds in the dark! Danger! Flee!

She slept in warm flannel pajamas, a remnant of her teen years and endless sleepovers with friends. Tonight's pattern was puppies. She shook her head to clear the fog of sleep as the footsteps thundered into her living room. There was a fire escape from her bedroom window to the back parking lot, one of those metal stair and ladder jobs.

She grabbed up her cell phone from its charger by the bed and ran to the window, but her time ran out as the footsteps approached the door. Maggie did not keep a gun. She believed the statistics that there were more tragic accidental shootings than incidents where crime was prevented. The rattling of her bedroom doorknob tested her faith in that assumption.

Heart pounding a million miles an hour in her chest, panic seized her as she punched in the access code to her phone and hit the redial button. She could not remember the last call she had made, and never even thought to dial 911. The volume on the device was turned low, as always when she slept. She preferred silence or the sounds of a sleeping city to the white noise that troubled sleepers used for comfort. She shoved the phone in her pocket as the door swung open and a flashlight beam struck her full in the face, forcing her eyes shut with its blinding light. She saw nothing more, because huge hands grabbed her and threw her onto the bed, face down.

Maggie tried to resist, to fight, but it was hopeless. All the self-defense classes in the world could not help a small unarmed woman woken from sleep in the middle of the night fend off a huge monster of a man. As her assailant landed on her, her breath left her body. Her mind was red with terror, arms pinned to the mattress, face buried in the fabric of the bed. She had no breath to scream.

WILLIAM MADE SHORT work of the woman. He found her at the window, panicked and trying to throw up the sash. He threw her small body onto the bed. He'd done it before; he knew what to expect. This time he would be more aggressive. He would not allow her to fight back. He threw his bulk atop her form and pinned her to the mattress. He heard the whuff of air leaving her body and his huge shoulder struck her back, and the fight left her. He quickly straddled her, and pinned her arms to the bed beneath his knees. He drew out tape, and pulled her head back with a fistful of her short hair. Around her mouth first so she could not scream, then around her eyes so she could not see. Finally, around her wrists so she could not strike.

The woman gasped and sucked against the tape, eyes wide with panic. He watched her buck and heave, but the air would not come. Her eyes dimmed as she lost consciousness. He reminded himself not to hurt her. They would not trade for a broken thing. Oops. He adjusted the tape to clear her nostrils as she struggled to breathe.

DERWOOD FLYNN'S PHONE blared trumpets into the night. He awoke immediately, long training sharpening his foggy mind, and quickly shook off the cobwebs of sleep. He picked up the phone. Four o'clock. An image of Lizzy popped into his mind, and fear gripped him. He had read somewhere that death was most likely at four a.m., when the body was at its lowest metabolic ebb. Not a good time for a phone call. Based on recent events, he had expected Martin Sinsley, but caller ID said Margaret Kidd was on the line.

"Yeah," he mumbled into the phone. No reply. He said it again, but still no reply. He nearly hung up the phone, but as he listened more closely, he heard strange huffing sounds, and a quiet whimper.

"Maggie?" he said. Nothing.

He dressed quickly with the phone on speaker mode, and hurried to his pickup. He drove fast through the night toward downtown Southern Pines. What the hell was going on?

Derwood connected headphones to his phone, the earbuds piping sounds from Maggie's phone directly into his ear. He could hear transmitted rumbling sounds and the occasional scrape. He thought he heard some indistinct mumbling but could make out nothing. What the hell was going on? He sped up through the night, and whipped around the Pinehurst traffic circle at seventy miles per hour, tires screeching as the pickup fishtailed out of the turn.

Chapter 32

WHEN MAGGIE LOST CONSCIOUSNESS, William hoisted her over his shoulder like a sack of feed and carried her out of the alley. The street remained deserted. The woman's small body fit easily into the trunk of his car, and he drove away. There was an all-night fast-food place a few miles away in Aberdeen, and he felt hunger stirring.

William soon pulled off the road into the all-night drive through and ordered breakfast. He liked to eat, and it took a lot of food to sustain his huge body. He ordered two sausage and egg biscuit meals, with two cups of coffee. Both were for him. He never considered ordering food for the woman in the trunk.

Losing consciousness had helped Margaret Kidd, from a certain point of view. Once she fainted, her gasping chest eased and her heart rate slowed. Before long, the flow of air into her lungs was adequate to deliver much needed oxygen to her suffocating brain and body, and she slowly regained consciousness. As awareness dawned, she felt panic rising once more, but this time she was able to control the emotion and keep herself calm. A hard object of some sort dug into her side as she lay in the dark. The pain helped clear her mind.

She lay still and felt motion, realized she was moving. She was in a vehicle. Her eyes were covered, but she could sense the smallness of the space. Had he put her in a trunk? It took little imagination to foresee her fate. With the bodies lining up, she pictured herself on a slab at the morgue, if she was lucky and her body was ever found. She tried not to think of the infinite hiding places for a small body in the woods. Where was the phone? Had the last phone call gone through? Was the line open? She struggled to speak, but only managed muffled grunts.

Maggie felt the car slow and turn, then stop. She heard the man speaking. It sounded like he was ordering food. What the hell? A drive through? The incongruity jarred her mind. What kind of nutjob kidnaps a woman in the middle of the night, throws her in the trunk, then pulls through the damned drive through at McDonald's? It hit her then, that she was at an all-night drive through. Those were all on the strip of U.S. Highway 1 in Aberdeen, south of downtown Southern Pines. She knew where she was! Now she needed to tell someone.

She twisted until her hands found the hard item that dug into her side. She felt cold steel and realized it was a tire jack. No sharp edges, but plenty of edges nonetheless. It would do. She worked her bound wrists back and forth over the edges of the jack, as the car pulled forward again and stopped. Maybe the car had reached the drive-through service window. Another human being might be just a few feet away. She tried to scream, but almost immediately the effort made her head spin as the increased effort to breathe forced her body back into suffocation mode. She tried to subvocalize, to kick, to make any sound that would alert the cashier that something was wrong, but the car pulled away again and turned onto the main road. She tried to imagine in her mind which direction it was headed, but she quickly became confused and disoriented. Instead, she focused on the tape on her wrists, and the jack.

Maggie worked at the tape on her wrists, and it finally began to part. After a few more minutes of struggle, her hands were free. She immediately ripped the tape from her mouth. There in the stale trunk, reeking of old groceries and spilled motor oil, she had never tasted sweeter air, and she drank it greedily.

She reached for her phone, and found it still in her pocket. The line was open, caller ID identified Derwood Flynn. She put the phone to her ear.

"Derwood. Derwood!" she whispered into the device.

DERWOOD SCREECHED TO a halt on Broad Street outside Maggie's apartment and dove into the alley. Her door was open, the lock splintered. He ran up the steps into the apartment. She was not there.

He should call the police, but Maggie had no land line. Could he call on his cell phone without disconnecting the active call to Maggie's phone? He did not want to take the risk. He ran back to his truck and sat, trying to come up with a plan. Where was she? What the hell was going on?

Suddenly, Derwood heard his name through the earbuds. "Maggie! What's going on, where are you?"

"Oh, thank God!" she breathed. "I don't know. Aberdeen, I think. I am in a vehicle. The trunk. On a road; the car is moving. I think the car just left an all-night drive through. Highway 1 in Aberdeen, I think."

"What the hell?" he said. "Are you sure?"

"No, I'm not sure!" she wanted to scream, but remembered to keep her voice low. "I'm in a goddamned trunk!" Then it hit her. Share your location. It could work, if there was signal, if they had similar phones, if the batteries lasted. "Listen, I am sharing my location with you right now. See if it works."

It worked. Derwood's phone pulled up a map, and he saw a blue dot moving south on Highway 1.

"I am on my way," he said. "Keep the line open."

"Screw that," she said. "I'm calling 911!" The connection ended but the blue dot glowed brightly. The car was headed out of town to the south.

Chapter 33

DERWOOD CALLED MARTIN Sinsley, who woke from a dead sleep and got on the road immediately. His next call was to Maggie's sister. Blanchard too came awake quickly, and after a brief exchange said, "Listen, Derwood, you are closest. Do not let that bastard get away. Do whatever you have to do. I will cover you. Go get Maggie. Whatever you have to do. Do you understand?"

Derwood understood perfectly.

He called Maggie back, hoping her phone was on vibrate mode. The blue dot was still moving south on Highway 1, through the small town of Pine Bluff.

"Hell, maybe Highway Patrol will be set up," said Maggie. Pine Bluff was a notorious speed trap. They should be that lucky. Except that Derwood was the only one actually speeding. The blue dot moved along near the speed limit.

Derwood's phone indicated and incoming call. Sue Blanchard. He reminded Maggie to share her location with the others, then answered the incoming call.

"We are going to connect you to the highway patrol. They have an officer near the last reported location, probably closer than you are," said the sheriff.

A moment later, Derwood's cell indicated a new incoming call. He answered, "Flynn."

"Yeah this is Officer Miller, North Carolina Highway Patrol. Dispatch said I needed to call this number ASAP. What's going on?"

Derwood laid out the barest facts. DA Margaret Kidd kidnapped by a suspected mass murderer, currently held in the trunk of an unknown vehicle, but in communication by her cell phone, on the road a few minutes ahead of Derwood's location on Highway 1 in Pine Bluff, moving south.

"I'm in Pine Bluff now, parked off Highway 1. Where is she, exactly?"

"Is this your cell number? I'm going to connect you directly to her. You can track her location."

A minute later, Miller called back to confirm that he had made contact with Maggie. The vehicle had passed his location probably while he was on the phone with Derwood minutes before, and now he was in hot pursuit, lights and sirens blaring. Dispatch had rerouted every available officer to the chase.

In the dark of the trunk, the road noise and soft vibration of the blacktop road were not uncomfortable. Maggie thought she could almost sleep, if not for the fear. So far she had kept control, but she could feel deep within her a well of panic trying to rise. She mercilessly forced it down. Do not think about it. Later, not now.

Her cell phone had a light, of course, but she was reluctant to waste the battery. She had no idea where the kidnapper was taking her, but she had a pretty good idea what would happen when they got there. She was still not certain who the kidnapper was, but the giant form suggested it was the man she had seen in Deloris Hitchcock's home several hours ago, her huge son. The bodies in the dam and in the lake and the strangled figure of Sarah Smalls motivated her. She turned on the light.

The trunk was fairly large but not meant for a person. It was littered with the sort of detritus one would expect. The only thing she could use as a weapon was a tire iron. A classic tool for a thug, she was not sure how much good it would do in her hands. Better than nothing, though. She saw a diagram showing how to fold the rear seat down into the passenger compartment of the vehicle, useful for fitting certain large items in the trunk. That would put her in the backseat area, right behind her captor, but she would not likely surprise him, much less overcome him. That direction was not her first choice for escape.

She saw a yellow plastic handle next to another diagram showing a stick figure leaping out of an open trunk. She realized that she was seeing an emergency release handle to open the trunk from within. All passenger vehicles sold in the United States since 2001 had them. They were supposed to prevent children from getting stuck in trunks, but they were good for kidnap victims, too.

She silently thanked the nameless engineer who had designed the handle. She reached for it, but then paused. What then? The car was moving down the road at what felt like highway speed. Jumping out was hardly better than staying put. Plus, as soon as she opened the hatch, William would know she was moving. What would stop him from simply pulling the car over and securing her more tightly the second time around? He might even decide it was safer all around to just kill her now, and be done with it. She released the handle.

William had finished his first egg and sausage biscuit, and was letting it settle before starting on the second when he saw flashing lights come over the hill in his rearview mirror. There were few other cars on the road at this hour. Had he made a mistake? How could they have found him? He was aiming for South Carolina and a place to keep the woman quiet while he arranged the trade for his sister. If the police followed him now, it would not work. Could they be after someone else? He still had about a mile lead on the chase vehicle. As soon as he topped the hill and the flashing lights were out of sight, he braked hard and turned aggressively to the left. The tires screeched as the car swung through the turn and he pressed the accelerator to the floor.

William continued to speed down the side road he had taken. Curves in the road blocked line of sight, and he could not see the lights of pursuit. Were they following? He did not know. After a mile or so, he slowed to a normal pace. He had been headed south, and the police might be looking in that direction. If he could break from the immediate pursuit, they might lose his trail. He continued east. If he could not make it to the Sandhills State Forest, there was another local option offering hundreds of square miles of unbroken forest shot through with dozens of roads. He would try to lose himself in the pine forest of the big army post near Fayetteville. Who would look for a fugitive there?

William sped the sedan forward to a sharp curve in the road. He jerked the wheel right, then left, and the car bounced over some railroad tracks. The sharp and rapid turns bled off much speed, but the crossing grade was uneven and the car bounced heavily across the tracks. The car's old shocks groaned in agony as the car bottomed out on the far side of the tracks. Sparks flew as metal chassis met hard asphalt.

Maggie had felt the car suddenly brake and turn left. The sudden change in speed and direction threw her violently around the small space, and her head and shoulder struck hard against the steel side of the trunk. Her head rang, and a sharp pain lanced through her right shoulder. She cried out in agony and fear, but the sound was drowned by the screeching of tires as the car jinked hard to the left and accelerated rapidly.

Maggie tried to assess her injuries. Her head sang and her shoulder ached, and she smelled wet iron in the close air, the smell of blood. She rubbed her hand to her head, and found a sticky knot beneath her hair. Her scalp was bleeding. Moving her shoulder sent bolts of pain into her upper chest. There was no way she'd be using the tire iron effectively.

As the car crossed the train tracks, Maggie bounced in every direction and picked up more bruises. She shrieked as the car barreled over a huge bump and her body flew upward from the floor of the trunk. She was able to turn her head so her face did not strike, but the side of her head crashed painfully against the underside of the trunk lid. Her shoulder screamed fire when she tumbled back to the floor.

A long sweeping curve finally brought William to a crossroads. The road sign pointing north indicated the way back to Aberdeen and eventually the Pinehurst traffic circle, but he proceeded straight, past a Mexican restaurant, shuttered in the hour before dawn. He slowed the car as he crossed the highway and drove on past open fields and pastures and modest neighborhoods with mobile and modular homes. Not far beyond the crossroad was a long straightaway, and the name of the road changed from Ashemont to Army Road.

Just then, far in his rearview mirror, flashing blue lights popped into view. He grunted and pressed the accelerator to the floor, and the car leapt forward. The police cruiser was still on his tail, and it had gained some ground. After he turned off Highway 1 and ran hard for a mile or so, he had slowed to avoid arousing suspicion, but he saw now that was a mistake. He had been lulled by the intervening distance hiding the lights of the chasing car in his rearview. He accelerated again, following the road toward the heart of Fort Bragg.

Chapter 34

AS THE CAR ACCELERATED, Maggie considered the trunk release handle. Was the time right? She had heard the stories of women too scared to run when they had the chance. She knew that escape was paramount, and she would not allow herself to be taken passively to slaughter, as many victims did, hoping their captor would show mercy in the end. No, she would run, fight, resist. But the time had to be right. Was that how it always happened? The abducted woman biding her time, hoping to choose the proper moment to flee, until all her moments were gone and her time ran out? She felt black dread rising and shook her head to banish the useless thoughts. Was now the time?

Maggie reached for the trunk release handle and grasped it in her left hand. As she began to pull, she felt the car accelerate and inertia slid her along the floor of the trunk, striking her right shoulder against the rear. She groaned again and released the handle as she clutched her wounded shoulder. Her phone flew and its light winked out. Darkness again overtook her in the tiny violent space, and tears from fear and pain finally spilled from her eyes.

William knew his options were shrinking fast. Soon, he would have nowhere to go. Ahead were traffic lights at another crossroad, but this time he did not slow. He raced through the intersection and across Highway 211 onto the outskirts of Fort Bragg itself. The lights behind him were intermittently visible depending on the shape of the road and hills. He could not tell if they were gaining. The roads were still deserted, but the Army was full of early risers. "We do more before nine a.m. than most people do all day," and all that crap. The roads would not be empty for long.

He slowed the car, and searched for a side road. He quickly found what he sought. This huge, empty part of Fort Bragg was loosely surrounded by roads leading to the controlled access parts of the installation behind gates where soldiers lived and worked, but the great body of the base was largely empty pine barrens laced through with sandy dirt roads and trails. William took one of these. As the car flew through the night, he had flashing glimpses of paths into the woods. As soon as he came to a road large enough for his car, he slammed on the brakes and jinked hard to the left. The car slid and skidded, but held the road tightly enough to make it through the turn. William doused the lights and aimed the sedan down the smooth sandy lane. He drove as quickly as he could in the dark without headlights, hoping that the dust from his passing would not leave a telltale cloud on the main road behind him. The sandy dirt lane was wide and smooth, obviously trafficked although currently empty. The wind was in his favor, gently moving the cloud of dust from his passing off the road and into the forest.

Miller saw the red taillights ahead in the dark, still far away but closer now. It was impossible to reckon distance in the night, but he had to be within a mile of the woman in the car. He had seen death many times. Twisted steel and shattered glass littered his mind as he thought of the dozens broken bodies he had seen in traffic crashes. But this was a living woman and the car was still on the road, and in sight just ahead of him. She would not die; he would not let her die. His radio chattered as updates came in, and he communicated his situation. He knew the authorities had vectored police from all directions toward his location, and he knew Highway Patrol had contacted the Military Police at Fort Bragg. Road Blocks would be arranged, reinforcements were coming. A helicopter was on the way, but right now it was just Miller alone on the road. He willed more speed from the car.

Miller flew down the road in pursuit, both hands gripping the wheel. He saw a form flash by on his right, then another. Aw, hell! Deer. They were thick on the ground in this part of the county. He did not slow until his high beam caught a large buck grazing just at road's edge. The buck leapt forward when pinned by the light. At speed, Miller's car bore down on the startled deer. Miller had no time to think, and instinct took over as he slammed the brakes and yanked the wheel. The car plowed into the deer with a sickening thump, its bulk splintering the shatter-resistant windshield, but the glass held. The deer flew into the air and out of sight as the airbag exploded in Miller's face. His seatbelt gripped him tightly as the car left the road, knifing across a ditch and into the trees.

After, Miller would count his blessings that he had not struck a tree, but as the car buried itself a hundred feet into the forest in a bank of sand, he cursed and shouted. He was out of the chase. He reached for his phone, but in the crash the device had flown out of reach and out of sight.

Derwood willed more speed from his pickup, and the big motor strained to respond, but the half-ton truck was designed for strength, not speed. He perceived the blue dot getting farther away. He had called Sue Blanchard, who was busy mobilizing every law officer within fifty miles, including the military police at Fort Bragg. She worked first to build a loose cordon of choke points and road blocks on the ground, then to tighten the noose as the men on the ground pursued. The bastard who took her sister had nowhere to go, he just didn't know it yet.

Derwood called Miller. The phone rang unanswered. Must be bad reception. Luckily, he could still see the blue dot that represented Maggie. It had turned off the road onto one of the spurs leading deep into the wilds of Fort Bragg. He tried to press the accelerator through the floor, but it would go no farther.

Derwood saw ahead off the road the still flashing lights of a police car in the forest. He surmised Miller had lost control in the pursuit and crashed into the woods. He did not even consider stopping. Margaret Kidd was the mission. He punched up Sue on his mobile and reported the accident, relying on others to rush to the officer's aid.

Driving a little slower now, Derwood switched screens back to Maggie's location and saw the blue dot was now behind and to his north, closer than before. They had left the main road. He braked the truck hard and pulled into a bootlegger's turn, just as the tactical driving instructors had taught him years ago. He had never tried the maneuver in a real-world situation, and he felt mild surprise that it actually worked. Going back the other way, he made a hard right onto the dirt road. The blue dot was not far ahead.

Chapter 35

CORPORAL JACQUELINE Lopez checked her watch. The digits showed 4:55. Firing would commence in five minutes. Lopez loved firing the big guns. The rumble shook the ground, and she could feel the percussion deep in her insides, like a living thing, a terrible thing, but a thing she controlled. She walked around her gun, performing her prefire check. She reached up and gently caressed the cool steel of the barrel, straight and very hard. It would not be cool for long.

When she grew up on the mean streets of Boyle Heights in Los Angeles, she never knew such power existed. The boys there, trying hard to be men with their 9mms and their .45s, the boys who thought they had the power? They had never seen anything like this. She crewed the M777 howitzer, the "Triple 7." Her gun was 155mm, and when it went off it belched fire and smoke a hundred feet into the air. The barrel pumped in and out to absorb the recoil, and feeling it swept away bad memories of boys with guns and the things they had made her do.

Lopez had joined the marines three years before, and she thought she would make sergeant soon. She never wavered from her initial request for combat arms, and she was thrilled to be assigned to the big guns of the 10th Marine Regiment, Second Marine Division at Camp Lejeune in Jacksonville, NC. The Carolina coast was about as far from Los Angeles as she could get and still speak the same language. Earning the respect of her teammates had not been easy. The work was hard and the shells grew heavy, but she had proved her mettle and now was just one of the guys.

This day the marines of the 10th Marine Regiment were at Fort Bragg. It had the only firing range in the region that could accommodate the big guns, and the 10th came up twice each year for a firing drill. This morning was a saturation fire drill, and they were firing high-explosive rounds. The guns had a range of up to twenty-five miles, more than enough to reach the target. Command had singled out a one-kilometer square area down range meant to simulate an enemy base and brought out twenty guns to reduce it, every gun firing five rounds per minute for a five-minute barrage, followed by three rounds per minute for the next half hour. Over two thousand rounds would fall, more than one round for every five hundred square meters. The target was broken into square grids about twenty meters per side. If they were accurate with the rolling fire, a round would fall on every grid in the zone. A few shrubs might survive, but no trees would. No buildings would survive. Any animal larger than a ground squirrel caught outside of a bomb shelter in the zone would be destroyed. Lopez didn't mind destroying animals. She learned long ago that no one and nothing was innocent.

William had found an even fainter path and forced the car down the vanishing road. The thin track faded and soon was not even a path as it led into the low scrub of second-growth forest. Pine saplings slapped the car, and it was forced to slow in the absence of a meaningful road. William leaned forward and urged more from the vehicle, but it was not designed for off-road travel, and it did not have the tires, suspension, gears or clearance for the rutted sandy ground. He pushed it as far as he could, but the car eventually churned to a halt, the saplings and ruts providing too much resistance to forward travel.

He slammed the automatic transmission in reverse, but when he punched the accelerator, the tires just spun until they were buried to the hubs. The car would not move. He cursed and leapt out.

MAGGIE FELT THE CAR slow, felt the strain of the motor, and eventually felt the car come to a stop. It jerked forward and back a couple of times, and she could hear the whine of the motor and feel the spinning of the tires. Her time had come and she yanked the hatch release handle. The trunk lid popped open.

Pain ripped her shoulder and a whimper slipped through her clenched teeth as she forced herself upright and over the threshold of the trunk. She landed on her feet and frantically searched the cavity for her lost cell phone. It had tumbled away from her in the trunk, and she had not been able to find it. Her cell phone. Her lifeline. She knew they were not far behind her. She knew Derwood was not far from her, but he was not here now. Only that big bastard. She had to buy time for someone to arrive. She turned from the trunk and began to run away through the scrub into the forest. She did not find the phone.

Derwood urged his pickup onward. The blue dot had come to a stop somewhere not far ahead, off the dirt road he now travelled. Not wanting to blow past another turn in the dark, he drove more slowly than before, but still as fast as he dared. He saw ahead a faded two-wheel track that turned off and headed deeper into the woods. There was no way to be certain, but judging by the position of the dot, it was probably the correct turn. In combat, you make the best decision you can in the moment, then you move on. No looking back, no second guessing. He turned.

Maggie ran as fast as she could, which turned out to be too fast. The dark forest was illuminated only by the night light leaking from the sky, and only a little of the milky light filtered to the forest floor. Limbs, saplings and brambles grabbed at her as she ran, but the forest floor was more open than she expected. There were few trees larger than her wrist, and there were large gaps between the trees.

The ground was sandy and in many places the sand was loose and deep, almost like a beach. Some force had turned the sand, plowing up roots and ground structure to leave a deep layer of shifting sand. No wonder the car had gotten stuck.

She ran on through the weird landscape. She did not see the limb that brought her down. It stuck out from the trunk of a fallen tree, ripped from its mooring and thrown across the landscape by some great unseen angry hand. She tripped on the branch and fell hard on the point of her right shoulder. Despite clenched lips and teeth, she felt the cry of anguish escape her mouth and fly into the night. Fresh tears leapt to her eyes as she struggled back to her feet, her shoulder an unbearable combination of wrenching ache and numbness extending down to her fingertips. She staggered up and on.

William saw the trunk was open and screamed in rage. He shined a flashlight into the cavity, but the woman was gone. Bitch won't get far, he told himself as he turned. He switched off the light and listened. The dawn forest was nearly silent. He heard a vehicle through the woods. Maybe it was coming for him. He needed to find the woman. As he listened, he smiled. The forest was nearly silent, but she wasn't. He heard her stumble and cry out. She was very near. He pointed the flashlight in her direction and began to move.

Chapter 36

DERWOOD'S PICKUP HAD the tires, suspension, gears and clearance for the rutted sandy ground, and the machine ate up the distance to the stationary blue dot. In the headlights Derwood suddenly saw the stranded sedan. He expected fire, so he stopped the pickup hard and dove from the driver door, his .45 at the ready.

But the sedan was silent and empty. Quick reconnaissance proved that the occupants had left on foot, deeper into the forest. He found Maggie's phone in the trunk, screen cracked but still functional. He pocketed the phone and studied the forest. They were on foot now, and close. They had to be. In this terrain, the few minutes that elapsed from the time the dot had stopped moving would allow them to go how far? A few hundred yards, tops? They had to be close, but which direction?

The forest was silent. Pine forests were like that. None of the cicadas that chirped in the hardwoods, and even the birds did not like the taste of pine sap and turpentine. Just the whisper of light wind in the low trees. His watch read 4:55 am. Still full dark, nearly an hour until the forest began to lighten and wake, and nearly two hours until the sun broke the horizon.

He reconstructed the scene in his mind. Maggie would be in the trunk, frightened but functioning. She had not been hurt, yet. She could have escaped the trunk when the car slowed, but William would have seen the lid pop open. She could have fled when the car stopped, and might have gotten away from the big man in the dark, if she just ran and got lucky. If she had run, she would have gone away from the back of the car, not around the sides closer to her captor. She would have run back the way the car had come in, toward her pursuit, her salvation. Except if she did that, she would be more visible on the path cleared by the vehicle, making her captor more likely to find her. She might have gone off into the woods at an angle, away from the car, alongside the track, but at an angle to it. That left about a ninety-degree search arc, if his reasoning was sound. He started to move.

WILLIAM QUICKLY FOUND his quarry. He did not speak but grabbed her roughly by the arm and kept moving into the woods. As he tugged her arm, she shrieked in pain. He had no time for this, and he needed silence not screaming. He grabbed her head in his huge hands and covered her face, muffling her scream. He stared at her terrified eyes. Holding her head between his hands, he thought how easy it would be. Just like the girl in the apartment, just like Mother. He liked watching them struggle, then came the quiet. He had not realized the joy of it, until that night in the redheaded girl's apartment. The struggle, then the realization that her time was up. How lovely and final, and to see it in their eyes. He felt he had finally connected. All those years, all those struggles to fit in, to understand, to really be with someone else. He had never been able to connect before. But now he understood. Now he could connect on the deepest possible level. He understood her, and she understood him. He felt joy rising.

Then the woman went limp in his hands, hanging like a rag doll. The sudden slack in her body nearly made William stumble, as her full weight came onto his outstretched hands. He held on for a moment, hanging her from his huge paws like an outlaw swinging on a rope, but then he released her with a start. If she died now, who would he trade for his sister? They would not want a broken thing.

She dropped to the ground in a heap. The joy faded. He threw her over his shoulder and lurched through the woods.

MAGGIE WAS NOT UNCONSCIOUS long, and when she came to her world was upside down as she swayed on the asshole's shoulder like a sack of grain. The fire in her shoulder had eased, or maybe her overwhelmed brain had just turned it off. She was grateful, able to focus for a moment on her predicament. Someone was coming for her. They were. What could she do to help them find her? The only thing she had left was her voice. She took a deep breath and screamed.

DERWOOD RAN IN A ZIGZAG pattern. As he got farther from the vehicles, his search pattern widened, but he tried to stay within the arc he had prescribed. He had not kept fit recently, and soon his legs and lungs burned, but there was no quit in him. He thought back to his selection and training long ago in West Virginia and the Long March over the endless hills, a walk without end. He would not stop now.

A scream split the air not a hundred yards in front of him and a little to the left. Derwood stopped the zigzag and ran straight ahead. He kept his pace just slow enough to avoid tripping. The scream cut off suddenly with an even higher pitched yelp, but he had zeroed in on the location as he bounded through the forest.

THE BITCH WOULD NOT shut up. Should have just done her a minute ago. William dropped her to the ground and kicked her savagely in the left side. That shut her up. He reared back and delivered another kick, this time aimed at her head, but she was able to dodge and took the blow on the left shoulder instead. He yanked her to her feet and kept moving.

William heard a sound behind him and turned just as a dark shape hurdled into view. He saw the glint of starlight off the dull matte finish of a pistol, and he grabbed the woman and held her in a choke hold before him. He could see in the dark a figure walking purposefully forward, hands outstretched in a firing stance. The figure did not speak or slow.

Derwood strode directly at the huge asshole in front of him. He was an operator, a shooter. He was the reaper. He would not miss, but he had to be able to see the outline of his target. In the dark, the figures blurred together. Easy day. Close the gap. He would fire when he rested the muzzle on the asshole's forehead if that's what it took.

Derwood kept his .45 raised and ready as he approached, eyes straining in the dark to separate the figures before him. He was not afraid to take the shot. He had spent enough time in the shoot house behind the wire at Fort Bragg conducting live fire drills with his teammates to be supremely confident in his marksmanship. He would not miss.

The outlines were becoming clear as he closed the distance. The large man tried to hide behind the smaller body of the woman, but the size discrepancy was too great. Derwood did not think of the man's name, or the woman's. They were not people to him. He was the target, she the hostage. He centered his sights on the target's forehead and began to squeeze the trigger.

Just then the forest exploded.

Chapter 37

THE 10th Marine Regiment brought their 155mm field howitzers and operation Rolling Thunder to the firing ranges of Fort Bragg twice each year, spring and fall. They set up in the night, in preparation for the day's festivities. Local Memoranda of Understanding with surrounding communities stipulated no firing between ten p.m. and five a.m., but at the stroke of five, the batteries would throw steel into the air with a great roar.

Corporal Lopez and her fire team loaded the high-explosive rounds into their Triple 7 just before five, and the fire command came as expected precisely on the hour. Lopez herself took the honors and yanked the firing primer. The gun recoiled with a tremendous blast, echoed all along the line as the entire battery shattered the still morning air and flame cut the darkness. The round left the barrel travelling faster than sound, faster than thought.

THE FOREST ERUPTED in violent noise, smoke and fire, and Flynn, Kidd and Hitchcock were thrown to the ground. Derwood was a combat veteran, and instinct took over as he held on to the pistol, managed to tuck it away as he rolled. As explosions filled the land, he realized immediately what had happened. The asshole had led them onto the firing range at Fort Bragg. The shells fell all around and the still morning became hell on earth. The sound overwhelmed sense and shattered eardrums. The percussion pressed on eyes, throats, and chests. The living air vibrated, pulsing with pressure and overpressure. For the first few seconds Derwood could not hear, see or think. Despite a long career under fire, he had never been under sustained artillery fire. Few modern U.S. soldiers had been. Not since the days of Vietnam had the U.S. faced a well-armed and coordinated adversary able to bring sustained artillery fire to the battlefield. Derwood buried his face in the sand and tried to burrow his body into the ground.

MARGARET FELT HER BODY go light as if she was flying through the air, and the forest lit up as a sudden sun erupted from the ground nearby. She found it oddly pleasant, floating weightlessly through the sky. It was beautiful really, as more little suns popped out on the forest floor all around. She smiled and thought of butterflies, until she crashed to earth in a deep crater blown out months before by a shell from a previous barrage.

WILLIAM HITCHCOCK ALSO flew through the air, but not quite as far. He landed in a heap on the sand, head ringing with explosion and light. He thought the man with the pistol must have pulled the trigger. He was hit. This wasn't so bad. It didn't even hurt. The girl was probably dead, though. That was too bad. It would not help Brandi. More explosions, the ground shook and sand rained down all around. He scrambled to his feet and tried to run, but every step brought another world-shaking boom dam light and smoke and noise and sand and dirt, and he fell again and he crawled. But it did not hurt. Another explosion and his left arm went. One moment he was crawling and scrambling and the next he tumbled across the ground like a scattered leaf before an autumn breeze, but then he could not feel his arm and it still did not hurt. He scrambled and he crawled and he was off balance and the world kept exploding and he saw he had no left hand and his arm stopped below the elbow and where is my hand but it does not hurt. And he scrambled and crawled.

AFTER THE FIRST MINUTE or so, Derwood had a tiny burrow around his body, and he tried to shrink inside it. Soldiers were taught to always improve their foxhole, and he dug for his life. The world around him and overhead was fire and pain as debris, rocks, dirt, branches, hot steel and everything under God's sun whistled death through the air. Two minutes in and his fingernails were shredded and bleeding, but he kept digging as shells rolled like thunder and split the air like lightning. Three minutes in and retired Sergeant Major Derwood Flynn had brought his body just below ground level. He knew he was lucky to avoid a direct hit, but the forest was large and he was small and the shells could not hit everywhere. He did not panic. Operators never panicked. Four minutes in he thought of Margaret Kidd, but he could not help her now. To search was to die. The only option was to pray that no shell landed too close. She was on her own. He kept digging. Five minutes in and Derwood remembered his cell phone.

Derwood punched redial on his phone and Sue Blanchard picked up immediately. It was impossible to hear over the roar, but Derwood shouted into the receiver. "Make them stop! Stop the barrage! Goddammit, make them stop. We are on the range. Repeat! Cease fire! Cease fire! We are on the range! Stop the barrage. Cease fire! Cease fire! Cease fire!"

MAGGIE AWOKE UNDERGROUND. She was inside a machine. The world was ending. The Earth shook and screamed, deep throated and raw and vibrating. She felt the tortured land moan and shake. It rattled in her bones, but she could not hear it. Loose sand filled her mouth and clogged her nostrils and plugged her ears. She tried to rise and her shoulder screamed and a giant hand slapped her back down. The hand pounded again and again and again, a giant fist crashing into the forest, into the earth, into her. She struggled to crane her neck and was able to free her head and her mouth from the embrace of the earth where she lay with sand caved in atop her by the barrage. She struggled to take a gasping breath, gagging and coughing as rough sand scratched her airways, but she lived. She did not have the courage to open her eyes.

SHERIFF BLANCHARD WAS coordinating the search for her sister, and she did not notice the distant boom of the artillery. It was a fact of life in the sandhills, like a summer thunderstorm. It never occurred to her that any human being could make it onto the firing range until she answered Derwood Flynn's incoming call. Cease fire! Cease fire! We are on the range!

How in hell could they be on the range? The range was guarded, gated, marked! Impossible! But Flynn kept shouting on the phone, his words indistinct but intelligible amid the terrible sounds of explosions coming through the tiny speaker. Like all local officials, Blanchard knew about the Marines' Rolling Thunder, and she had points of contact, both Army and Marine public relations officers. She called immediately and demanded a cease fire.

To the everlasting credit of the United States Marine Corps, the officer on the phone understood immediately that a police chase had somehow ended with personnel down range in the hot zone of the artillery exercise. He immediately called headquarters and within moments was speaking directly to Colonel Roberts, commanding officer of the 10th Regiment. The ceasefire order went out, and the big guns fell silent. The gun crews looked at one another in confusion, but followed orders like good Marines.

IN THE FOREST, THE woods quieted once more. Darkness crept in, but was held back by dozens of small fires burning in the scant undergrowth and scrub pines. Derwood Flynn rose from his foxhole and began to hunt. He found William Hitchcock on the ground a hundred meters away. The huge man crawled and slid, continuing to run, but he was not going far. His shattered body did not have much left. He was covered with dirt, he bled from both ears, and his left forearm was severed below the elbow. Hitchcock had not gotten below ground. That he had survived at all was a miracle. As he approached, Derwood remembered the sheriff's words. "Do whatever you have to do. I will cover you."

He stopped over the broken man and pulled out his pistol. The man seemed oblivious to his presence. Maybe his mind was gone. Artillery could do that. No matter. Flynn pointed the pistol at the back of the man's skull and pulled the trigger. The tiny crack of the .45 was barely audible in the forest after the roar of the artillery. It popped almost like a joke, a tiny firecracker. What had they called them when they were kids? Ladyfingers? Derwood smiled. The pistol sounded like that. But the bullet was no joke as it tore through the big man's brain and dug into the loose sand beneath. The body dropped instantly to the ground, face buried in the sand. Derwood squeezed the trigger again, another round ripping through the man's head. He turned to search for Maggie.

IN THE DITCH BURIED in the sand, Maggie clung to life while the world ended around her. She focused on breathing. Her mind was empty of thought and then the explosions stopped. She felt the earth stop shaking. She shook sand from her face and hair and pushed up on her good arm. She felt no pain as she was able to come first to a sitting position, then to her knees and finally to struggle upright. The forest around her was lit by dozens of small fires. She staggered forth, no direction in mind but feeling she had to move. Ahead she saw a figure moving slowly in the flickering light. The figure paused and raised an arm. In the smoky gloom, she saw two bursts of flame and light, but nearly deafened by the artillery fire, she heard nothing and could not make sense of them.

DERWOOD AND MAGGIE met in the clearing. Maggie looked as if she had returned from the grave. Her face and hair were streaked with dirt and sand, she cradled her right arm with her left hand as she shuffled along. Derwood looked little better, but was uninjured. They looked at each other for a long moment, and Derwood said, "Let's go home, Maggie."

"What?"

"Let's go home, Maggie." A little louder.

Maggie saw Derwood's lips move, but heard only rushing and ringing in her ears. "What?"

"Ah, jeez," Flynn mumbled. Ruin the moment why don't you? He jerked his head and they walked side by side back to the vehicles. Neither vehicle would drive again. Both William's sedan and Flynn's pickup had made it inside the hot zone of the range, and the bombardment had done its work. The sedan had taken a direct hit, and was blown into a thousand pieces of twisted metal. The truck was laced with shrapnel holes, dented, bruised and shattered.

They followed the path back toward the main access road, and after a few minutes were met by others—cops mostly, but finally by EMTs and an ambulance. They rode to the hospital together. Given the proximity, they were carried to Womack Army Medical Center. That was a lucky break, because the Army doctors in the ER there had experience with battlefield trauma and were not rattled to receive two victims from an artillery barrage. They had seen it all before.

Chapter 38

LATER, AFTER SHE WAS sure her sister was out of immediate danger, Sue Blanchard got back to work. She coordinated the moving parts of the ongoing investigation. Sinsley discovered the dead body of Deloris Hitchcock. He found a home office with bookshelves lined with psychology textbooks and scholarly works by researchers dating back years. Two shelves held dozens of leather-bound journals, the kind with unlined blank pages, within which Deloris Hitchcock had systematically documented her own research going back decades. She considered herself a scientist, and her records were meticulous. The case broke quickly once the investigators began to read the journals. The journals would be discussed and studied for years to come, both in law enforcement and in psychology circles, but not with the reverence that Deloris Hitchcock had craved.

She was a disciple of Burrhus Frederic Skinner, the great psychologist. She finished high school as his *Schedules of Reinforcement* was published. She made it her mission to study with the great man. During her time at Harvard, she was able to cultivate his acquaintance and work in his lab. She found his ideas on operant conditioning as true as they were applicable. She used her great beauty and her body as stimulus for both positive and negative reinforcement, and the willing students and faculty of Harvard University proved an ample laboratory to perfect her own version of operant conditioning. By the time she left Cambridge she was an accomplished practitioner of Skinner's theories, although her subjects were not rodents in a box. She practiced her craft on men.

As her skills grew, she sought more experimental subjects. Her husband, whom she met while in her last year in Cambridge, was one. The date of their meeting was recorded in her journal, and she immediately designated him a prime test subject. It did not take long to bend him to her will, and she carefully recorded the results of her experiments. She was the force behind his rise and financial success early in their marriage. However, as their marriage evolved, she saw cracks forming in their relationship. He began to chafe under her yoke, and her control over his behavior became more erratic. She struggled to perfect and apply new techniques. It fell apart when he defied her influence and lost most of their money gambling in the market.

Deloris had no tolerance for men she could not control. Her husband of twenty-five years was found dead in his car one Sunday morning, an apparent suicide. He had run a long dryer vent from the exhaust pipe of his car into the passenger window and sealed the gap with acoustic foam. A bottle of cognac and a few sleeping pills on the seat beside him ensured that the suicide was painless. She collected the life insurance, and sought another subject. She cultivated Willem "Rosie" Smits, and he turned into a convenient replacement. She applied her method, and before long Smits was smitten by the beautiful seductress. He kept no secrets from her.

She considered her quarter-century experiment with her husband a limited success, but he had been unduly influenced by preexisting stimuli that existed before she met him, and over which she had no control. Rosie was convenient but similarly tainted. She needed to start with younger subjects less influenced by poorly controlled environmental stimuli of all sorts. Her ideas and notes were recorded in black ink in an elegant hand in her journals.

She decided on a two-pronged approach. She would acquire a young subject for experimentation through the foster care system, and she would also create her own. She applied to be a foster parent and went through several unsuitable subjects before William. His lack of social skill reduced the likelihood that he had been subject to excessive outside influence in his early childhood. He represented as close to a blank slate as possible given that he was already six years old when she found him.

Creating her own subject was more problematic, and it was expensive. She was nearly past child-bearing age, and multiple attempts with multiple men failed to impregnate her. She was forced to turn to an in-vitro fertilization clinic at the research university in Durham, about ninety minutes up the road from Woodlake. Eventually that was successful, and she delivered a healthy baby girl. The test tube baby had no father. She named the girl Agatha Brandywine Hitchcock.

Her methods reached their apogee in late summer 2002 when Amanda Hinrichs ran for the Woodlake board of directors. It was during those months preceding the election that Willem Smits confided to Deloris the fate of Fred Akers, and she saw an opportunity to apply her method for the greater good. That was what science should be about, after all. She could preserve the peaceful lake experience for everyone. Once everything was revealed, the people would be grateful. She had perfected Behaviorism, and she would finally publish her work and receive her just recompense. She doubled her efforts to teach her adopted son William, and Wagner rang throughout her house, her laboratory.

A few weeks before the Woodlake election in August 2002, she identified the perfect effectiveness trial. She had conducted many efficacy trials at home and around town, and William had performed well under ideal conditions. How would he perform on real task, requiring complex decision making under uncertain conditions? The election provided just such an experiment, and Deloris released the boy upon Amanda Hinrichs.

She did not mean to involve the husband and the child, but you cannot make an omelet without breaking a few eggs. When it was over, she was ambivalent about William's performance. He had taken many risks. It was all documented in her leather-bound journals in her neat hand in black ink.

William had carjacked the Hinrichs family in the morning as they got into the car for school. A .22 pistol held to the back of Jason Hinrichs' head as he sat in the passenger seat was all the threat needed to encourage Amanda to drive the car to the Hitchcock home and park in the garage. Two shots to the back of two heads eliminated the need to fix anything for the guests to eat.

Deloris considered bringing eleven-year-old Brandi into the experiment at that time, but ultimately decided it would be better to wait for her flowering. She would not ask a child to do the work of an adult. Childhood was sacred. No. She herself pulled the trigger that fired the bullet into the brain of young JJ Hinrichs. However, she allowed Brandi to sit in the car with her dolls to play with JJ that day. Deloris noted in her journal that Brandi had been uncomfortable at first, but when William joined her, she calmed and eventually seemed at ease with the dead boy, appearing to view him as an extension of her dolls and other play things.

In the small hours of the next night, William had driven the car off the dam into the deepest part of Lake Surf. The car had bounced down the riprap at water's edge with no trouble and floated long enough for its momentum to carry it to the deep water. William had arranged the parents in the front seats, and left the boy in the rear. The hardest part was getting the driver's side window back up, but he had managed.

In her write-up after the experiment, Deloris blamed herself for leaving too many factors uncontrolled, making it difficult to judge the effectiveness of her interventions. William had been lucky to overcome the family so easily. The car had settled perfectly into the deep water. She drew several important conclusions. Too much luck. Plan more thoroughly. Further research required.

Overall, she considered the experiment a success. She wrote a detailed letter to Professor Skinner, but of course she never posted the letter. Into her files it went. The only cloud on Deloris' horizon that summer was the reaction of her lover Willem Smits. The man had completely lost his nerve and in truth, she reflected in her journals, he had never shown much of an investigative spirit. He saw merit in Deloris' methods, but he could not reconcile himself to the murders. Of course, he did not realize that he himself was yet another experimental subject. Deloris was too subtle.

And yet, she trusted the fate that had brought them together. She had grown fond of him. She could not eliminate him. Eventually Brandi provided the solution. Ever the scientist and teacher, Deloris guided Brandi through independent study until the girl hit upon a simple yet elegant idea. Lead acetate was once used as a sweetener, and Willem Smits loved tea. It was easy for the girl to combine hydrogen peroxide, vinegar and lead metal in the kitchen and create crystalline lead acetate, which would then dissolve in an aqueous solution, such as tea. She took to serving Willem Smits tea every evening. Such domestic bliss! He was grateful. Over time this experiment, too, was successful as Smits' mind began to come undone. The experiment with lead had an unexpected but delightful side effect. Brandi Hitchcock developed a lifelong fascination with chemistry and pharmacology.

Brandi's coming-out party occurred in her twentieth year. By that time, James DeVaney had descended far into the depths of depression and alcohol abuse to numb his heart to the loss of his daughter. His only comfort was his granddaughter Sarah. Then a new factor entered his life. By that point he was a hopeless old man, but the new factor was young, lithe and beautiful, and she had a name: Brandi Hitchcock.

Deloris had taught her daughter everything she knew and sent her off to college to pursue traditional education in chemistry and nontraditional education in the great laboratory of the undergraduate campus. Students there were easy picking for Brandi, men and women alike.

One summer while Brandi was back home, Deloris encouraged her to spend some time with her old acquaintance DeVaney. She had never forgiven the man for his betrayal over the powerboat issue. She thought when she engineered the car crash that killed his daughter and son-in-law, that would have been retribution enough to destroy him, but the presence of his granddaughter had allowed him to see just enough hope for the future, and he clung to that hope with all his might. Brandi could finish the job.

The drunken old man was easy prey and could not resist Brandi's nimble mind and supple body. After Brandi's intervention, it was easy for William to enter DeVaney's bedroom and squeeze the man's life out of his neck. Deloris showed William just where to put the body in the dam. It had worked so well for Smits—why change a winning formula? DeVaney lay undisturbed for over eight years.

When Willem Smits discovered what they had done, he grew anxious and specifically asked that they leave DeVaney's granddaughter out of it. Let the child alone. In his growing confusion, he went so far as to contact an attorney in Raleigh to set up a small trust fund for the girl. It was another betrayal, but Deloris loved Willem Smits in her way, and Brandi loved him in her way, and together they left Sarah Smalls out of their studies.

But as Smits' mind receded far beyond conscious filters, they saw a dilemma. As Smits' mind faded, his filters might fail. What if he said the wrong thing to the wrong person? And yet they could not kill Smits. You do not kill those you love. Nor could they ignore him, for he knew too much. They resolved to set watch upon him, and

Sarah Smalls was the perfect unwilling accomplice, the solution to their dilemma.

Deloris was getting too old for field work, but Brandi was entering her prime, and she had become proficient and persuasive with the Hitchcock Method. Applied technical visits to Cranston ensured he gave them what they wanted. He thought it was a fair trade.

As Deloris largely aged out of effective field work and entered semi-retirement, she passed the baton to her daughter. Her journals had correspondingly fewer entries. When the body washed out of the dam after Hurricane Miranda, perhaps an instinct of self-preservation had prevented Deloris from penning further entries. Her notes were silent on the events of the week leading up to her murder.

Luckily for the investigators, she had taught her daughter well. Brandi had taken meticulous notes of her own, starting from a young age. The detailed journaling generally followed her mother's template, and included complete records of her own experiments through high school, into college and beyond. She was peculiarly fond of symmetry in her journal as in all aspects of her life and her work. Later, forensic psychologists would say obsessive compulsive disorder drove much of her behavior, but she carried no such diagnosis as she detailed her life, plans and experiments in her journals. A recent entry detailed her nocturnal visit to Pinelands Estate after the exposure of Willem Smits. She had tried to ease his passing by reading from a work by his favorite author and her own namesake.

It turned out that she had been deconditioning William for many months leading up to the murder of Deloris. Brandi's journal recorded her expectation that Mother would not long survive the attentions of her beloved son.

Brandi had remained silent in jail for a time, but when confronted with the reality of her mother's journals and her own, her attorney advised a different tactic. Unfortunately for her, defense by brainwashing rarely succeeded. No matter what defense she tried, she was looking forward to many years behind bars.

Chapter 39

One Week Later

DERWOOD FLYNN HAD HAD a good morning. He awoke before dawn with a clear head, his sleep undisturbed by nightmares of the killers he had not killed. His dreams, unwelcome visitors in the night, had left him to haunt other uneasy souls. The bourbon had not strayed from the cabinet since the murder of Sarah Smalls. The fresh ground coffee was hot, his tablet was charged, and prepped with *The Times*.

The story published in the *Town Crier* was picked up by national news over the weekend and was the lead in the Sunday supplement of the *Times*. The writer called it "The Florist, the Warrior, and the Witch." It began twenty years ago, when a flower merchant and a soldier disagreed about motorboats on a private lake. The florist bashed in the head of the soldier in a fit of pique. The story wove through two decades of murders and cover-ups, with detailed documentation gleaned from eyewitness accounts and meticulous record keeping. By the time all was over, there were nine dead bodies and one seriously banged-up female district attorney.

The story read like fiction, but a rusty lump of metal in the shape of a crowbar was pulled out of the muck at the bottom of Lake Surf, a task made easier after the Corps of Engineers drained the lake. The old crowbar contained no traces of evidence, but it lay exactly where the informant said it would.

Audiences love a hero, and Margaret Kidd was made for the role. Young, strong, tenacious, tough, honest. And so photogenic. Hollywood could not have cast a more suitable heroine. She deserved the accolades. The reporter got it mostly right, but Derwood Flynn was curiously omitted. The secret soldiers behind the wire had ways of avoiding the media.

The coming week was full of funerals, but Derwood dressed and attended only one, the funeral of Fred Akers. Unit guys take care of their own, and he went out of respect for his former comrade-in-arms.

The morning of the funeral, Derwood sat with Lizzy and Maggie over breakfast at Greenbow's. Maggie's hearing was returning and Lizzy's belly was on the mend. She had moved in with Derwood after her operation. She said her mother was driving her nuts, and that it would only be for a little while. Kate was furious and blamed Derwood, but he did not mind. He liked having Lizzy in the house. Who would have guessed?

He ordered the Lumberjack Special. When he saw Lizzy's disapproving stare, he said, "Breakfast is the most important meal of the day."

"Mmm-hmm," Lizzy said, and shook her head. Maggie did not even try to swallow her grin.

"So, Smits killed Akers?" Lizzy said.

Maggie nodded. She and Lizzy were on one side of the table, Derwood on the other.

"Looks that way. That's what Deloris' journals say. Sounds like he didn't plan it. Just a sudden impulse. Almost an accident, in a way," said Maggie.

"And the guy sold flowers?" Lizzy said.

"Yeah. Apparently, he was a florist to the mob in New York," said Maggie.

"Made a killing," said Derwood.

Maggie and Lizzy looked at one another and rolled their eyes. "Did he really say that?" said Lizzy.

"Pathetic," said Maggie.

"Funny, though," said Derwood as he shoved a forkful of eggs and bacon in his mouth.

Later, at the funeral, he greeted old colleagues by name. Lawrence Simpson showed up in full dress uniform, row after row of decorations and medals weighing down his jacket. There were other soldiers, too, some he knew and some he did not. Mostly Unit guys, but he was surprised to see several members of Thirteenth group Special Forces, Akers' original special forces group before he joined the Unit. Some of them were obviously too young to have ever known Fred Akers, but soldiers liked to honor their own. Derwood was glad to see it.

AFTER THE CEREMONY, Derwood and Maggie paid their respects to Jill Akers, but they did not linger. They did not notice the small group of soldiers who gathered in a corner of the graveyard. Lawrence Simpson was surrounded by the men from Thirteenth Group, and he spoke quietly and with authority.

"That's him. That's Derwood Flynn," said Simpson.

"You don't think we can bring him in, then?" asked another soldier. "We could use him. We've got another shipment next week, straight from Chiriquí. Got to get them settled and working. The last batch is about worn out. Time to turn them over for processing. We need another man on the ground, someone reliable."

"Oh, Flynn is reliable, all right, but he is incorruptible," Simpson said. He shook his head. "Stay away from him. Find someone else."

THE GATHERING BROKE up. A few mourners lingered. Derwood and Maggie tried to make small talk as he drove her home. Her damaged hearing made for difficult conversation over the road noise. They shouted about the weather, about the future. Maggie mentioned there might be an upcoming opening on her staff for an investigator, but Derwood said he already had work. He was a deputy sheriff and a consulting detective. Conversation lagged and Maggie, who had been having some trouble sleeping since her ordeal, dozed in the comfort of Derwood's pickup.

As he drove, he surreptitiously glanced at the strong beautiful woman next to him. Finally, he found a dream he did not want to escape. He smiled and hummed a tuneless ditty to himself as he drove. Things were looking up.

The End

About the Author

TB Brown is a reformed farmer and physician. He can sometimes still be found wandering the halls of the hospital, or the forests and fields near his home. An avid if mediocre amateur musician, on a good day he will be found in jam circles around North Carolina.